BY JOSÉ RAÚL BERNARDO

Silent Wing

The Secret of the Bulls

SILENT WING

A NOVEL BY

JOSÉ RAÚL BERNARDO

SIMON & SCHUSTER

SIMON & SCHUSTER
Rockefeller Center
1230 Avenue of the Americas
New York, NY 10020

SIMON & SCHUSTER and colophon are registered
trademarks of Simon & Schuster Inc.

Designed by Amy Hill
Manufactured in the United States of America

1   3   5   7   9   10   8   6   4   2

Library of Congress Cataloging-in-Publication Data
Bernardo, José Raúl.
Silent wing : a novel / by José Raúl Bernardo.
p.   cm.
1. Cuba—History—Revolution, 1895–1898—Fiction.   I. Title.
PS3552.E7275S55   1998
813'.54—dc21   98-10521   CIP
ISBN 0-684-84389-7

ACKNOWLEDGMENTS

My thanks to Richard J. Riordan, mayor of the city of Los Angeles, and his associates: Adolfo V. Nodal, general manager of the Cultural Affairs Department, and Marlene Dermer, chair of the Literary Committee, for inviting me to participate in a literary panel honoring José Martí, the eminent nineteenth-century Cuban poet and patriot. During the discussion, after all the other panelists effusively eulogized Martí—and deservedly so—I stirred great controversy when I opened my remarks by saying, "I came here not to praise Martí, but to talk about his one tragic flaw." I then read excerpts from the libretto of my first opera, *The Child,* inspired by Martí's guilt-ridden autobiographical poem "La Niña de Guatemala." It was the audience's enthusiastic response to the story that gave me the impetus to transform the libretto of my opera into this work of fiction.

My thanks to the people who read the first draft of the manuscript and provided me with excellent comments and questions: My agent, Owen Laster, and William Clark, A. J. Hernández, Helen Breitwieser, Carol Bowie, Amy Hill, Barbara Raynor, José Badué, and Rosario Rexach.

After I revised the manuscript, I sent it over to my editors, Michael Korda and Charles F. Adams, who over lunch kept making one brilliant suggestion after another on how to better the novel. My thanks to them and to Carol Catt and Gypsy da Silva, who lovingly copyedited the work.

My thanks to Phyllis Throgmorton and the Pepacton Arts Center, for the support they have given me, allowing me to complete this novel.

But my final and most expressive thanks must go to the two people whose help has been invaluable to me: My father, José Bernardo, whose love of books I inherited; and my partner, Robert Joyner, whose love of truth transformed my life.

To all of you, my deepest thanks.

De corazón, as we Cubans say.

From the heart.

To A.J.

and

To the Quetzal

CONTENTS

SOULS WOVEN TOGETHER BY THE GODS

CAN NEVER BE UNRAVELED

Ancient Mayan Saying

PROLOGUE

Guatemala, 1877

SOL, A BEAUTIFUL YOUNG WOMAN with dreamy dark eyes and long golden hair that falls in gentle disarray over her naked shoulders, is sitting at the dressing table in her bedroom, pen in hand, looking intently at her diary, opened wide in front of her.

Minutes ago, the hundreds of bells of the great City of Guatemala had begun to peal softly in the faraway distance, calling for vespers, and announcing to the world that the day was ending. It was the sounds of those bells that awakened Sol from her late afternoon siesta, triggered her thoughts, and made her run to tell her diary about all the incredible things that happened to her in the little church she visited today at noon, hoping that by writing it down she might be able to make some sense of that visit. A visit she certainly had not intended to make, and yet, a visit she does not think she will ever be able to forget.

Barefoot, wearing nothing but her semitransparent cotton camisole and petticoat, she has just jumped out of bed, grabbed her diary from under her mattress—where she keeps it—and has rushed to her dressing table, anxious to share her innermost feelings with her best friend, her diary. And yet, now that she is sitting at the table, totally oblivious to the last beams of the setting sun that, filtering through the open shutters, casts amber lines across the blank page of the diary facing her, she just stares at it, not knowing exactly where—or how—to begin.

Then, decisively, she begins to write with a swift yet elegant hand.

At first I didn't want to do it, but you know how impossible and stubborn Xenufla can be. Ever since she nursed me when I was a little baby she thinks she is my real mother. How can I ever say no to her?

XENUFLA, an older Mayan Cakchiquel Indian woman, has taken care of Sol since the moment her "niña"—her little girl, as Xenufla calls Sol—was born. Xenufla knew how unattractive and silly Sol found the eligible young men of marriageable age Sol had met so far. So Xenufla kept on insisting and insisting, day after day after day, "Niña, please, listen to me. You must go to the little church of the sacred village of Jocotenango on a Thursday—right at noon—and ask Santa Rita there for a husband. The Saint is good, she will listen to you, I know she will, and she will find the right man for you, the one the gods mean you to have always by your side."

Every time the old Mayan woman said it, Sol would smile back at her and say, "Xenufla, I am too young for that kind of thing—I am not even eighteen! I am not desperate for a husband, Xenufla, not quite yet."

But Xenufla could not—or would not—accept Sol's answer. Every time Sol said that, the old Indian woman would retort, always trying to sound stern and severe, though never quite being able to achieve it, "Why, niña, do you want to die an old maid? When I was your age I already had two children and a third one on the way! And besides, you know very well that most of your girlfriends are, if not married, at least officially engaged by the time they come of age."

A week ago, after one more such confrontation, Xenufla lowered her voice and confidentially told Sol, "A man can be a lot of fun, niña. Believe me. You may think I am just an old Indian woman now, but, niña," she said, raising her voice just a little bit as she touched her ample breasts, "I am still a woman. And this woman knows what she is talking about. Men can be a lot of fun! They take you and make a girl into a woman. And once a girl becomes a woman, and she finds out what it is to feel like a woman, believe me, niña, she is never too young—or too old—to enjoy what a man is good at!" she added, winking at Sol just as she started to laugh, loud belly laughs that made Sol join in the laughter as well.

How could Sol ever say no to Xenufla?

Sol had never seen Xenufla so happy as when she told her old nurse, "All right, Xenufla, all right. Next Thursday I'll go with you to the little church of Jocotenango to see Santa Rita—right at noon—and we'll see what happens."

The minute Sol agreed, Xenufla told Sol to sit down and then started to instruct her in all the things the young girl was supposed to do.

"First, you must eat nothing after midnight of the day before. Nothing. Not a thing. You must not even drink water. And you must not say a single word either, not to me, not to anybody, not until after you have petitioned the Saint. We'll leave early in the morning, to make sure we'll get to Jocotenango with plenty of time. Then, after we arrive, before you start the long climb up the hill to see the Saint, you must drink a glass of sacred balche in the Saint's honor. Don't make that face, niña, it is a delicious drink! It is made of fermented honey and the bark of the bacab tree, and it makes your head spin and readies you for the Saint—you'll love it. Then you must climb up the entire hill slowly, very slowly, step by step, without rushing. And you must do it quietly—just as if you already were inside the church—with your head covered and your eyes cast down and looking at the ground, while you hold firmly with both of your hands a magic *cirio*, one of those long, thick candles they sell at the bottom of the hill to the young women who go up the hill to petition the Saint, the kind that is perfumed with the most sacred incense of them all, *pom*," Xenufla said. "Then, when you get up to where the Saint is, you kneel in front of her, light the candle in the presence of the Holy Lady, and offer it to her, looking her in the eye and keeping your body as rigid as you can make it while you deeply inhale the magical scent from the *cirio*, which will send you into the world of the Saint. When the heavy smoke starts to make your eyes cry, do not close them. Keep them open for as long as you can, and even if tears do come out, keep staring without blinking at the Holy Lady. And then, if you have asked the Saint with faith in your heart, the Saint will answer your prayer and give you a sign."

"A sign?" Sol asked. "What kind of a sign?"

"Different signs to different people," Xenufla answered. "My oldest niece, Machuela, you now the one I am talking about? The one with the little mustache? She was almost twenty—and *still* unmarried—when she went to the Saint. And when the Saint answered her, she fainted. She never told me what happened, what she saw. But two months later she was already with child! After marrying Torcuato, the blind man, of course."

Smiling to herself as she remembers Xenufla's words, Sol goes back to writing in her diary.

The truth is I didn't know what to expect. I just went to see the Saint to satisfy Xenufla and get her out of my hair. I did exactly as she told me to do, exactly what I saw a lot of Indian women do. I was the only white woman there, and I must confess, I felt a little intimidated—and embarrassed—by the whole ritual. I lit the cirio and I offered it to the Saint, and I let the musky scent of the magic candle embrace me until my eyes started to tear. I kept them open, as Xenufla had told me to do, and I looked up at the Saint. Then, all of a sudden, I felt a tremor under my feet. I thought we were going through an earthquake, so I looked around me. But not a thing was moving, and yet I was shaking badly. I got so scared, I did not know what to do. It was then I looked up at the Saint again and noticed that her eyes were changing form and color, little by little becoming dark blue instead of brown until they became the dark blue eyes of a handsome man with dark, thick eyebrows—piercing dark blue eyes that were now dreamy, now teeming with desire, as they stared at me, through me, making me feel something I had never felt before, my entire body both burning hot and shivering cold at the same time.

Sol puts down her pen and shivers again as she remembers those piercing eyes she saw this afternoon. She closes her eyes and she can still see them, vividly, as vividly as she saw them then, when they stared at her in the church. She shakes her head, still disbelieving what she saw, what Santa Rita had shown her: those piercing dark blue eyes that have been following her ever since, even into her bed and into her dreams; deeply penetrating dark blue eyes that seem to be filled with both an unimaginable pain and an indescribable joy at the very same time.

Eyes like those cannot exist, she tells herself.

Or can they?

Sol remembers what it was like to leave the church afterwards. How shaken she was as she walked down the hill toward Xenufla.

Xenufla knew, just from looking at Sol, that something had happened, that her niña had received a wonderful sign from the Saint. But Xenufla did not say a single word, she did not ask a single question. It was Sol who asked it, as they both climbed into the carriage that would take them back home.

"Xenufla," she said, "did you feel the earthquake?"

When she heard that, the old Indian woman just looked at Sol, and as she shook her head from side to side, she smiled knowingly at her niña. The gods had spoken and had given her niña a wondrous sign—just as Xenufla knew they would. The man meant by the gods to be always by her niña's side had been chosen and was on his way to her.

Now all there was to do was to wait for him.

PART ONE

CHIRILINGO

CHAPTER I

THE TIRED OLD WHISTLE of the small steamship manages to let out a piercingly loud blast soon followed by another, then another. Julián is suddenly awakened by these raucous sounds. Startled, he opens his eyes, and from where he is, lying right on the ship's deck, he can see through a misty early morning fog what appears to be a lush tropical shore gently gliding by.

Guatemala at last? he asks himself.

Eager to take a closer look, he quickly begins to stand up, and then he has to smile at himself. Since he is a young man of just twenty-six, strong, muscular, with broad shoulders, and with a body chiseled by hard labor, he had thought that sleeping on the ship's deck—something he has been doing for the last twelve nights—would not be too hard on him. But, Was I wrong! he tells himself as he stretches his sore muscles. His entire body seems to be aching all over. To save money he has been sleeping *a costilla pelada*—on nothing but his ribs—on the deck of *El Futuro*, the small freight steamship that is bringing him from the port of Veracruz, in Mexico, to this new land, Guatemala. Having been exiled nine years from his home in Cuba, he now seems to be always on the move, constantly going from one place to the next, with no country—and with no job—rarely being able to afford a comfortable bunk, not even on this very inexpensive freight steamship.

He quickly unfolds the jacket to his black suit, which he had been using as a pillow, and, after he brushes it carefully and smooths out the wrinkles as best he can, he puts it on, hurries to the railing, and looks intently at the shore of this land he is about to enter, wondering what it is that makes it seem so different from the shore of his native Cuba. Certainly one sweats as much here as one sweats there, he thinks. It is still very early in the morning, and yet, the heat is already stifling, even though it is not quite the end of March. So far 1877 is turning out to be a very hot year, Julián tells himself, as he wipes his forehead with his handkerchief while his eyes focus on the pale blue mountains barely visible in the far distance, framed by the luxuriant greenery of the rain forest near the shore.

And then, all of a sudden, Julián realizes what makes this place seem so different from his own Cuba. Where are the tall slender royal palms of his native land? he asks himself as he turns his head, scanning the opulent tropical shore of Guatemala, looking for—dreaming of—a Cuban royal palm. And as he does, while he stretches his sore arms once again, and again massages the back of his neck, he asks himself the very same question he has been asking from the moment he set foot on another ship, a ship very much like this one, a ship that nine years ago took him away from his homeland: When will I be able to go back home?

Suddenly, the tired old steamship whistle of *El Futuro* lets out a second set of piercing blasts, and a bell begins clanking and clanking loudly. Responding to its urgent call, sailors appear all over the ship, as if from nowhere, scurrying around the deck, shouting orders to each other, and throwing ropes to the men on shore, who shout back at them as the steamship begins its docking operations.

Leaning against the railing of the ship's deck, his face covered with thick drops of sweat, Julián admiringly watches the ship's crew helping each other, each of them knowing exactly what to do, each of them a piece of a very complex and well-oiled machine.

One of the men rushes by Julián's side, and as the man reaches for a rope, he accidentally bumps into Julián. Julián quickly moves out of the man's way and mechanically, almost unconsciously, pats the small leather bag he hides under his vest, next to his revolver, to make sure he still has the little money he was given by Señor Fermín—a Guatemalan man Julián had befriended in Mexico City.

Ten weeks ago, Julián decided to leave Mexico behind. Or, rather, it was decided for him. After the latest military coup d'état in Mexico City, three and a half months ago, the members of the new conservative Mexican regime did not like at all what a young liberal Cuban writer in exile with the burning passion of individual freedom running wild through his veins was saying about them. Before things got worse, Julián's friends begged him, "Please, Julián, either quiet down or get out of Mexico." But quieting Julián down was totally out of the question. After all, his own family had not been able to quiet him down in Cuba; that was why he was in exile in Mexico City—where Julián had barely been able to eke out a living by writing political essays for *La Revista Universal,* an ultraliberal literary publication. It was then that Señor Fermín suggested that Julián try his luck in Guatemala.

"I believe there's a future in Guatemala for you, Julián," Señor Fermín said. "I took the liberty of writing to a friend of mine, Professor Saavedra, about you. He is an exiled Cuban man, like you. He was teaching in New York City when the consul of Guatemala hired him and he is now the principal of the Escuela Central, the most exclusive girls school in Guatemala City." He paused as he extracted an envelope from one of the inner pockets of his impeccably tailored, elegant, silk faille frock coat. "And here's his answer," the old man added, showing Julián a letter from Professor Saavedra, in which the professor said that a full-time teaching position was open at his school for a man with the proper credentials, and that he would try his best to hold it open for as long as he could to help his fellow Cuban, Julián, get that position. But, the professor stressed, it was essential—and in his letter Professor Saavedra underlined that word *essential* not once but twice—*essential* that Julián got to Guatemala City as soon as he could, and definitely prior to the end of the current school year, for by that time teaching appointments for the next school year had to be proposed, approved by the minister of public instruction, signed, sealed, and completely settled.

After reading him Professor Saavedra's letter, Señor Fermín gave Julián, in addition to some money for the trip, a letter of introduction recommending Julián to the new liberal president of Guatemala, Gualterio Rubios, a former schoolmate—and a personal friend—of Señor Fermín. "Being in the right political circles can never hurt a young man," Señor Fermín added as he winked at Julián.

Still leaning against the ship's railing, Julián sees Yubirio, an older Cuban sailor who works on this small steamship, rush by. Effortlessly and with almost animal perfection, Yubirio, who is tall and black as ebony, and who has huge, bare, muscular arms glistening with sweat, throws a thick rope to one of the other sailors already on the shore, who grabs it and ties it to a wood post just as Yubirio begins to sing at the top of his lungs one of those bawdy Cuban songs popular at the time.

> *The man who doesn't know how to drink*
> *and doesn't know how to make love,*
> *What good is a man like that? Eh?*
> *What good is a man like that?*

Julián smiles at the way Yubirio puts an emphasis on the word *Eh* as he sings, creating a lilting syncopation that puts rhythm into his movements, making what he is doing seem more like a pleasant dance than the strenuous job Yubirio and all the rest of the sailors are undertaking. The power of music! Julián thinks. Leave it to a Cuban man to put rhythm to everything so he can dance through life. Julián remembers when not yet seventeen he was imprisoned in La Habana, sentenced to forced labor, and had to work the stone quarries of San Lázaro just for publishing in his school paper a poem saying that Cuba should be free from Spain. Barely a man then, and already a political prisoner! Quarrying the heavy stone had seemed so much easier when the men sang as they worked, he remembers. Yes, the power of music! Julián repeats to himself. It makes life so much easier.

Standing nearby on the shore and watching the ship as it docks are dozens of men—stevedores. These men are short and stocky, of Mayan descent. They all have slightly slanted, almost Oriental eyes; long, black, coarse hair; huge, muscular arms; and their dark-honey skin has been made darker by the scorching sun. Barefoot and wearing nothing but well-worn white cotton pants tied around the waist by thick jute ropes, and old wide-brimmed palm-leaf hats sheltering their heads, they are waiting expectantly for the ship to dock so they can begin to unload its cargo.

Julián looks at them as Yubirio, with the help of another sailor, places a large gangplank noisily into position and gives a loud commanding whistle, making Julián turn to Yubirio, who smiles at him.

"Hey, Julián," the black man shouts, a smirk in his voice as he points to the Guatemalan shore with a nod of his head, "don't get too drunk down there."

"I'll try not to," Julián shouts back, a matching smirk in his voice, and pauses briefly just to add jokingly, "unless I have to," which makes Yubirio laugh a loud belly laugh.

Yubirio waves good-bye to Julián, a powerful, manly wave, and gets back to work, dancing as he sings.

Julián nods his head and, admiringly, smiles back at Yubirio, for he sees in the old Cuban sailor a proud Negro man who has managed to escape from the infamous whips and shackles of Spanish slavery. He must have had it a lot worse than I ever had, Julián tells himself, and yet, look at him, singing and dancing. Then, unaware that he is doing it, Julián begins to hum the catchy tune of Yubirio's song as he begins to exit down the ramp, limping ever so slightly—a limp he owes to the heavy iron ball he had to wear while in prison.

Still humming, Julián goes to the corner of the dock where he retrieves his battered leather suitcase, a suitcase that has accompanied him to so many places in his constant and useless search for an adopted home: Isla de Pinos. Madrid. Zaragoza. París. London. Progreso. Ciudad México. Veracruz. Contoy. Isla Mujeres. Belize.

And now, Guatemala.

It seems to Julián that all he has been doing for the last nine years of his life is packing and unpacking, just to repack everything once again. Not that he has that much to pack and unpack. The worn black suit he is wearing has been everywhere, as well as the companion twin suit—his "better" suit—which he carefully keeps, neatly folded, inside his suitcase, waiting for "special" occasions. A few changes of underwear. Toiletries. A bottle of quinine to fight malaria. A flask of gin to make the quinine palatable.

And his books.

He picks his suitcase up. He had forgotten how heavy it has become. That is why it is so heavy, he thinks, because of his books. He has tried to leave them behind but he has found out that he cannot. In moments of despair—and he has had plenty of those—it has been only his books that have provided him with the strength to live through one more sleepless night and face one more hopeful dawn. Thucydides. Plato. Plutarch. Cicero. Cervantes. Shakespeare. Whitman.

His books are his friends—the friends who talk to him.

Just as his diaries are his friends—the friends who listen.

As if all his books were not heavy enough, Julián also carries in his old suitcase his voluminous diaries—nine of them by now—each page filled top to bottom, front and back, including all spaces that might have been margins, using the finest pen and the smallest handwriting, the letters as tight to each other as he can make them, so small and so tight against each other that at times he himself cannot decipher what he has written. But paper is so expensive and so difficult to find! And memories are so valuable! How could he leave his diaries behind? Besides, he uses most of the material in those diaries to write articles about his trips. That is how he has been making a living, by writing travel articles for magazines and newspapers. Barely enough of a living for himself—and definitely not enough of a living to support a wife.

And yet, having a wife is what he yearns for. Having a woman by his side to share his bed, his life, and his dreams.

Lost somewhere in the early pages of last year's diary, he wrote,

> The night is long and silence presses painfully over my heart.
> Why does this emptiness weigh so heavily upon my soul?
> But even the longest of nights must come to an end.
> The sun calls me to work. I must let go of my pain
> and fold over my tired shoulders the wounded wing of the poet.

Less than a month after those lines appeared in his diary, he was rereading them, and it seemed to him as if those lines had been written by someone else. The desperate loneliness he saw in them overwhelmed him.

It was then he said to himself, All right Julián, *When* are you going to marry?

After all, he told himself at the time, he was already a man of twenty-five, and a man that age is supposed to start thinking seriously about getting a wife, starting a family, and settling down. Everybody knows that.

That very same night, after supper, he called on Lucía, the daughter of a well-to-do exiled Cuban lawyer who for the last eleven years has been living in Mexico City, and the only unmarried Cuban woman he knew in that city.

In her house, Lucía, her father, and her two aunts had provided a Cuban oasis for Julián. There, Julián no longer felt a foreigner in a strange land, because there he no longer had to feel embarrassed about his speaking Spanish with a Cuban accent. During the few moments he spent there, at Lucía's house, he could close his eyes and feel that he was back home, with his sisters, with his mother. Even with his father, his Spaniard-to-the-core father, who would no longer talk to his rebellious son because Julián, through his writings demanding liberty for Cuba, had shown great disrespect for the Spanish Crown—and thus for him. But a father whom Julián loved and admired, a man who taught Julián about what it takes to be a man: about integrity. And honor. And truth. And about keeping to one's word, no matter what.

Lucía was not expecting Julián to call on her that night; he never called on Thursdays. But if she was surprised by his appearance—and at such a late hour—her face did not show it. She welcomed him politely with a smile, the same way she had always welcomed him, accompanied him to the parlor, gently asked him to have a seat, and told him she would be right back. Moments later, she came back and began to pour the divine-smelling hot chocolate she had the family's Mexican Indian cook prepare for Julián. With it, Lucía served a large tray of churros—crisp deep-fried pastries covered with powdered sugar—which she knew Julián loved so much.

Julián took the cup of hot chocolate she offered him and began to stir the hot drink to cool it, his eyes fixed on the swirling liquid. Still not daring to look up at her, standing tall by his side, he blew gently on the steaming chocolate, as if gathering his strength, and then he said, his tense voice barely audible:

"Lucía, would . . . would you marry me?"

Not pausing, not even for the briefest moment, Lucía answered, "Why, of course," her voice calm and firm. Then, without adding another word, she proceeded to pour herself a cup of the hot chocolate, after which she sat quietly on the rocking chair opposite Julián's, the way she always did when he was there calling on her.

Julián had not expected her quick response.

Almost spilling his cup of chocolate, he raised his eyes to her, looked at this tall, thin, rather prim woman stiffly sitting across from him as she delicately sipped her steaming hot chocolate—a woman of whom he knew very little, almost nothing; a woman whose eyes had seldom if ever met his—and wondered, What have I done!? He had asked her on an impulse. On an urge. Out of desperation. The nights of a man with no country can be very, *very* long, and very, *very* lonesome—books or no books.

But what was done was done.

And now that he has done it, he cannot wait to have Lucía in his bed, by his side. That is the reason he is here now, in Guatemala. To get that job he has been offered so he can send for her. A teacher may not make that much, he knows, but the security of a monthly salary will allow him to marry her. That is precisely what he told Lucía he would do when he left Mexico City over two months ago, the day he gave Lucía his most sacred word of honor that he would come back for her to make her his wife.

Anxious to get started on the long journey that remains to get to Guatemala City, the inland capital of Guatemala, Julián picks up his battered old suitcase and asks a stevedore on the dock where he might purchase one of the palm-leaf hats such as the one the man is wearing.

"*Allí, señor,*" the short, stocky Mayan stevedore answers, pointing to a small palm-leaf-roofed stand, just a little past the customs house.

"*Gracias,*" Julián says.

Minutes later, wearing his badly wrinkled three-piece black suit, a Guatemalan stevedore's wide-brimmed palm-leaf hat, and carrying an old battered suitcase, light with clothes but heavy with books and diaries, Julián enters the small Mayan village of Puerto Dulce, by the Caribbean Sea, the first stop on his long, long way to his future: The wondrous, mysterious, and magical Guatemala City, which lies way up in the mountains, miles away to the west.

He takes a deep breath, raises his eyes, looks ahead of him, smiles broadly, and then, walking as fast as his limp will allow, he decisively starts for the center of the village, looking for an Indian cantina where he has been told he can make arrangements to catch the next train of mules to leave for Guatemala City. And as he does, he begins to sing Yubirio's bawdy Cuban song to himself, heavily underlining the *Eh*, just as Yubirio did, and letting the power of music—that makes life so much easier—put a rhythmic lilt to his steps.

> *The man who doesn't know how to drink*
> *and doesn't know how to make love,*
> *What good is a man like that? Eh?*
> *What good is a man like that?*

CHAPTER II

I T IS PAST NOON of the Friday before Easter, and Julián finds the tiny village of Puerto Dulce incredibly crowded with Mayan Indians who have come from near and far to join in a yearly ritual essential to pacify the two gods they fear the most: The god who spurts tongues of fire from the mountaintops, and the god who shakes the Earth. This is a spring ritual long practiced in their own Mayan religion that by powerful magic the Catholic white priests have transformed into a different one: the elaborate procession that takes place every year on Good Friday.

Mayan men, women, and children—all of them wearing black mourning cloaks over the most incredibly embroidered and colorful garments Julián has ever seen—stand shoulder to shoulder, two or three deep, lining both sides of the village's only street, which is exceedingly muddy because it had been raining almost incessantly for the last two days.

Barefoot, hats in hand, watching in stoic silence, they focus their emotionless eyes on a Mayan boy, barely seven, who, also barefoot but dressed in a black cassock topped with an almost transparent white cotton surplice, is leading the procession, walking tremulously along the muddy, narrow, little street, carrying in his hands a tall, thin, silver cross lifted way up high. Two older Indian boys, similarly attired, follow him, walking side by side. One of them holds in his raised hands a silver chalice that glitters in the midday sun, which has finally appeared from behind frighteningly dark clouds, and which has begun to shine dazzlingly bright and excruciatingly hot. The other boy carries a silver censer that he constantly swings in a gentle pendulumlike action, creating clouds of a strong-smelling myrrh incense around him. A priest—the only white man Julián can see in the entire crowd—follows them. Robed in a thick black velvet cape embroidered with a silver skull and bones, he is sweating heavily, while his booted feet trample with difficulty through the muddy street as he utters strange words in a strange language nobody seems to understand. Following the priest, a dozen short, stocky, and powerfully built Mayan men who have been chosen for this great honor carry on their shoulders a large float, obviously heavy. They are wearing white cotton pants, folded up to mid calf, and white long-sleeve shirts, folded up way above their elbows almost to their armpits, revealing their dark-skinned, thick arm muscles, which, like their foreheads and tight neck muscles, are glistening with thick drops of sweat as their bare feet sink deeply into the mud under the heavy weight of the float they are carrying.

On the float there are three life-sized statues: Two of them are images of white women, both of them with pale blue glass eyes and long curly wigs made of real blond hair, and both of them dressed in heavily embroidered purple and brown robes made just for this occasion. The statues of the two women are kneeling down on the floor of the float, their polychromed wooden faces weeping carved tears. Their suffering faces are turned up toward the third statue—the standing figure of a tired white man with a long curly beard and with the saddest eyes Julián has ever seen. This man, crowned with thorns and dressed in a real red-velvet robe, appears to be struggling hard to carry on his sagging shoulders what must be a very heavy cross. He seems to be moving painfully and slowly—as painfully and as slowly as the float moves—toward the little whitewashed church located at a small plaza at the other end of the street.

Something does not look right to Julián as he looks at the figure of the man carrying the cross on the float, but he is not able to point his finger at exactly what it is that seems so wrong to him.

As the float passes in front of the crowd, the Indians kneel down on one knee and cross themselves, as they have been taught to do by the white priest, and then they stand up and throw large, colorful paper flowers to the figure of the sad white man bent under the weight of the cross while they shout words of prayer in their own Mayan language. Once the float has gone by them, the Indians join in behind it, slowly walking along the muddy street, heavily treading on the colorful paper flowers and burying them into the mud, their stoic faces showing no trace of any emotion whatsoever as they follow the float all the way to the small church at the end of the street. When the float finally enters the church, all the Indians who are following it crowd themselves inside. Then, after the float is placed on a high altar at the far end of the small nave, the priest begins to waft a little cloud of incense and sprinkle a few drops of holy water on the face of each of the Indians, who wait patiently in line to get this token of hope coming from the representative of God himself.

Julián, from afar, holding his heavy suitcase in his hand, follows the Indians with his eyes as they go into the church and line up for the blessing. Then, walking on the mud-spattered boardwalk along the opposite side of the street, now almost totally empty, he goes to a small one-story-high building, painted pale yellow, that is located right across the plaza from the church. A large, hand-painted sign hangs over the louvered swinging doors, which are painted a deep green. Spelled out in big bold red letters, the sign reads CANTINA, each letter heavily ornamented with colorful painted flowers.

In strong contrast to the blinding brightness outside the cantina, it is very dark, almost pitch black, inside the small tavern, which smells of rancid oil, lard, garlic, cilantro, tequila, mescal, and sweat; and once Julián enters, he has to wait for a long while until his eyes adjust to the sudden darkness and are able to see.

"*Buenas tardes,*" he finally says, politely addressing his greeting to all of the few people inside, all of them older Mayan men dressed in white who, not believing in the magic of white priests, have not joined in the procession. "Has the mule train come in yet?" Julián asks the man behind the counter, a thin old Indian man, also dressed in white, whose sharp black eyes look distrustfully at Julián as he shakes his head from side to side. "When is it due?" Julián asks, as he places his suitcase on the floor, takes out his pocket watch from one of the pockets of his vest, and looks at it.

The thin old Indian man raises his head and looks at Julián, studying him. No white man has ever joined the mule train—that he knows of. Not when there is a comfortable—though expensive—stagecoach that leaves every day right after the last ship arrives in port. Julián smiles at the old Indian man and places his pocket watch inside his vest pocket. Still distrustful of this pale young white man in the black suit, the old Indian, not saying a word, makes a gesture with his head, pointing out toward the plaza, indicating the mule train's arrival.

Julián turns his head and sees, at the far end of the small plaza, a train of mules that is just arriving from La Ciudad, as people refer to Guatemala City. Julián then turns around again, leans against the counter, and asks the old Indian man for a shot of gin, which he later follows with another as the mule train arrives in front of the cantina and as the muleteers begin their long task of emptying their baskets filled with city goods.

It is only after serving Julián a third shot of gin, followed by a local dish made of fried squid wrapped in banana leaves, that the cantina man takes a more friendly stance toward Julián and answers his questions, telling him that his mule train is led by Anacleto, an older half-Mayan, half-white man who, Julián notices, seems to be led by his much-younger wife, Ixhula, the only woman in the group, an all-Mayan Indian woman who orders not only her husband but every one of the other muleteers around.

As the muleteers unload their mules, Julián, enjoying still another shot of gin, looks at Anacleto's wife closely, admiring her handsome face, which could have been carved on the walls of Mayan temples. Her profile is elegant; her nose, small; her mouth, brief; her forehead, well modeled; her chin, sharp; and she wears the long braids of her black hair as a crown above her head in an almost classic Greek style. And yet, despite all of these perfections of form, this woman handles, ties, cinches, and uncinches a mule with such a cruelty that it would disgust anyone looking at her, Julián the first. She hits the poor beast, smacks it, flogs it, whips it, shouts at it, screams at it harsh words after harsh words, adding insult after insult to injury after injury, while the poor animal keeps recoiling and recoiling from her in abject fear.

How can a woman be capable of this much cruelty? Julián asks himself. He has never seen a woman behave in such a way, be so cruel to anything, anybody, certainly not to an animal. He has seen a man be cruel, oh yes, many a time. He has a limp to show for man's cruelty. But a woman? Never. What could make a woman behave like that? he wonders. And yet, that muleteer, Anacleto, must love that woman, Julián tells himself, he simply must. After all, Ixhula is his woman, his wife. Julián, puzzled, shakes his head. The ways of men, he thinks. How difficult they are to understand! Would he love Lucía should she ever turn out to be as cruel and as demanding as this Indian woman is? Could Lucía ever be anything at all like this other woman?

He shakes his head once more, and then, catching himself, has no choice but to chuckle to himself. Here I go again, he thinks, wondering about married life. He orders another shot of gin, and as he tastes it he tells himself, I'm sure all men tremble and shake when they think of spending the rest of their lives with the same woman. Will we run out of things to say to each other?

For Julián, talking to Lucía has never been easy—she has always been so elegantly distant, discreet, even aloof. He certainly can't understand her. But then, who can ever understand women? he has been told by all of his men friends. And if he can't understand Lucía, how could he expect Lucía to understand him? Every time he begins to talk about his dreams of freeing Cuba from the enslaving Spain, she dismisses it, waving her hand gently, and saying, "Oh, yes, yes, yes, Cuba," as if she had heard it all before, which probably she has. What else do Cuban men in exile talk about? But still, he has seen other Cuban women talk eagerly about the revolution and the guerrilla war that has been going on in Cuba for such a long time, and wondering why more has not yet been accomplished. Soon it will be ten years since the criollo revolutionary war was started in 1868, and still nothing has been achieved. Negroes are still slaves; Cubans, despite paying exorbitant taxes to Spain for what the Spaniards call "protection," still lack representation in the Spanish courts; and the jails keep filling up with men of all ages, of all races, of all classes, whose only crime is that they believe in freedom.

Before their engagement, Julián thought Lucía did not want to talk about serious things, that she thought, like most women in her class do, that women should not talk about war. "War is man's talk." Julián often heard his own mother say that to his sisters whenever one of them brought up the topic of the continuing war between criollo Cubans and Spain. But Julián knew that his mother had to say things like that whenever that topic arose, to avoid unnecessary confrontations between him— the only son in his family, a born-in-Cuba criollo man who strongly believed in Cuba's freedom from Spain—and his father, a former Spanish army lieutenant living on a Spanish army pension.

Still, Julián hoped that after his engagement to Lucía, things would change between them, that she would listen to him talking about his dreams and agree with them and support them. And yes, things did change. But certainly not in the direction he expected.

Since the moment he proposed to her and they became engaged, over a year ago, all Lucía talks about is either the wedding this, or the wedding that. Things need to be bought, sewn, knitted, quilted, and embroidered. Scores of sheets, and of pillowcases, and of tablecloths, and of napkins, and of . . . of *everything!* There seems to be so much an engaged woman must do before she becomes a wife! The few minutes they share together are spent talking about things Julián finds inconsequential, if not boring. Who cares what color will be in fashion when they finally wed? He smiles to himself. The husband-to-be still doesn't have a steady job, and all the wife-to-be can think about is her trousseau. Women! he tells himself, as he orders one more shot of gin. But things will change when they marry, that much he is sure of. Lucía has Cuban blood. He knows with total certainty that she will agree with his dreams and support them any way she can, as a wife must. As soon as all of this business with the damn wedding is over, he tells himself. As soon as they get married. But for that to happen, the first thing he must do is to secure that teaching job Professor Saavedra is supposed to be holding for him in Guatemala City. And to get that job, the first thing he must do is get there. As soon as he can. Right away. Before someone else gets it.

That thought awakens him.

He looks out over the louvered swinging doors leading into the cantina, and realizing that Ixhula, Anacleto, and the rest of the muleteers have almost finished the emptying of their cargo baskets, he pays for his drinks and food, and goes to where the half-Mayan man and his all-Mayan wife are. After he greets them and a few words are exchanged, Anacleto gladly agrees to take him along, back to the city, for a few pesos.

"We'll start out first thing tomorrow morning," Anacleto says. "And I mean *first* thing tomorrow morning, señor," he adds. "We always leave way before dawn, because, otherwise the heat of the sun will—"

But Julián, who is desperate to get to Guatemala City—and to that job—interrupts Anacleto. "Couldn't we leave this afternoon?" he asks. "Please," he says, "it's urgent." Julián pauses. "*Really* urgent," he adds.

It is the way he says it.

Anacleto looks at Julián and sees in Julián's eyes the same intensity he heard in Julián's words, a pressing intensity that implies severe need. The old half-Indian man stares deeply into Julián's deep blue eyes, trying to decipher the reason behind his earnest request. "Well, if you insist," Anacleto says, after a while. "We will leave this afternoon, right after the siesta."

"But that's going to cost him two pesos more, no?" interjects Ixhula, who, standing next to her husband, is looking intently into Anacleto's eyes.

Anacleto looks first at Ixhula, a hint of anger on his face, then at Julián. "Two pesos more?" he asks, with a hint of an apology in his voice.

"Two pesos more," Julián answers, nodding his head and smiling at the old Indian. "Is there anything I should get for this trip?" Julián asks Anacleto.

Ixhula answers for her husband. "A good strong jute hammock," she says, staring deeply into Julián's eyes, as if she were measuring him, this broad-shouldered pale white man with the deep blue eyes and the eagerness in his voice, whose face is made to seem even paler by the dusty and wrinkled black suit he is wearing. "You can get it from Zecuato, the cantina man," she adds, pointing with her head to the cantina.

THAT NIGHT, the first night Julián spends in the Guatemalan jungle, is also the first night he ever spends in a hammock, which he hangs between two of the several tall trees that outline one of the large clearings muleteers use as designated stops on the way to and from Guatemala City.

Surrounded by the fantastic sounds of the rain forest, he shares the muleteers' meal, a little bit of beef jerky and dried bread, which he accompanies with swallows of the bitter quinine water they all drink to ward off the dreaded malaria, followed by longer swallows of the sweet-smelling gin he has begun to love, because it covers the taste of the quinine.

After a while, more than slightly inebriated, he finds his way back to his hammock, where he lies down. And though he is dead tired, and his thighs—unused to riding a mule—are painfully throbbing with incredible cramps, he gets ahold of his last diary, and under the little bit of light of the full moon that pierces through the heavy canopy of the trees above him, and the light of the distant fire in the center of the clearing, he manages to scribble down a few words for the magazine article he is planning to write about this exciting, adventurous trip.

Julián looks up one more time at the tropical night that envelops him and smells the intriguing scents of the intoxicating jungle that surrounds him, and, for the briefest of moments, he stops worrying about how little money he has and about that job he hopes to get, as he inhales deeply the perfume of the lush tropical vegetation enfolding him.

Then, right before passing out, he scribbles other words in his diary, words so intimate that he will excise them from the magazine article.

> *Half asleep in my hammock, more than meditate, I dream.*
> *There, in my dreams, I am embraced by the ones I love:*
> *my friends, my family, my beloved mother,*
> *all of them still crying in Cuba for me.*
>
> *And I see behind them all, in the faraway distance,*
> *my Cuba, glowing radiantly with the bliss of freedom.*
> *Then, as wings get lost, and as a spirit or a cloud goes by,*
> *lifting away the heavy pressure on my lonely soul,*
>
> *I hold tight against my heart the one I love, the one I dream of.*
> *And with her body pressed tight against my body,*
> *and with her lips pressed tight against my lips,*
> *I slowly fall asleep, dreaming of love.*

CHAPTER III

B UT THAT WAS THEN, a week ago last Friday.

Since then, Julián has spent the longest eight days he has ever spent in his entire life, riding on Pellejuda, pronounced Pay-a-hoo-dah, a name that means Bag o'Bones—"the skinniest, the oldest, the meanest, the most rebellious, the most recalcitrant, and the most stubborn mule the mountains of Puerto Dulce have ever seen"—words he wrote in his diary last night while thinking that Ixhula, Anacleto's wife, was probably not that cruel after all.

This morning, as Julián reaches the top of yet another mountain and stops to take a deep breath, he lifts his wide-brimmed palm-leaf hat, which he has been wearing as low on his head as he can, trying to elude the direct heat of this incredible sun—which he is sure is much hotter than the sun of his native Cuba. And then, taking his handkerchief from one of the pockets of his vest, he wipes his forehead once again with it; a useless act because the handkerchief is as wet as his shirt, both of them as soaking wet as the rest of his clothes. He closes his eyes and dreams of cold water embracing him.

Lord, what he would give for a bath!

He is glad he decided to take off his black coat when he started on this exhausting trip along this narrow trail that goes first across the low wetlands and then up the mountains, and wishes he could have done the same with the rest of his black clothes: his vest and his pants. He should have gotten some thin white cotton pants, like the muleteers wear. But, where would he have carried his revolver then? He pats it, loaded and ready to go, carefully concealed under his vest. Again he rubs his eyes with the handkerchief, hoping—and failing—to catch with it the thick drops of sweat that hang from his dark, thick eyebrows. Then, after shaking his head forcefully so the thick drops of sweat fall heavily on the forest floor, he opens his eyes and glances down through the dense jungle of the mountaintops to look at what lies ahead of him.

And what he sees startles him.

There ahead of him, framed by the thickest, the darkest, and the most exuberant of rain-forest greenery, and surrounded by the conical peaks of distant volcanoes, is a broad valley, through whose center runs a meandering river that shimmers in the sparkling early morning light as if it were a glittering ribbon of silver. The valley is shrouded by a thick, pale gray mist that hovers over it, moving very languidly. And piercing through that mist there appear to be dozens of tall, white, pointing spires, almost obelisks.

Julián shakes his head. Traveling through the Guatemalan jungle must have done something to his sense of vision, he thinks. Or to his sense of reality. It must be this incredible heat and this unbearable humidity, he tells himself. He takes his handkerchief, wrings the moisture from it, and pats his forehead again, wondering if, despite all the quinine he's been drinking, he has caught malaria.

He has been told malaria begins with a very high fever, after which follow one hallucination after the next, hallucinations so vivid and so realistic that people swear they have actually lived them—if they are able to survive them. Is this the first of such hallucinations? He glances again at the vision in the distance, focusing his eyes on the distant white spires, trying to make sense of what he sees.

What *are* those pointed things? he asks himself as he squints, sharpening his focus.

Bell towers . . . ?

Julián rubs his eyes once again as he looks down at the distant, shrouded valley in front of him. Could those things really be bell towers? He shakes his head in disbelief. Then he looks at them again. They *are* bell towers! That's what those white, pointing spires really are. Bell towers! Dozens, hundreds of them! Is that possible?

He is not the only one who has seen them.

Pellejuda, his mule, must have seen them as well, for her normally arduous trot suddenly becomes first a soft gentle gallop, then a full-blast run as she—and the entire mule train—aim for their eagerly awaited destination, the great City of Guatemala, lying on a high plateau, up in the mountains, close to the clouds; a magnificently beautiful place where spring is said to be perennial.

And so it seems.

Yes, Julián tells himself as he enters this wondrous place where the weather has suddenly become dry and wonderfully pleasant. He is no longer sweating as he had been. He takes his black coat, which he had neatly rolled and tied on the left side of his intractable mule, next to the machete he had there, under his left thigh, and as he puts the jacket on, he again feels his revolver hidden under his vest, next to the leather bag where he keeps the little money he still has left. Then he smiles expectantly as he looks all about him.

Proudly upright amidst the cloudy mist that envelops them, the dozens of bell towers dotting the landscape look to Julián almost like the tall white masts of dozens of great ships, anchored to the dry earth. As he gets closer to them, Julián notices the broad, inflexibly straight streets that delineate the city, as if those streets—made of hard, well-compacted dirt edged with wide stone sidewalks instead of boardwalks—were the perfectly symmetrical lines of a colossal chessboard. And as the mist begins to lift and the atmosphere begins to clear, Julián realizes that he is indeed within a wonderful place: a white, calm, peaceful, and majestic city, where groups of glossy, dark green magnolia trees catching the sun seem to glow brilliantly among bunches of immaculately white buildings. "Like dark emeralds amongst white opals," he will note in his diary.

All of the buildings, except for the slender bell towers which strive hard to reach the sky, are only one story high. This is because of the frequent earthquakes; earthquakes so powerful that, centuries ago, they leveled the former great city of Guatemala, now called Antigua, the *Old* Guatemala City—a city twice built and twice destroyed, first by a volcano, then by an earthquake, Julián remembers reading. This new Guatemala City Julián is admiring was rebuilt a third time, this time miles away from Antigua, in an attempt to elude both the dark clouds of volcanic ash coming from above and the thick tongues of seismic fire coming from below. But still hardly a year goes by that the new city does not shake and quake while the Mayan Indians who serve the white folks rush to pray to their ancient gods for help, and while the white folk and the Ladinos—the half-white, half-Mayan people who inhabit most of the city—rush to pray to the all-powerful Christian God introduced by the Spanish conquistador Pedro de Alvarado more than three centuries ago.

Julián lets Anacleto and his wife, Ixhula, lead him to a house they know of, in the Mayan part of town, where an older Mayan woman will let him have a room for very little money. Once there, Julián is shown to a small room, almost a cell, painted pastel pink, with a tiled floor, a small window, and a crucifix on one wall. The room has a bed in the corner. A *real* bed with a *real* mattress! Julián thinks as he looks at it and smiles. No longer a hammock or the hard planks of a ship's deck!—and next to the bed there is a small table, where he places his old, heavy suitcase. He opens it, and as he begins to take out the neatly folded black suit he keeps inside, he asks the nice, barrel-chested older Mayan woman with the long black braids tied above her head who has rented him this room, "Please, señora, could you tell me where may I go to take a bath? I have been on a mule for the last eight days of my life, and I think I'm beginning to smell like her. Don't you think?" he adds, as he sniffs the sleeves of his coat.

There is something about Julián that women find very attractive, almost irresistible. He is a good-looking young man, true, but that doesn't quite explain it. There's something else. It may be his eyes, deeply blue and deeply set, sparkling dreamy eyes that seem incapable of lying. Or it may be his voice, deeply soft and mellow. Or it may be his smile, always genuine and sincere. Or it may be nothing more than his sexuality, an innocent sexuality that is that much more attractive because it is understated, not obvious as it is in most young men his age. In every one of his gestures, in every one of his smiles, in every single action he takes, he is attractive. Even when he is doing nothing but joking about the way his dusty black clothes smell.

It is to this innocent sexuality that the nice older Mayan woman responds, despite her knowing that she is not supposed to respond at all to a white man—no Indian is ever supposed to notice how white folk behave.

And least of all to notice how white folk smell!

But when she sees him sniff at his own clothes and joke about it, she is surprised by his candor, and despite her better judgment, the older Mayan woman begins to laugh, loud belly laughs totally out of control.

"Aha!" Julián says, looking at her reaction. "I knew it! I must smell *worse* than a mule! Much, much worse than what I even imagined!"

The woman, who finds it difficult to stop her laughing, finally manages to say, "Forgive me, señor. I did not mean to be disrespectful."

Julián looks at her, feigning indignation, and flashes his bewitching smile as he says, "I'll forgive you as soon as you tell me where to go for a bath."

The Mayan woman smiles back at him. "There's a barbershop right around the corner, on La Calle de las Flores—the Street of the Flowers," she says. "The barbershop has a bathroom in the rear," she adds, "and the barber, Cholito, is supposed to be very good." She pauses, deeply embarrassed. "And he's not too expensive," she dares to add.

"Now you're telling me that on top of a bath I also need a haircut?" Julián says, jokingly, making the woman laugh again, though this time she covers her mouth with her right hand.

Julián turns around and looks at himself in the small mirror above the table next to his bed. He has not looked at himself since he departed Veracruz, in Mexico, and when he sees himself he does not believe his own eyes. He had removed his palm-leaf hat when he entered the house of the Mayan woman, as a gentleman is supposed to do, and now, as he looks at himself in the mirror, he sees that most of his face is darkly tanned, almost blackened, by the sun, except for the part of his forehead that was under the hat, which is as white as it can be, a clear-cut line separating dark and light areas. His hair, normally unruly and difficult to tame, has grown in wild ringlets behind his ears, and he certainly could use a shave. Beards are not in fashion for young men, he knows. He caresses his mustache, thick and dark, like his hair. I'll keep the mustache, he thinks. He unpacks his clean suit, to take with him to the barbershop, to change into after his bath.

"Did you say the Street of the Flowers?" he asks the Mayan woman.

"*Sí, señor,*" she answers. "Right around the corner. As you exit, turn right and then right again. You cannot miss it."

.   .   .   .

"DON'T TELL ME, let me guess!" says Cholito the barber, jokingly pinching his nostrils closed with his fingers as a way of welcoming Julián into his tiny barbershop, which is totally open to the street, the bifolding louvered doors neatly folded at either side of the entrance archway. "Just in from the Caribbean coast, right?" Cholito adds, rolling his eyes as he looks up and down at Julián. He does not let Julián say a word. "On a mule, right?"

Cholito, who is as short and as stocky as he is spicy, is a half-white, half-Indian Ladino man who takes great pride in his light, white-man's skin, though he has very little facial hair and a more-than-thin Indian mustache. Dressed totally in white—except for his slippers, which are heavily ornamented with colorful stars and roses—Cholito stands by an old, water-stained cane barber chair located deep inside his shop. He is wearing a large, beautifully tailored straw hat trimmed with an elaborately embroidered ribbon band, similar to the hats for sale that hang on the back wall of his shop, below which, on a low shelf, there is a collection of old books that have lost their covers piled next to a lot of yellowing newspapers thrown one on top of the other in a jumbled disarray. Cholito, ever so elegant, lets his fancy hat hang fashionably in back of his neck and proudly lets his long hair, which strongly smells of perfume, hang loose; hair that has the shiny black color of his Indian mother's and the long soft curls he inherited from the white man who fathered him, a man Cholito never got to know.

Still pinching his nostrils, Cholito points with a manicured index finger to the back of the barbershop, where Julián sees a door with a sign hand painted on it, the big bold red letters reading: BATH.

As soon as Cholito heats the water and fills the large tin tub, Julián gets in and lets the warm water embrace him. The room Julián is in is tiny, almost a closet. Papered with full-color prints advertising this hair tonic or the other, it shines with sparkling cleanliness, just as Cholito does, and it is next to the kitchen of the cantina next door, from which emanate delicious smells of food—*real* food, no longer the dried beef jerky or the dried bread that has been Julián's diet for the last eight exhaustingly long days.

Julián takes the soap in his hands and, after he luxuriates in the way it smells and feels—a sandalwood soap that, to him, speaks of all the wonders of civilization—he decides that as soon as he can, this very afternoon, after the siesta is over, he is going to go to the Escuela Central and introduce himself to Professor Saavedra. I hope that job is still available, Julián thinks, as he rubs and rubs himself as vigorously as he can, trying hard to eradicate the smells of Pellejuda, his mule, which he thinks may have gotten deeply under his skin. He surely does not want to smell like a mule when he finally gets to meet the man he hopes will be his future boss.

After his bath, all dressed up in his clean black suit, cleanly shaven, his unruly hair cut and tamed, his thick mustache neatly trimmed, Julián, feeling like a brand-new man and smelling of sandalwood soap and hair tonic, rushes to the cantina next door, where he savors a succulent dish of pepián, a delicious Guatemalan Mayan stew that gets its flavor from toasted pumpkin and sesame seeds, cilantro, hot chiles and burnt tortillas—his first hot meal in over a week.

After this delicious meal, Julián goes back to his room.

There, the siesta silence of the sleepy city surrounding him, he takes off his suit, folds it carefully, places it on the little table by the side of his bed—he does not want it to get wrinkled—and wearing nothing but his underpants, he lies on his bed: a real bed that despite its thin, cotton-stuffed mattress feels heavenly.

Then, closing his eyes, he starts to daydream about what it will be like to have Lucía lying naked on his bed, by his side, her long, black hair enveloping him.

But every time he is about to create her image in his mind, something happens, the way it always does when he starts to think of her. Lucía's face begins to evanesce little by little and, superimposed on Lucía's face, another face begins to appear, a face he has often seen in his dreams, but a face he has never seen in his life: the face of a woman who at times looks somewhat like Consuelo, the young Cuban woman who, when Julián was not yet fifteen, showed him, for the first time, what a great thing it was to be a man to a woman.

This mythical woman now in front of him, this woman of his dreams—whom in his diaries he calls his "idealized, unattainable beauty"—looks him in the eye with an intimate look that mixes Lucía's modest, shy, ethereal kind of love, with Consuelo's sensual, bold, bodily passion.

It is this mysterious woman of his dreams who, for years, has inspired him to write poems in his diaries; the latest one, written only two nights ago, while he lay in his hammock, deep in the Guatemalan jungle.

I dreamed it. Did you dream it as well? Your hair,
unpinned by love, was falling in loose drapes
around my wounded head, cradled within your lap.

I look for you, search for you. My love bursts out of me and lives
outside myself knowing that you are near: Every womanly shape
I see stirs my soul while my lonely body yearns for you.

To the divine love of souls I place my claim,
while our naked bodies immolate themselves with a fiery love!
So, please, come alive! Become real! Soon!

Let your hair, unpinned by love, weave through my fingers.
Let the bed shelter us. And let the loose waves
of your hair soothe my pain and cradle us into life!

Caressed by the ethereal yet sensual look of this mythical woman of his dreams, Julián, for the briefest of moments, stops worrying about tomorrow and escapes into a different world. And in that magical world, after the ardent mouth of this woman of his dreams avidly tastes his, and after her ardent body avidly opens up to his, Julián, released, falls asleep with a smile on his face.

CHAPTER IV

"A S YOU CAN SEE, Julián," says Professor Saavedra as he shows Julián around the Escuela Central, "this is a monumental building. Very well built too. Look at the thickness of those pillars," he adds, pointing toward the colossal Ionic marble columns that border the immense central patio of the school. "Not long ago this was the home of a very wealthy group of Spanish priests who were expelled from Guatemala by Don Manuel, the general who liberated Guatemala from Spain," Professor Saavedra adds. "Don Manuel had to expel them because those priests, whose salaries were paid by the Spanish Crown, did not believe that church and state should be separated, as Don Manuel proposed, and had begun to interfere in politics, where—as I'm sure you'll agree—priests do *not* belong."

After going across the patio, totally empty because the school holds no classes on Saturdays, they arrive at Professor Saavedra's office, a large room that has a very high ceiling, coffered and heavily ornamented, and that is lined by magnificently bound books, floor to ceiling, placed inside Honduras mahogany cabinets behind filigreed bronze-and-glass doors. At each corner of the room there is a black granite pedestal holding a white marble bust of a famous historical figure: Plato. Cicero. Washington. Bolívar.

"A year after those priests left," continues Saavedra, "when President Rubios was elected, he expropriated their vast properties, and the mansions they lived in, like this one, became either hospitals or schools. Did

you happen to go by the Correos building on your way up here?" he asks
Julián. Julián nods. "Well, that huge building used to be a convent,"
Saavedra says, "benefiting only the select few. Now, as a post office, it
benefits all."

With a gesture, Professor Saavedra offers Julián a seat by the elaborately carved mahogany two-sided partners desk with its dark green
tooled-leather top that is in the center of the room.

As he sits down, Julián feels the smoothness of the leather with which
the high-back chair has been upholstered, while he turns his head in all
directions, looking at the collection of books in the cases, trying to make
out their titles.

But Professor Saavedra's words demand his attention.

"Since then, most of those priests have come back and have learned to
keep their business where it belongs: inside the churches," Saavedra says,
"and their salaries are now paid by the Vatican. But, as you can imagine . . ."
Saavedra offers Julián a cigar from the large silver-and-ebony humidor lined
with cedar he keeps on his desk. "*Cuban,*" he interrupts himself as he points
to the cigars, "like us. *The best!*" he adds with pride as he chuckles.

"As I was saying," he continues, "as you can imagine, the name Don
Manuel, to this day, cannot be mentioned in the presence of those priests,
because, even though they were handsomely compensated, they still think
they lost all of this"—he points to the magnificent room he and Julián are
in—"because of him. Something which, of course, makes the general
laugh every time he hears it, because making this building into a school
was President Rubios's idea, not Don Manuel's."

After Julián takes a cigar in his hand and smells it, closing his eyes the way
Cuban men do when evaluating a cigar, Saavedra takes another cigar in his
own hand and, pulling out of the top drawer of his desk a silver cutter, snips
the end of his cigar and passes the cutter to Julián, who does the same.

"By the way," says Saavedra as he takes a tall, cylindrical, leather-topped
silver box from his desk, opens it, takes a large wooden match out of it, and
then offers the box to Julián, who takes another match, "one of Don
Manuel's daughters, the middle one, still comes to school here. Her older
sister did too. She graduated—when was it? A couple of years ago? Those
girls . . . Wait till you meet them. They are very much like their father."

Saavedra strikes his match against a pumice stone sitting on top of his desk and lights his cigar, turning it around very slowly in his hand, while Julián does the same.

"Don Manuel—that's how the general likes to be called—Don Manuel is truly a man worthy of our century, Julián," Saavedra says admiringly, as he watches how the flame of the match begins to ignite his cigar. "With a group of only thirty-three men—all of them with balls as big as the general's—he started a revolution in Comitán, right at the Mexican border." His cigar now lit, Saavedra blows gently on it, to stop the flames, and still with the cigar in his hand, he smells the delicious aroma that emanates from it. "And in less than a month, Guatemala, as big a country as it is, was free from Spain, without losing a single battle!"

Saavedra takes his cigar to his mouth and for the first time he tastes it, his eyes closed in total ecstasy. After a while he exhales. "Nothing like a real Habano, eh, Julián?" He smells it again. "Now the general wants to unify all of the Central American countries into one large federal country, like the United States, so we can all help each other. And he'll probably get his way, if he lives long enough, I can bet you on that!" He pauses and looks at Julián. "Do you know, Julián, that Don Manuel himself told me that if he were a young man again, nothing but *nothing* would stop *him* from going to Cuba and teaching those damn Spaniards a thing or two!"

Saavedra, who has been standing by the side of his desk, moves behind it and sits.

"Well, enough said about politics and our school. Now let's talk about you. There are ten million questions I would like to ask you, but I'll settle for just one."

He faces Julián and smiles at him.

"What can I do to help you?"

LATER ON, as Saavedra walks Julián across the patio, back to the entrance door, he has his right arm on top of Julián's broad shoulders, which are sagging.

"Don't look so worried, my friend," Saavedra says. "I'm sure Minister Andrújal, the minister of public instruction, will approve of your joining our school full time next year, when school begins again. By then the copy of your diploma that you requested from Zaragoza in Spain should have arrived here. Those things take a lot of time, you know. I wish I had the power to override the rules, but the minister is the only one who can officially appoint you, a foreigner, as a full-time teacher." He pats Julián's shoulder gently. "But until the next school year begins, teaching part-time, a couple of classes a week for the remainder of this school year, won't be so bad. Sure, you won't make as much, but you'll have lots of free time for your writing. I'll tell you what. Tomorrow . . . No, tomorrow is Sunday. I mean Monday. Monday, after we go to the ministry, I'll take you to El Ateneo. That's a very exclusive club where only the most influential—and the wealthiest—men in Guatemala gather. You know: to play billiards, talk about politics and women, and fight an occasional duel—the usual stuff. A lot of these men are very interested in the future of Cuba, Julián. They are looking forward to trading freely with Cuba without having to pay Spain those outrageous taxes the Spanish Crown demands. A lot of money could be made by those men once Cuba is free, Julián, a lot of money. You should get to know them and talk to them. And once we are at El Ateneo, I'll introduce you to some of the newspapermen in town. Let's see if we can begin to spread some of your ideas and get some of your writings published here, Julián. The money may not be great, but the reputation . . ." They have reached the entrance door to the school. Saavedra looks Julián directly in the eye. "Julián," he says, placing both his hands firmly on Julián's shoulders, "right now, that's what you need to do: Get to know Guatemala, Julián. And what is more important, let Guatemala get to know you. Let people get to know you well, and the rest will be easy." He shakes hands with Julián and stays at the huge entrance door to the school as Julián begins to go slowly down the hill in the sharply slanted rays of the late afternoon sun.

It is only then Saavedra notices Julián's slight limp.

He had not noticed it before. He had been looking at Julián with kind eyes all afternoon. But now, after noticing Julián's limp, he looks at Julián with even kinder eyes.

At the bottom of the hill, right before turning the corner, Julián turns back to look up toward the immense school building once again.

Saavedra, still at the door, waves at him. "Cheer up, Julián," he shouts. "Everything's going to work out for the best. You'll see, you'll see," Saavedra adds, aiming his remarks apparently at Julián.

But in reality, Saavedra knows, he is aiming them primarily to himself.

We'll need all the luck we can get, he tells himself. And then some. He sighs. But we're going to do it. We're going to get that boy the full-time appointment he needs, and I'll be damned if we don't. That boy *will* teach here. This school needs great teachers, and that boy—that young man— has inside him the makings of a great teacher if I've ever seen one!

Saavedra stays at the door until he sees Julián turn a corner at the bottom of the hill and disappear from his sight. Then he closes and locks the door behind him and starts slowly across the patio, back to his office, musingly caressing his neatly trimmed long beard, which is white in places.

Julián seems to have the ideas, Saavedra tells himself, repeatedly nodding his head unconsciously as he crosses the patio. He seems to have the dreams. No question about it. And he's good . . . No, not good—*excellent*—with words. The way he sounded whenever he spoke of Cuba; the way his voice quivered when he told me of the almost-inhuman atrocities he saw there while he was in prison, the outrageous depravities he himself was forced to endure, and for so long. And yet, despite all of that, the controlled passion he used when, in a voice totally free from hate, he discussed Cuba's need for men of action, "led by reason," as Julián said. That young man, Saavedra repeats to himself, he certainly knows how to use words well. But . . .

Saavedra pauses as he reaches the door to his office. Is he—will he become—another one like me? He enters his office.

Or does he have the balls, the *cojones,* to leave all of this behind—Saavedra asks himself as he looks around the exquisitely appointed room—to go to Cuba and fight to set her free, as Don Manuel did with Guatemala?

He shakes his head, doubtfully.

Maybe, he tells himself. Maybe.

He sits in his chair behind his desk, still caressing his beard. Then he lights the polished-brass, swinging-arm kerosene lamp at his desk, pulls from a drawer some student papers, places them on the dark green leather pad that covers most of the heavily burnished top of his huge desk, and he is about to begin to grade them when he pauses and starts to nod his head up and down as he thinks again of Julián.

We shall see, he tells himself. We shall see.

CHAPTER V

THIS IS NOT EXACTLY what I had in mind, Julián thinks, as he walks down the hill where the school is located and where most of the wealthy folk live, and starts across the flat part of town to the house of the Mayan woman where he is staying.

My plans to send for Lucía will have to be put on hold, at least for a time. I wonder if my diploma will get here in time so I will be able to get a full-time appointment? he asks himself. Still—he remembers the old Cuban saying, *De lo malo, lo mejor*—From the bad, make the best. At least I have a part-time job, even if it is only teaching two afternoons a week. That should provide me with enough money to get by until the official appointment comes. It will come—he assures himself—*it will!* I am determined to do whatever it is I must do to get it. I have the knowledge, the know-how. I did graduate from law school with honors, in Zaragoza, as I told Saavedra, and even though I have yet to receive the actual diploma, I have already taught school, both in Spain and Mexico. So I know I can do the job. And I am sure I can do it well—I certainly will do my very best to do it well. All I need to do now is to convince the minister. He sighs. I hope he will be as easy to convince as Professor Saavedra.

He smiles to himself when he thinks of Saavedra.

Saavedra seems to be a really *good* man—Julián tells himself—honestly interested in the future of Cuba. And still very much a Cuban, even if he has been living here for so long that he has lost his Cuban accent and is married to a Guatemalan woman. I wonder what she is like? he thinks, and then he smiles again. No doubt Saavedra was born to be a teacher, Julián thinks and chuckles. Those mannerisms of his! The way he loves to enumerate his points, treating me as if I were one of his pupils. Which, in a way, I guess I am. I have a lot to learn about Guatemala. From Saavedra *and* from everybody else. A lot!

He raises his eyes and looks about the city in front of him.

Julián hears distant marimbas and *chirimías*—Mayan flutes—singing soulful Indian melodies filled with longing as he sees, all across the city, column after column of white smoke rising up to heaven, now tinged the color of embers by the last rays of the deep red-orange setting sun; columns of smoke that rise from outdoor cooking pits, which smell as heavenly as the smoke's final destination. Everywhere, Mayan men guarding the streets have begun to go around with long wooden poles, a torch at one end, which they use to light the tall gas lanterns located at every other corner. To Julián, the flaming lanterns look like flickering stars shining bright amongst the white buildings that little by little are turning blue as night begins to fall and as the moon starts to become visible. He remembers the way La Habana, the city where he was born, looked at night: hundreds of flickering gaslight stars, a necklace of lights outlining the entire edge of the bay, reflecting on the dark deep waters. And then he remembers the flag that *still* flies over his Cuba, a flag not her own, but of Spain.

Remembering that flag brings his thoughts back to Saavedra.

And to himself.

Will I end up like the professor? Growing old teaching in a foreign land and losing my Cuban accent? Julián asks himself. Will I end up an old man sitting behind a fancy desk, smoking expensive Cuban cigars, an outsider watching how the world transforms itself, like the old professor? Will I end up with a beard that turns whiter year after year, and with a waist that gets thicker and thicker year after year, while I wait, year after year, like the old professor, for someone to come and do what I always dreamed of doing but did not have the guts—the balls—to do?

Julián shakes his head.

No. That is not how I am going to end, he tells himself. That is certainly *not* how *I* am going to end. If that's what a comfortable job does to a man, well then, I do not want any part of it. In this world, Julián knows, there are dreamers. And there are doers.

And he, Julián, was born to be a doer.

Oh, sure—Julián tells himself—I'm sure Saavedra has dreams. All men have dreams. All women. All people. But dreams have to be made into reality, at whatever the cost. At whatever the sacrifice. Or else they remain nothing but dreams. And nothing, *nothing,* can dry up anybody faster than not taking any actions, however small they may seem to be, to make dreams into reality. *Nothing!* and *I*—Julián reassures himself—I am *not* going to dry up. I am *not* going to sit behind a fancy desk and enjoy a Cuban cigar while somebody else is fighting to free Cuba. If it is true that only the blood of martyrs feeds dreams, well then, Lord, please, let me feed dreams, even if that means that I'd have to become a martyr myself.

No sooner does Julián think this than, all of a sudden, he realizes what was wrong with the image of the man on the float that he saw in the Good Friday procession the day he disembarked in Puerto Dulce: the image of a man who, crowned with thorns and wearing a red velvet robe, carried over his sagging shoulders a heavy wood cross.

His eyes. That was what was wrong with the image of that man.

His eyes.

The artist who carved that image did not know, did not understand— in the least—how that man with the crown of thorns felt. In the *very* least. Because if he had, because if that artist had understood how the real man crowned with thorns felt as he carried a cross to his glorious death, the eyes of the man carrying the cross would not—could not—have been the saddest eyes in the world, but on the contrary, they would have been the most exultant eyes in the world, enraptured with joy. Because, by his action, that man was feeding dreams. And by feeding dreams, he was making his own dreams come true and fulfilling his own destiny.

Suddenly Julián remembers the reason why he came to Guatemala: to get a job, to marry Lucía and start a family. That is my dream, a dream I cannot wait to make true. But, is that dream more important than my dream of freeing Cuba? he asks himself. Freeing my homeland is my dream. My life's ambition, my life's cause. My destiny. The reason why I think—the reason why I *know*—God placed me on Earth. To achieve the liberation of my homeland. And if not to achieve it, to work diligently, as hard as I can, incessantly and for as long as need be, to help achieve it. Do those two dreams—having a family of my own and freeing my home-land—do they *have* to be in opposition to each other as I've been led to believe by Lucía's friends and family?

"That's what you need to do, Julián," Lucía's friends and family kept telling him. "Get an honest-to-goodness job so you can finally get married and start your own family. With a woman and children under your care, you'll have no choice but to give up those childish dreams of yours and start living a *real* life, where paying rent and buying food is all that counts. Think about it, Julián," Lucía's friends and family kept urging him, "and come to your senses. Who's ever heard of a little guy like you, a poet, with no money and with no weapons but for your 'pretty' words, daring to face that huge Goliath, the Spanish Empire, Eh? So come on, Julián, give up those childish dreams. They may sound good on paper, but they do not put food on the table. And food on the table is what you need now, if you're ever going to marry and start a family. So come on, Julián," Lucía's friends and family kept egging him on, "set aside those silly dreams of yours and grow up, Julián. *Grow up!*"

Julián didn't realize it, but he had been so immersed in his thoughts that, after he noticed the columns of smoke rising from the cook fires and after he watched the Mayan guards lighting the street lanterns, he had kept his eyes cast down as he walked. When he raises his eyes, he realizes that he is walking next to the wall that outlines the famous cemetery of Guatemala City, a large complex partly hidden behind high, white, stuc-coed walls. His readings about Guatemala have told him that this ceme-tery is filled with outstanding marble statuary. Curious, when he goes by the main entrance, with its huge filigreed bronze gates, he glances through the openwork and sees that his readings did not lie. Everywhere inside are white marble angels, frozen in time and space, some of them kneeling, some of them standing, atop elaborate marble crypts, looking up with hopeful eyes toward the sky above them, now dark blue, while their silent wings, lit by the nascent moon, cast long dark blue shadows on the surface of the Earth.

Suddenly, an uncontainable cry, a cry of the most unimaginable pain, the deep wailing cry of a man beyond control, makes him look across the street.

There, opposite the main entrance gates to the cemetery, he sees a cantina. And through the open turquoise-color shuttered doors of this small stuccoed building, painted pale ocher, Julián sees, lit by the dim glow of a few kerosene lamps turned very low, several Mayan men, dressed totally in white, who wear black ribbons of mourning around their arms. They are silently passing around a bottle from one to the other, each of them taking a deep swallow as they gather around one young Mayan Indian man, not much older than Julián himself, who is the one Julián had heard, and who is beating his chest in utter despair as he sobs.

Julián raises his eyes to the sign above the entrance door to the cantina. El *Último* Adiós, the sign reads—The *Last* Good-bye.

Those men must be saying their last good-byes to someone they loved, Julián thinks. And that poor young Mayan man, he must have lost someone very dear to him. A mother? A best friend? A wife? The mother of his children? The girl of his dreams? The love of his life?

Julián sighs as his thoughts turn back to Cuba and he remembers the day, years ago, when placed aboard a ship and sent into exile, he looked back and saw his beautiful homeland disappear little by little behind the horizon line. He felt then that perhaps he was bidding Cuba, his beautiful Cuba, the love of his life, his *last* good-bye.

But that will not be the case—he assures himself. I will not die without stepping once more on Cuban soil. I swear it. I will *not!* And with that resolution, Julián straightens his back and decisively steps across the empty street. This calls for a celebration, he thinks, as he enters the cantina and asks the stocky, wrinkled old Mayan man behind the counter, who is also totally dressed in white, for a shot of gin.

To tomorrow, Julián toasts silently as he shoots the gin down his throat. When my homeland will be free.

Still with the shot glass raised in the air, he waves it at the cantina man, signaling him for a second shot of gin, which the old Mayan man immediately pours. And free she will be, Julián assures himself, as he shoots this second shot down his throat. I just have to take a step at a time. That's the only thing a man can ever do, Julián tells himself, take one step at a time. But—Julián reminds himself—a man must always keep his dreams in clear focus ahead of him as he takes those steps. A man does not ever want to get sidetracked, he tells himself. Like the old professor.

"I won't," he says aloud, "I won't."

Thinking that Julián, leaning against the bar, has called him again, the wrinkled old man behind the counter comes over to him.

Julián, puzzled, looks at the man behind the bar, who is looking back at him with a question in his eyes.

"Another ginebra?" the old Mayan man finally asks.

Julián smiles at him. Why not? he asks himself.

He nods yes and orders another shot of gin, which he follows later with another, and then another.

A while later, after Julián's eyes have begun to acquire the hopeful look of the angels across the street, he finally bids the wrinkled old Mayan man behind the counter good evening, and, leaving El *Último* Adiós behind, resumes his walk back to his lonely room at the far end of the city, where the poor Mayan folk live.

CHAPTER VI

A S JULIÁN WALKS BACK to his room, in a daze, the gin running wild through his veins, little by little he begins to forget about Cuba, and almost unaware that he is doing it, he begins to breathe in little by little the intense beauty of this, his first night in Guatemala City.

The streets of the city, lit by the dim flickering gaslights placed at every other corner, are now shrouded in almost total darkness, since the half-risen moon has decided to hide behind clouds. The flowering magnolia trees scattered all over the city have been in full bloom for several days. Some of the large petals of their huge, pale cream flowers have already fallen off and are now lying all over atop the stone sidewalks, which are busy with people going every which way, trampling carelessly over the petals. This makes the petals release a wonderful smell that perfumes the pleasantly cool night with a heavily musky scent.

Quietly enjoying the intense, dreamy aroma of the fragrant Guatemalan night as he walks, Julián thinks he hears distant Cuban music. Surprised, he stops and listens. His ears have not fooled him. Incredible as it seems to him, somewhere in Guatemala City an organ grinder is playing a habanera, one of those sensual Cuban dances that evoke with their lustful rhythm the way women from La Habana walk.

Trying to locate where the music is coming from, Julián turns corner after corner until he turns one more and comes across a small park—El

Parque de La Victoria—dedicated to the victory of Guatemala over Spain. In its center, standing on a high pedestal, there is a marble sculpture of a larger-than-life tall and handsome white woman—The Spirit of Guatemala—wearing a torn classic Greek robe that lets her beautiful bare breasts show. Proudly looking up to heaven, she is breaking the opprobrious chains of slavery as she steps, defiantly, over the Spanish Crown, which lies crushed at her feet. Julián pauses for a moment to look admiringly at the beautiful statue from afar before he starts across the busy street toward the music that seems to be coming from somewhere within the park.

Beautifully lighted with closely spaced gaslights, the park is incredibly crowded, the way it is on every Saturday night. Accompanied by their ever-vigilant chaperones, dozens of beautiful young girls—*niñas,* as unmarried young women are called—wearing their very best, are parading around the square park, walking lazily in one direction along the broad sidewalk that outlines it. At the same time, dozens of young men, also wearing their very best, are also parading around the park, walking equally as lazily along the same broad sidewalk as the girls and their chaperones—but in exactly the opposite direction. And as they walk, the young men keep staring audaciously past the chaperones at the niñas, hoping to catch their sparkling dark eyes.

Oh Lord!—Julián says to himself, sighing deeply as he watches the young men and the young girls smile surreptitiously at each other while he cuts across the park—How soon will I be able to have Lucía next to me, here, by my side, with me?

Suddenly the sound of loud laughter interrupts his thoughts.

Searching for the music, Julián has managed to cut across the park—no easy task—and now he stands behind a large group of people, all of whom are laughing loudly. The people are circling the organ grinder, a Mayan Indian man who, as he plays, stands in front of a large wooden case that has hundreds of tiny slots, each holding a tiny rolled piece of paper. The case is divided in three panels. The left panel, painted pale blue and holding rolled pieces of pale blue paper, has a sign above reading MUCHA-CHOS—Boys. The next panel, painted a pale cream color and holding rolled pieces of pale cream paper, has a sign above reading SABIDURIA—Wisdom. And the right panel, painted pale pink and holding rolled pieces of pale pink paper, has a sign above reading MUCHACHAS—Girls. Above all these signs, there is a large sign done in brilliant red, bold, circus-baroque letters reading EL FUTURO—The Future. The Mayan man keeps turning the cracked wooden handle of his old musical instrument as he keeps on excitedly shouting over the music. "Go, Chirilingo, go! Find out who would like to know the future! Go, go! *Go!*"

Chirilingo is a tiny Guatemalan monkey. He has long, skinny arms and legs, covered with short, red fuzzy hair, and huge black eyes deeply set in a small, narrow face, outlined by sparkling white muttonchop whiskers. Dressed just like his master, the organ grinder, Chirilingo is wearing a colorful and heavily embroidered vestlike garment—a *huipil*—over white shirt and pants, his long, curly tail sticking out. On top of his head he is wearing a tiny red straw hat covered with glittering red beads. The tiny hat is held in place by a barely visible black elastic cord tied under Chirilingo's chin.

Chirilingo goes around the group of people, a tiny tin cup in his hand. Whenever a person drops a penny into his cup, Chirilingo, following the verbal instructions the organ grinder gives him, rushes to where his master is, drops the penny in the organ grinder's hat, which is lying on the ground, rushes to the case with the hundreds of slots, selects one piece of paper, takes it to the person who gave him the penny, and hands it with one hand to the person at exactly the same time as he lifts his tiny hat with his other hand, making everybody laugh. And he does all of this in a split second. If one were to wink, one would miss it all.

Thinking that this would make a great subject for a newspaper article, Julián moves to the front of the line, to take a closer look at Chirilingo and at his Mayan master.

Urging his tiny companion on, the Mayan Indian organ grinder shouts, "Hey, Chirilingo. Who in this entire crowd do you think needs to know the future the most, eh, Chirilingo? Who?"

Chirilingo, responding to his master's voice, goes excitedly around the laughing crowd of families and couples until he stands in front of the only young man in the entire crowd who is alone. Dressed in his vested black suit, the tall young man with the broad shoulders, the chiseled face, and the thick mustache—Julián—is confronted by the tiny monkey, who extends his long, skinny arm, holding his tiny tin cup out toward him.

Still heavily under the influence of the gin, Julián smiles at Chirilingo and looks for a penny, first into the right pocket of his pants, then into the left one. But finding none, he pulls the lining of his pockets out, shows Chirilingo his pockets are empty, and shrugs his shoulders, which makes everybody in the crowd laugh even louder.

This delights the organ grinder.

"Never you mind, señor," he tells Julián. "Chirilingo will bring you a little bit of wisdom about the future, even if you don't pay for it. Won't you, Chirilingo?" And mindful Chirilingo rushes to the case with the hundreds of slots, picks up a rolled piece of pale cream paper, rushes back to Julián, and extending his right arm, he hands the paper to Julián, lifting at the same moment his glittering tiny red hat with his left hand.

Julián, laughing with the rest of the crowd, unrolls the paper and reads to himself:

> *When honor and truth are at odds,*
> *let truth prevail.*

Puzzled by the ancient Mayan saying written on the tiny piece of paper, a serious piece of wisdom he certainly was not expecting to get from someone like Chirilingo, Julián shakes his head as he ponders it, not able to understand it.

How could honor and truth ever be at odds? he asks himself.

People around him look at him, this young white man with the thick mustache, the deeply suntanned face and the pale forehead, dressed in a vested black suit, who all of a sudden is not laughing anymore.

The organ grinder, who does not want to scare his customers away, wisely makes a joke of Julián's puzzled face. "Oh, Chirilingo," he says, "the señor did not like the little bit of wisdom you brought him. Isn't that a shame?" He turns to Julián. "Never you mind, señor," the organ grinder adds, "Chirilingo will gladly bring you a *happy* future." He addresses the tiny monkey. "Chirilingo," he shouts, "run and make sure you bring the señor a *happy* future this time." The organ grinder smiles broadly, then he immediately adds, shouting it as loud as he can, for all the world to hear: "AS IF HE HAD *PAID* FOR IT!"

When people hear this, they begin to laugh uproariously, wondering if perhaps Julián is part of the act, while Chirilingo rushes to the case of the thousand slots, picks up a rolled piece a paper—this time pale blue—rushes back and hands it to Julián, again lifting his glittering red hat.

Julián unrolls the tiny piece of paper, not realizing that the expectant eyes of everybody are on him, and reads it. And what he reads makes him smile, a broad smile that illuminates his face. He looks back at Chirilingo and nods his head several times to the tiny monkey, thanking him as the rest of the crowd sighs with relief.

"Well done, Chirilingo!" his master says. "You brought a *happy* future to this nice señor." Then he shouts again, "Go, Chirilingo, go, go! Find out who else would like to pay handsomely for a bright, happy future! Go, go! *Go!*" And when they hear that, all of a sudden, a lot of the people in the crowd raise their hands, beckoning for Chirilingo and asking him to bring them a bright, happy future.

Julián, still substantially-more-than-slightly inebriated, resumes his walk back to his lonely room at the other end of the city, where the poor Mayan folk live, but he feels a lot better now. After all, now he knows what tomorrow will bring him. Chirilingo himself has given him the good news.

When he gets to the next street corner, he takes from his pocket the rolled piece of pale blue paper, unrolls it, and reads it again, by the flickering light of the corner gas lamp.

Don't give up hope.
The girl you've been waiting for
is just around the corner.

Wouldn't that be great—he asks himself, hopefully—if all of a sudden I were to turn one more corner and I were to find the girl I've been waiting for there, the girl I've always dreamed of? Wouldn't that be *just great?*

Julián smiles at himself as he delicately rolls the tiny piece of pale blue paper again, and, not ever wanting to lose the bright, happy future Chirilingo brought to him, he places it carefully inside one of the pockets of his pants.

But as he does, the first piece of paper Chirilingo gave him, the pale cream one, falls out of his pocket without him realizing it.

And as Julián starts back to his lonely room at the far end of town, that tiny piece of paper, a pale cream piece of paper full of wisdom that told Julián, "When honor and truth are at odds, let truth prevail," that tiny piece of paper now lies on the surface of the sidewalk next to dozens of trampled pale cream petals of the wonderfully scented magnolia flowers. Unnoticed. Totally unnoticed.

Forgotten.

PART TWO

EARTHQUAKE

CHAPTER VII

WHEN JULIÁN FIRST HEARS the pealing of the dozens of bells of Guatemala City calling the faithful to early Sunday Mass, he is sitting at the tiny table in his lonely room, writing by the light of a single candle, now almost all gone. He raises his head, looks out the little window above his bed, sees that the sky is still dark, the sun not risen yet, and goes back to the letter he is writing to Lucía, a nine-page letter filled with details about his incredibly long and exciting trip—a letter Lucía receives twelve days later and which she reads aloud to her coterie of friends and family the following Saturday night, at her home. Enclosed in that letter, Julián included a picture postcard of Guatemala City, printed in sepia on heavy cardboard. On its back, Julián had written a few words, words so intimate Lucía did not dare to read them aloud to anyone, not even to herself. Not wanting anyone else to see those words or read them, she pasted the postcard in her album the minute it arrived, and underneath she scribbled in her small, delicate handwriting:

Guatemala, April 16, 1877.

That, and nothing more.

Making it look as if she found the postcard somewhere.

As if Julián had not sent it. As if the fiery words written on the back of the postcard were not there. As if those words had never been written. As if Julián's torrid words needed censoring.

Friends and family members who got to see the postcard pasted in her album would just look at it and say, "Oh! So that's what Guatemala City looks like?" And then they would invariably face each other and say, "It does not even remotely compare to Mexico City, does it?" And as they made that comment, they'd look at Lucía with pity in their eyes for they knew that, sooner or later, she would have to move to that remote small town in the picture postcard, *if* and *when* she married that boy, the poet—the poor-as-a-rat poet—who, they all thought, had no future. Certainly no future to speak of. These were the same people who had told Julián: Get a real job. Get a wife. Start a family. Drop those silly dreams. The same people who looked at Lucía as if she were already an old maid, because at her advanced age of twenty-nine most women in her social class already had at least three or more children. The same people who would find Julián's words to Lucía uncalled for and rude, if not plainly obscene.

It was from these people that Lucía had hidden Julián's words.

And from herself as well.

She was afraid of the passion hidden in those words, a passion to which she thought she might not be able to respond. A passion she did not know if she would be able to match. And yet, though she did not let anyone else read Julián's words, and though she herself would never be able to read them again, those words had been engraved within her heart.

And that night, the night she read Julián's letter to her coterie of friends and family, that night, when alone in her bedroom she unpinned her hair and went to her bed, as she felt her loosened hair over her naked breasts, she felt him there as well, his body pressing hard against hers as he whispered in her ear the words he had written to her, the same words she had so carefully hidden from everyone else.

> *It is for you I yearn. For you, and for your hair, so dark,*
> *that the world of shadows must envy it.*
> *I place a point of my life within that darkness and pray*
> *that soon your hair—and you—will be mine.*

Since the time he wrote those words, over two and a half weeks ago, Julián and Professor Saavedra have gone to the Ministry of Public Instruction twice to meet with Minister Andrújal and apply for Julián's official appointment to the school. And twice they have gone back to the school without having been able to see the minister. They were received very cordially, and after waiting for not too long a period of time, they were told that the minister would not be able to see them because of one reason or another.

Saavedra told Julián not to worry. "This happens," he said, "because people in government do not know how to handle their time." But he didn't mean it. He knew what was going on. The game of power the minister was playing. Some of his friends at El Ateneo, the private men's club, had told him.

The Monday after he met Saavedra, Julián, accompanied by the old professor, went to the presidential palace and delivered to President Rubios himself the letter of introduction Julián had brought from Señor Fermín in Mexico, which President Rubios read in Julián's presence.

"Any friend of Señor Fermín is a friend of mine," Rubios said after he read the letter, welcoming Julián to Guatemala with a firm handshake. But after Julián and Saavedra left, the president asked one of his assistants to find out who this Julián was, and to report back to him personally with any and all the information found.

The minister of public instruction was aware of this ongoing search. And until the president was given all the information he asked for concerning this Julián, he, the minister, would do nothing. So the minister of public instruction kept being polite to both Julián and Professor Saavedra, kept apologizing for not being able to see them, and kept telling them to please wait, which was all Julián and Saavedra could do.

In the meantime, Julián has started to teach part-time at school. Twice a week, he teaches courses in philosophy and the history of civilization, two subjects which Julián adores.

Professor Saavedra has made his office available to Julián at all times, letting him share the huge partners desk, and has shown Julián where the keys to the bookcases are kept, giving Julián the great opportunity to browse at his will through the magnificently leather-bound books in Saavedra's personal library while working on his lectures. It is there, inside that office, that Julián can almost always be found, the top of his side of the desk covered with piles of books, his head bent down, working on a political essay he hopes to publish in a Guatemalan paper, scribbling word after word in his tight, elegant handwriting, still leaving no margins in his notebooks, even though Saavedra has told him repeatedly that paper is abundantly provided by the government.

With the help of Saavedra, Julián has been able to find a room in the private house of a Ladino widow, located much closer to school than the one where he first stayed, which was on the opposite side of the city, the side where poor Mayan folk live. The house of this Ladino widow is in the vicinity of the cemetery, and though the room there is a little more expensive, the location of the house saves Julián a lot of time, since he still walks to school. Now, every evening, on his way back from school, he stops at El Último Adiós, the bar across the street from the cemetery, for a shot or two of gin, after taking his daily dose of the bitter quinine.

Panoplo, the wrinkled old Mayan man behind the counter who serves Julián his shots of gin, has begun to know this young white man with the unruly hair and the thick mustache who comes to his bar late every day, wearing a clean black suit and limping ever so slightly, and who treats him like an equal, something Panoplo sincerely appreciates and likes. He has begun to think of Julián as a friend, even though he doesn't know his name. He just calls him *Ginebrita*—Little Gin Boy—because of Julián's predilection for that drink.

Julián, inquisitive by nature, and wanting to get to know more about Guatemala—as Professor Saavedra told him he should do—is constantly asking Panoplo about Mayan life, and Mayan food, and Mayan art, and Mayan lore, and, specifically, about Mayan religion. And Panoplo, who comes from the tiny Mayan village of Chirimacotengo, located on the west coast of Guatemala, right by the ocean, answers Julián's myriad questions, something the old Mayan man truly enjoys doing. He loves to tell Julián of the many gods of the coast, especially about the *Chacs,* the four great gods of water, one of whom—the powerful god of the sea, he who controls the raging waves of the Pacific Ocean—is the god to whom Panoplo was dedicated at birth.

Recently, however, with the advent of the new legal codes of Guatemala, Panoplo and Julián have begun to talk more and more about politics and about how those new codes will affect life in Guatemala and, particularly, Indian life.

. . .

DURING AN early afternoon visit to the club El Ateneo, Professor Saavedra introduces Julián to Señor Gostiero, the Attorney General of Guatemala, who is the man responsible for the new legal codes just issued by the administration of President Rubios. Gostiero, impressed by Julián, tells the young Cuban exile that he will have his office send Julián a copy of the new codes. "I will be very interested to know what you think of our new laws," Gostiero tells him.

The next day, a leather-bound set of the new legal codes is delivered to Saavedra's school, addressed to Julián. After his work is done, Julián takes the volumes to his room and spends all night long studying them in detail, poring over the new codes in amazement. The codes are almost unbelievable, managing to break new ground almost on every single page. They even make women into people, giving them the same rights as men, including the right to own property in their own name, and to testify in court—something Julián thinks has been long overdue in all American countries.

Highly impressed by these new laws, the next morning Julián sends Señor Gostiero a letter commenting on the codes; a letter so brilliant Señor Gostiero has it excerpted and published the following day in *El Progreso*, the newspaper of the Reform Party.

Dear Señor Gostiero,

You wanted to know what I thought of the new codes. They are not perfect, because we do not yet live in a perfect world. They are codes of transformation for a country in transformation. In their spirit, they are modern; in their definitions, clear; in their style, concise; in their vast reforms, sweeping. Written by those who do not want and who will not accept tyranny, the codes provide weapons to fight and master tyranny. Finally the new spirit of the new Americas has taken form and become law! With these legal codes Guatemala has laid over the ruins of the past the foundations for a new nation, alive and glorious.

The day after the letter appears in the paper, Saavedra and Julián go a third time to see the minister of public instruction, and this time the minister *himself* welcomes them into his office.

Nothing tangible actually comes out of this meeting.

When Saavedra brings up the subject of Julián's appointment to the school, the minister just keeps to his noncommittal bureaucratic way and keeps saying, "We'll see, we'll see what we can do," as he escorts Julián and the professor back out of his office. The minister, himself appointed to his job by the president, has no choice—like all professional bureaucrats—but to wait and see, and to take his lead from the president himself, whose response to Julián's letter is not yet known.

But even if nothing tangible actually seems to have come out of that meeting, a lot has been accomplished by Julián's letter. With the publication of his letter, Guatemala has begun to find out about him.

All of a sudden, Julián has become a topic of conversation among all the people of Guatemala.

And that includes all the young teenage girls who go to Saavedra's school.

AT THE FIRST lecture given by Julián at the school, several weeks ago, the girls felt a little bit ill at ease in the presence of this new professor who spoke with a strange accent, and yet, a young professor who, despite being dressed in just a plain black suit, was surprisingly attractive. But after that first incredible lecture, in which Julián was able to recreate with words the world of ancient Greece and made it so real that the girls felt they were actually inhabiting it, the girls discovered that this new teacher with the deep set dark blue eyes was able to transform history—up to then the most boring of subjects—into the most exciting and the most wonderful topic. Since then, the girls have become so enthused about Julián and about his teaching techniques that they cannot wait to return to his next class.

"Do you study history with the new Cuban teacher?" they all ask each other. "Isn't he really cute?" they whisper to each other, giggling as they say it. "Do you know if he is married?" they all want to find out. "Who *is* this man?"

It doesn't take long for rumors to start.

One of the girls finds out that the new teacher is a poet who was thrown out of Cuba, she says, because of a poem he wrote demanding the freedom of his homeland.

But Gabriela, the middle daughter of Don Manuel—the general who liberated Guatemala from Spain—has already made of Julián a romantic hero and tells the rest of the girls at school that what that other girl said is not true in the least. "I definitely know," she says, "that Professor Julián left Cuba in his hope of finding the ideal woman of his dreams." And then she adds, with authority in her voice, "I know for a fact that he is not married, and that he has no intention of ever getting married, until he finds the exact woman for whom he so desperately yearns. It is *precisely* because of his quest for the woman of his dreams that he has been traveling for years and years and years, all over the world."

"If that is true," the other girls says, "I certainly would like to find out more about *that!*"

The next morning, Gabriela shows the girls one of the many poems written by Julián that have appeared in *La Revista Universal,* a Mexican literary publication her father, Don Manuel, receives and keeps bound in his library; a poem Gabriela—unbeknownst to her dad and to anyone else in her family—has daringly ripped from the bound set of journals.

After proudly showing her trophy to the rest of the girls, Gabriela commands them all to sit down on the tiled patio floor, and shaded by the lustrous, leathery, dark green leaves of the large magnolia tree in one corner of the huge patio of the school, she reads the poem aloud, her trembling voice quivering with the virginal passion of a not-quite-yet-fourteen-year-old girl.

I close my eyes and there, in front of me, I see her.
I extend my hand, and within the dark shadows
of my dreams she hides away. And my sighing
sends her shadow a missive of my painful longing.

Thus, my beloved and I walk for eternity:
She hiding within the shadows, me following her.
But soon, within the world of shadows, we will make love
with a light so immense it will surpass all the stars.

After Gabriela finishes reading the poem there is a moment of silence, broken first by one long sigh, and then by another, to be followed by a large chorus of sighs, interrupted by one of the girls, who says, "Oh, poor, poor, *poor* Professor Julián! He must be in such a great need of love!"

And all the others girls knowingly nod their heads in agreement.

Then, yesterday, to top it all, Julián's letter appeared in *El Progreso,* the newspaper of the Reform Party, which most of the girls' fathers read.

This morning, the girls, now aware that Julián is not only a lovesick young man but a celebrity as well, have flocked to his class, not daring to miss a single moment of his company or a single word the new teacher has to say while each of them stares at him, hoping to catch his eye.

But this young new professor never looks at any one of them.

His eyes just look up toward the ceiling and sparkle with unparalleled intensity as words flow like uncontained torrents from his mouth, creating vivid worlds where heroic men and their courageous women fight indefatigably to make their dreams true, even if this entails dying valiantly in their search for liberty.

THAT NIGHT, after dinner, Gabriela waits until she sees that her mother and her two sisters have gone to their rooms, and then she tiptoes surreptitiously into her father's library, where she finds Don Manuel asleep in his huge wing chair, an open book on his lap, an emptied cut-glass brandy snifter and a half-filled decanter on a small mahogany side table next to him.

Not saying a word, Gabriela gets close to him and pats her father's bald head, abruptly awakening the general with a start. Not giving him time to say a word, she kisses his bald head and then, jumping on his lap, tells him, "Daddy, did you know that you are the nicest, the bravest, the most handsome, and the most wonderful man on Earth?" Then she kisses him on both cheeks and, as she does, she reaches inside his open vest and tickles the poor man into uncontrollable laughter.

Don Manuel, who married late in life to a woman twelve years younger than himself, is a fifty-seven-year-old man who has controlled armies of rebellious men, subjugated armies of enemies, and fought armies of bureaucrats to get his way and bring freedom and peace to Guatemala. His body, which has lived through thirst, hunger, and deprivations of all kinds, proudly wears scars caused by Indian arrows, and by

Spanish bullets, and even by treacherous knives. He has heroically confronted, resisted, and survived all of that.

But he is totally incapable of dealing with Gabriela's tickling.

"All right, all right, all right!" he screams, "I give up, I give up! What do
you want this time?"

Gabriela stands there, her impish eyes looking up at heaven, her
mouth open in total amazement. "Who? Me . . . ? Can't a loving daughter
come to her father and tell him she simply adores him just because he is
the greatest, the nicest, the—"

Her father will not let her finish. He just says, "Gabriela . . ." his voice
trying to sound as severe and as stern as he can make it, while he looks her
in the eye.

Gabriela caresses his bald head once again. "Daddy," she says, "is it too
late to invite someone to next week's party? Or did you send all the invitations already?"

"Who do you want to invite this time?" Don Manuel answers.
"Another one of your girlfriends?"

Gabriela, sheepishly, kisses her father on the cheek and, hugging him
tight to her, says, "Daddy, did I ever tell you about the new Cuban teacher
at school . . . ?"

THE FOLLOWING MORNING, while working at his desk, Professor
Saavedra receives an engraved invitation from Don Manuel—signed by
the general himself—inviting the professor and his wife to a formal ball to
celebrate the coming of age of the general's oldest daughter, Soledad,
Gabriela's older sister, who will be eighteen a week from Wednesday—
and requesting the courtesy of an answer.

Underneath his signature, the general added:

Esteemed Saavedra,

*Feel free to bring with you any other Cuban man that you know. It is time
we all get together and do something for Cuba.*

Saavedra, pleasantly surprised, leans back in his chair and slides the
invitation over to Julián, sitting across the partners desk.

"How about that!" the professor says, interrupting Julián, who raises his eyes and glances at the invitation, noticing the signature at the bottom. "Will you come?"

"To Don Manuel's?" Julián asks.

"To the house of Don Manuel *himself*," Professor Saavedra answers, grinning from ear to ear. "Next Wednesday."

There's a short pause.

"I don't think I will be able to go," Julián says, hesitantly, after a while, looking down at his notes, evading Saavedra's eyes. "I . . . I have a very difficult lecture to prepare for my Thursday class and I . . . We're getting to Imperial Rome and, you know . . ." Julián raises his eyes, looks at the professor, and smiles embarrassedly. "I just have to reread my Cicero," he says, and immediately gets back to his note taking.

Julián does not lie to Saavedra.

However, though it is true that he does have a class that Thursday that he has to prepare for and that he does have to reread Cicero, that is not the real reason he does not think he can go to Don Manuel's formal ball. The real reason is that he knows he does not have the proper attire to go to such an event, and that he doesn't want to make a fool of himself. Nor of the Saavedras.

"It won't harm you to get to know Don Manuel, Julián," the professor says, matter-of-factly. "I'm sure President Rubios will be there, and several if not all of his ministers. Nobody ever says *no* to Don Manuel, Julián. He is still a very powerful man." Seeing all the hesitation in Julián's eyes, he adds, "We could use his influence in getting your full-time appointment to the school, just in case your diploma does not get here in time." He pauses. "Besides," he adds, a twinkle in his eye, "Don Manuel's reception will take place"—he counts with his fingers—"five. No, not five. Six. Six days from today. I'm sure that between now and then you will be able to find some time to reread your Cicero. And, Julián, even if you didn't, I'm sure that even Cicero can wait if—"

He leaves his sentence incomplete on purpose while looking intently at Julián, who does not look back at him.

Then, after smiling, the professor completes his sentence.

"—if it is for the good of Cuba."

When Julián hears this, he drops his pen, raises his eyes, and looks doubtfully into Saavedra's eyes.

Then, after a while, when he sees the twinkle in the old professor's eyes, he has no choice but to shake his head and smile.

"Cicero can wait?" Saavedra asks, chuckling.

"Cicero can wait," Julián answers.

CHAPTER VIII

THE FOLLOWING EVENING, Saavedra, with the help of Julián and all the other teachers at the school, is making sure the school auditorium is properly set up for the debate that is to take place that night. This debate promises to be quite heated, since the two scheduled speakers are Colonel Germán Corrientes, a personal advisor to President Rubios and a member of the Reform Party, and Rabbi Salomón Mordecai, a Hebrew scholar of Sephardic origin and one of the most notable historians in Guatemala, who is a member of the opposite party, the Traditional Party. The two men are to discuss:

Which is mightier, the sword? Or the pen?

Four and a half years ago, when Minister Andrújal, the minister of public instruction, hired Professor Saavedra, the exiled Cuban teacher, to head this school, the minister warned him. "The Escuela Central has a lot of enemies," the minister said, "because it is housed in a building that a lot of people think was stolen by President Rubios, since it once belonged to priests who were expelled from Guatemala for interfering in politics. Now that the priests have been allowed back, a lot of their sympathizers, the members of the Clerical Party—most of whom are religious fanatics—have become acerbic enemies of the school. You must make the school palatable to them so the school will be able to grow."

At the time, Saavedra was stupefied by this request—this order—given to him by the minister himself. How could Saavedra make the school palatable to a bunch of angry religious fanatics? But, by the time he stepped on Guatemalan soil, he had formulated a plan. With the help of his wife, a Guatemalan woman, Saavedra started a series of monthly concerts and evenings of poetry to entice Guatemalan ladies to the school. Then, to attract their husbands, Saavedra recently started a monthly debate that takes place in the main auditorium of the school. In those debates, Saavedra invites two or more men of different backgrounds and opposing points of view to discuss a given topic, and he then lets the audience decide who the winner of the debate is by their applause.

Though this program is not quite a year old, already through the doors of the school have passed some of the most famous names in Guatemala if not in all of Latin America. Writers and poets have debated the merits of the poetry of Walt Whitman; newspapermen and lawyers, the Reconstruction process in the United States; artists and sculptors, the paintings of Claude Monet; scientists and educators, the theories of Charles Darwin; priests and economists, the writings of Karl Marx; and musicians and conductors, the operas of Richard Wagner.

THE APPOINTED TIME for today's debate is still half an hour away, and the auditorium of the school is already almost filled to capacity, something Saavedra cannot believe. Normally there are still audience members straggling in when the debate is half over! Saavedra is looking at the door when he sees Doña Lucrecia Suárez-Villegas arrive.

Doña Lucrecia, a tight-lipped, skinny old woman who always wears a tightly laced corset that keeps her as straight as an arrow despite her abundant years, is a malicious, gossipy old lady who always insists on sitting in "her chair," right in the front row, only to fall asleep. But she has the ear of President Rubios—something everybody knows—so she is respected, if not feared, by everyone. That is why she is treated like royalty by all, Saavedra being the first to do so. He knows that the old lady thinks the world of his school and that she has said so to President Rubios and all of his ministers. So the minute he sees her standing at the door, Saavedra himself rushes to her and escorts the old lady to "her" chair. After he sees that Doña Lucrecia is comfortably seated, he espies more people arriving. Saavedra begs Doña Lucrecia's pardon and excuses himself. He asks his teachers and their assistants to bring whatever other chairs they can find to the auditorium. They place these chairs against the back wall of the hall first, and they are quickly filled, and then along the side aisles, and those also are soon taken. More people keep coming in, and Saavedra, seeing that few seats are available, begins to place additional chairs on the stage while he tells the others to bring still more chairs and to start placing them in the large central aisle. "Make sure there is room for people to enter," he tells his men, all of whom, Julián included, are helping out on this occasion.

Suddenly the room bursts into applause, and people stand up. When he hears the applause, Saavedra, busy on the stage placing chairs, turns around and cannot believe his eyes.

President Rubios has just come in, unannounced, accompanied by his wife and his three eldest sons. He is not wearing his uniform, just a black frock coat. Saavedra rushes down the stage steps to where Rubios is and invites him and his family to come sit on the stage, but Rubios shakes his head. "I did not come here as Rubios the president, but as Rubios the citizen," he says, and then, despite Saavedra's pleading, Rubios and his family sit on one of the side aisles, in the back row. Saavedra makes sure they are as comfortable as he can make them, and, hearing a round of applause, he rushes to the entrance door. Colonel Corrientes, one of the speakers, a tall, commanding man with a thick black mustache and a pointed goatee, has just come in, in full-dress uniform, his chest crowded with medals, his sword gleaming in the flickering gaslights of the auditorium. He is accompanied by his wife, a handsome blond woman wearing a brilliant red evening suit.

The professor greets them and is accompanying them toward the stage when another round of applause lets him know that Rabbi Mordecai, the other speaker, a thin, short man with a full white beard, has arrived. Saavedra asks Julián, "Please, Julián, escort Colonel Corrientes and his wife to the stage." Then he turns and goes to Rabbi Mordecai, who has arrived alone, dressed in a simple frock coat, wearing a black silk yarmulke on his head. Saavedra greets him and escorts him to the stage.

Then, after catching his breath, Saavedra turns around and looks at the room. He sees that *all* the gaslights have indeed been lit, as he told the caretakers to do, and that *all* the tall windows are indeed open, letting the breezes cool the room, which is hot in anticipation. Then, moving to the center of the stage, Saavedra says a few words, greeting the audience and introducing the speakers. "And now, ladies and gentlemen," he finally says, "let our illustrious guests help us decide the question that tonight is our concern. In this century of ours, in this America of ours, what is more important? The pen?" he says, pointing at Rabbi Mordecai, who, sitting at one side of the stage, stands up and bows to the audience. "Or the sword?" he adds, pointing at Colonel Corrientes, who, sitting at the opposite side of the stage, also stands up and bows to the audience.

The two men approach Saavedra, who takes a coin from his pocket, tosses it in the air, catches it, and places it on the top of the back of his left hand, covering it with his right hand. "Heads or tails?" Saavedra asks. Colonel Corrientes takes the initiative, answering first. "Heads," he calls. Saavedra uncovers the coin. "Heads," he says. "The sword comes first." Still not believing his eyes, Saavedra proudly scans the room, filled beyond his wildest dreams, and steps aside. Saavedra sits on the steps at one side of the stage—not realizing that Julián is standing right behind him—and eagerly waits for Colonel Corrientes to start his dissertation.

But no sooner does the old professor sit than another round of applause is heard.

Saavedra looks to the main door of the auditorium and there he sees a handsome older man with balding head and a short gray beard, who, despite his wearing a simple frock coat, gives the impression he is wearing a military uniform.

"Don Manuel!" Saavedra utters, almost to himself, in total disbelief. "The general here too?"

When the crowd realizes who is at the door, everybody stands up and applauds. *Everybody*, including President Rubios, who stops his own applause welcoming Don Manuel only to signal the great general to come sit by his side. Don Manuel begins to walk to where Rubios and his family are sitting, on one of the side aisles in the back row. Rubios signals his eldest son to move out of his chair and stand behind him. Don Manuel reaches the place where the Rubios family is sitting, shakes hands with Rubios, and politely nods to Rubios's wife and children. Rubios then moves out of his own chair and offers it to Don Manuel, who refuses it, insisting that Rubios sit where he was, while Don Manuel sits on the chair Rubios's son was occupying, by Rubios's side. The applause has not ceased. Don Manuel stands up, nods politely to the entire crowd, and then sits down again, quietly facing the stage.

Little by little the room becomes silent again, as all faces turn to Corrientes, onstage.

Colonel Corrientes does not know what to do. Whom to greet first. For a second he is tongue-tied. He doesn't want to break protocol. Don Manuel is the older man and he is both the liberator of Guatemala and the first president the nation ever had.

But Don Manuel, Corrientes tells himself, is no longer the president, Rubios is. And he, Colonel Corrientes, works *for* Rubios. So, after taking a deep breath, he opens his remarks by greeting Rubios first. "President Rubios," he says. Then, after a brief pause, he adds, "Don Manuel. Professor Saavedra. Rabbi Mordecai. Distinguished audience," and starts his dissertation defending the sword.

After a brilliant presentation, received with a great round of applause, Colonel Corrientes withdraws and lets Rabbi Mordecai take the podium.

Rabbi Mordecai, who does *not* work for Rubios, and who had invited his personal friend Don Manuel to come to this debate, opens his remarks by greeting Don Manuel first. "Don Manuel," he says. Then, after a brief pause, he adds, "President Rubios. Professor Saavedra. Colonel Corrientes. Distinguished audience." And then he proceeds with his presentation defending the pen, which is no less brilliant than Corrientes's, and which, like Corrientes's speech, is also received with a great round of applause.

The applause is still going on, and Saavedra is about to stand up from his perch on the steps at one side of the stage and say a few final words before letting the audience decide who is the final winner, when Julián, standing behind him, leans over and, whispering, asks, "Saavedra, may I say a few words?"

Saavedra turns around and looks at Julián with puzzled eyes. He knows Julián is a gentle young man, discreet, knowledgeable, with good manners, and fluent with words. And after his letter commenting on the new legal codes of Guatemala, the letter that was published in *El Progreso,* he knows that Julián has the makings of a very good writer. But a man needs a lot more than that to be a good orator, to speak to an audience, *any* audience. And to speak to *this* audience, after the two excellent presentations made tonight, a man following would need to be more than brilliant. He would have to be incandescent. What could Julián add to what was already said? He begins to shake his head. But Julián insists.

"Please," Julián says. He does not ask, he does not beg. He simply says, "You told me that the most important thing I could do is to let Guatemala know me, didn't you?" He looks around the scintillating room, "Well, Saavedra," he says, "all Guatemala is here." He faces the professor. "Let them know me." He pauses. "The essay I've been working on deals precisely with this topic," he adds and pauses again. "Please," he repeats.

It was the way he said "Please." The way a man with guts—balls—would say it.

Saavedra accepts Julián's dare.

The professor stands up and moves to the center of the stage. "Ladies and gentlemen," he shouts over the applause—still going on—demanding to be heard, as he gestures the audience to quiet down, which the audience politely does, little by little. He lowers his voice. "We have here a young man exiled from Cuba," Saavedra says, "where he wore the opprobrious shackles of a political prisoner when he was but a boy of seventeen because he dreamed of freedom for his beloved country, which, as you all know, is also mine." He turns around and points to Julián, who begins to move toward him. "And he would like to say a few words," Saavedra adds and begins to applaud as he moves out of the way, letting Julián occupy the podium.

The audience, surprised, takes a moment before they join Saavedra in welcoming with their polite applause this young man with unruly hair and a thick mustache, who, dressed in a plain black suit, moves toward the center of the stage. After a few seconds the audience quiets down to an expectant silence.

"Citizens of Guatemala," Julián begins, his voice clear, sure, and fearless. "We are honored this evening with the presence of not one but two of the greatest men in our century." He points to the back corner of the auditorium. "President Rubios and Don Manuel," he says, pointing to them in that order. And then he immediately adds, "Don Manuel and President Rubios," pointing to them in that new order. The audience stands and bursts spontaneously into another round of applause. Julián, shouting over the crowd, continues. "Two great men who—whatever differences they may have set aside—now sit, and will *always* sit, side by side, for the benefit of this great country, Guatemala."

The audience responds with even bigger applause.

Julián waits for them to quiet down. "Thus," he proceeds, his voice now soft and mellow, his eyes sparkling with light, "sit Pen and Sword. Not on opposite sides of the stage," Julián says, pointing to Colonel Corrientes and Rabbi Mordecai, who are sitting on opposite sides of the stage, "but side by side," he says, pointing again at Don Manuel and President Rubios, "the one no stronger than the other; the other no weaker than the one." The audience, now in silence, stares at him, captivated by the quiet sonority of his voice. "For without the sword of Don Manuel, whose valor brought freedom to Guatemala, and the pen of President Rubios, whose new legal codes are making that freedom legendary all over the Americas, this Guatemala we have today would not be the Guatemala to which all the other countries of Latin America look, for guidance and for courage."

The audience as a whole stands up, applauding enthusiastically.

Julián moves on with his thesis, a thesis of brotherly unification. He enraptures everyone in his audience, speaking with simple words, using simple images everyone can understand. And yet every word he utters is branded with the stamp of greatness and truth.

Julián brings his message to a conclusion.

"Separately," he says as he raises his hands made into fists and keeps them apart from each other, "either pen," he looks at his right hand, "or sword," he looks at his left hand, "can help us conquer the world," he finishes his sentence, his voice calm, the voice of a person who is simply stating his case. "But united," he adds, his voice becoming exultant as he starts to bring his two hands together closer to each other, "pen and sword, checking and balancing each other, like mind and heart, like body and soul . . ." he says, looking at each and every one of his audience as he brings his two hands closer and closer together. "United," he repeats, "pen and sword make each of us into that ideal poet-warrior the ancient Greeks dreamed about. And then, all of us, together"—he clasps his two hands together in one powerful entity—"will bring about a new world where nobody will need to conquer anybody else, because we will all be at peace.

With each other. And with our *own* selves. Ladies and gentlemen," he says
as he faces his audience, his eyes aglow, "it is up to each of us to make that
world of tomorrow come true. Today."

For a second the audience is in a state of shock.

Julián's body seems somehow to be resplendent, as if it were radiating
its own light, a light that has permeated every body, every soul in the
room, causing in everyone that overwhelming emotion people experience
only when confronted with an enlightening experience.

Colonel Corrientes and Rabbi Mordecai are the first ones to react.
They both rush to Julián, at the same time, and they both embrace him
first, and then, brotherly, they each embrace each other, as the whole
room bursts into an explosion the likes of which had never been heard in
the whole of Guatemala. Saavedra thinks he sees the walls shake. Never
has he heard such spontaneous applause. Never.

Two weeks ago nobody knew Julián. A week ago Guatemala read him.
Tonight Guatemala heard him.

And now all of Guatemala knows him.

Saavedra rushes to Julián and shakes hands with him, then embraces
him, and then, not being able to contain himself, and not knowing what
else to do, he kisses Julián's cheek. And his kiss brings Julián back to reality,
awakening him, and transforming him, making him again into the Julián
he was before the oration, a rather shy young man with unruly hair and a
thick mustache who stands, dressed in a plain black suit, in the center of
the stage. But a young man who is being showered with a standing ovation
that seems to go on forever.

While the world around Julián shouts and cheers, President Rubios
and Don Manuel, the two of them standing up side by side, are, like the
rest of the crowd, applauding heartily as each of them is asking himself
the very same question: Who *is* this man?

Except that Rubios's eyes seem to be puzzled as he asks that question.

While the eyes of Don Manuel are filled with admiration as he looks at
Julián.

MOMENTS LATER, as Julián walks back to his little room in the house of
the Ladino widow, he stops by El *Último* Adiós and finds the place totally

deserted, except for Panoplo, the wrinkled old Mayan man who runs the cantina.

Outside, the night is cool and dark. No moon can be seen. No stars. A thick evening fog has embraced the city. Julián has found his way to the cantina almost by instinct, his will more than his feet guiding him through the tortuous and steep shortcut he takes every night to go back to his bed.

Panoplo welcomes Julián, even though he was about to close, and both Julián and Panoplo sit at a tiny turquoise-painted wooden table, opposite each other, Julián having one shot of gin after another, while Panoplo drinks straight from a bottle of mescal that has no label.

The place is lit by a single kerosene lamp, located on the scarred wood of the counter behind them. And though the flame of the lamp is turned really low, it casts huge shadows of Julián and the old Mayan man on the roughly stuccoed ocher walls inside the cantina; shadows that, flickering constantly, make the large, colorful flowers painted on those walls seem to come alive. The musty smells of men's sweat and of alcohol inundate the small room that, with its welcoming warmth, makes Julián feel as if he were home—the only home Julián has known in a long, long time—perhaps because in that room he finds in Panoplo not only listening ears but an understanding heart.

Still in a daze, unable to believe that he did as he did, Julián tells Panoplo everything that happened in the school's auditorium. And with his eyes fastened on the shot glass in his hands—which Panoplo, listening quietly, keeps refilling the minute it is empty—as if searching on the surface of that tiny shot glass for an explanation, Julián talks. And talks. Apparently to the old Mayan man. But Panoplo knows Julián is talking to himself. And when a man is talking aloud to himself, the old Mayan man knows, one sits, and one listens in silence, as Panoplo does, his eyes fastened on Julián, whose hands have not ceased to tremble as he speaks.

Julián is still shocked by the experience, so new to him.

"Not by the applause," he tells Panoplo. "No, not by that. But by the experience itself, when something happened to me I do not yet quite understand. It was," he tells Panoplo, "as if all of a sudden I had been possessed by something stronger than myself. I had no intention of doing what I did, Panoplo, I swear I really didn't. I just wanted to say a few words and thank the people there for being who they were, for achieving in their own country and during their own lifetimes the liberty that I dream of day and night for my own country," he says.

The old Mayan man keeps listening in silence and keeps nodding his head up and down. He knows well what Julián is talking about. He understands. He, like Julián, also fervently dreams of liberty, not only for his own people, but for himself as well. What would it be like to be free, he asks himself, free to speak again his own language, free to practice his own religion, free to be proud again of being who he is, a Mayan man living on Mayan land? What would it be like to be governed by Mayan men sitting side by side with white men, just as he sits side by side with Julián, both white and Mayan men equally sharing the destinies of this great country? How much would he give to achieve that?

Julián shoots the cool gin in his shot glass down his throat again and then, staring at his again empty glass, sees reflected in it the face of Panoplo, who keeps on nodding and nodding. Julián raises his head and looks at the old Mayan man, his eyes searching for Panoplo's eyes until Panoplo's eyes meet Julián's squarely across the tiny table.

"You understand, don't you?" Julián asks.

Panoplo nods his head. Then, slowly, deliberately, he shoots some more mescal down his throat. And then, after wiping his mouth, he stares in total silence at the bottle in his hands for a long while.

There's a long pause.

"Yes, Ginebrita," Panoplo finally answers, "I do understand. It has happened to me." He raises his eyes and again stares deeply into Julián's. "It is frightening, isn't it? When the gods take hold of you and decide to speak through you?"

Julián nods silently, in agreement.

Panoplo continues talking in a soft voice, almost as if talking to himself. "And since the gods do not know how to lie . . ." He sighs, a deep, deep sigh that seems to come from the innermost part of his soul. "Well, you know . . ." he adds after a while, "when you tell the truth, people listen. Truth is so difficult to find that, when one hears it, it shines through, no matter what." Panoplo pours some more gin in Julián's shot glass while he himself shoots more mescal, that firewater he likes so much, down his throat, straight from his bottle.

They both are silent for a long while.

Then, after he shoots the gin in his shot glass down his throat, Julián stands up and begins to take out his leather bag, to pay for his drinks.

"I cannot accept money from one who has been chosen by the gods," Panoplo says.

Julián insists, but the old Mayan man raises his eyes to Julián and looks up at him with the saddest eyes Julián has ever seen.

"It's painful, very painful to be chosen by the gods," Panoplo continues. "You may not know it yet, but it is very painful," he adds, lowering his eyes.

But then he raises his eyes again to Julián, and this time they are suddenly beaming with an incredible joy, becoming sparkling, as his forehead shines as if lit from the inside. "And yet, it is exultant," he continues, "when one is riding high on *Xocomil,* the wave of the gods. The crest of that wave is taller than the tops of the tallest mountains!" He smiles as he looks at Julián. "Maybe that is why the fall is that much more deeply felt," he says as he stands up and gives Julián's shoulder a friendly pat.

"Prepare for the fall, my friend. But do not ever, *ever,* let the fear of falling keep you from praying to ride high again atop the wave of the gods. Pray for *Xocomil,* my friend. Pray for the wave of the gods. And when it comes, ride it, ride it as high as you can and for as long as you can, and let the gods speak and tell their truth through you. What people will do after that . . . the pain they will make you go through, that will not matter, for the gods have spoken through you, and the gods speak only the truth."

CHAPTER IX

OWERFUL NEW ORATOR, proclaims the headline on the front page of the following morning's *El Progreso*, the newspaper of the Reform Party, which along with *El Estandarte*—the paper of the Traditional Party—is placed daily on Don Manuel's breakfast table. Below the headline appears a review of last night's debate at the Escuela Central. Running alongside the review there is a large pen-and-ink drawing showing a young man with unruly black hair and a thick mustache who, wearing a plain black suit, is standing at the podium, his two hands apart, made into fists and raised above his head, as he is speaking to a room bursting with people.

As usual, Gabriela is the last one to enter the dining room.

She sees that everyone is seated, that coffee has already been served, and that her father has *El Progreso* opened wide in his hands. She looks at the paper and, from across the table where she stands, she is able to read the headline of the paper and thinks she recognizes the young man in the drawing. Could that be a drawing of our new teacher, Professor Julián? she asks herself.

"Let me see, let me see, let me see!" she shouts as she rushes to her father and grabs the paper out of his hands.

"Gabriela!" her mother, Doña Rosaura, admonishes scoldingly and perhaps even a little bit too loudly. Doña Rosaura never likes to raise her voice. Elegant, decent women never do. So she never does. Or at least tries not to. But there are times when a woman, no matter how decent and elegant she is, has to show some strength and determination. And that time is almost any time Gabriela is around. "Watch your manners, young lady!" she says, decisively. Then turns to her husband. "Manuel," she says, "you cannot let Gabriela do this to you! You are spoiling this girl, making her into an unbearable brat! What kind of an example is she going to be to her younger sister!"

Gabriela's kid sister, Carola, who is sitting opposite Gabriela's place at the beautifully set breakfast table, covers her mouth with her embroidered linen napkin so as not to be seen laughing at her mother's predicament. It is a known fact that Gabriela can do anything she wants to or get anything she wants from Don Manuel.

"When are you going to learn good manners and behave as a young lady must, like your older sister!" Doña Rosaura continues, pointing to the young blond girl who, sitting silently by Doña Rosaura's side, is trying to hide a smile. "Sol has never once in her entire life given me a single headache! But you, Gabriela, *you* . . . !"

The youngest girl, ten-year-old Carola, Doña Rosaura's "baby," interrupts her mother's diatribe, her voice small and tentative.

"What about me, Mommy?" she says, plaintively. "Have I ever given you a headache?"

Doña Rosaura turns to her and pats her delicately on the cheek. "No, my love," she says, "of course not. You have never given me a single headache. And you won't either, will you? You are never going to behave like Gabriela, are you?"

Little Carola looks at her mother with teary eyes, shakes her head, and says, almost whining, "Oh, no, Mommy, I promise you I won't."

Then, as her mother faces her husband again, Carola faces Gabriela and, after making sure her mother is not looking at her, she first gives Gabriela a big, meaningful grin, and then she sticks her tongue out at her sister.

"Manuel," Doña Rosaura says, addressing her husband, who is trying hard to concentrate on his breakfast, "are you just going to sit there, drink your coffee, and do nothing, as usual? What do you expect me to do with Gabriela if you insist on letting her get away with everything!" She turns to Gabriela. "Gabriela," she says. "Give that paper back to your father right now, and apologize for what you just did. *Now,* I said!"—hitting the white linen covered table with her index finger several times—"and I mean now, Gabriela. *Now!*"

Gabriela, of course, never listens to her mother. And certainly not today. While Doña Rosaura has been going on and on, complaining and complaining about her to Don Manuel—something that happens more than once daily—Gabriela, after sticking out her tongue in reply to her kid sister, started to read the review, and upon reaching a certain point, ignoring that her mother is still complaining to her father about her, she raises her voice, and hurt, almost in anger, interrupts her mother.

"Daddy!" she says, her voice quivering almost to the point of crying as she points at the drawing on the front page, "why didn't you take me with you last night? It says here you were there, and that President Rubios brought his three eldest sons. And you didn't even tell me about it! And you *know,*" she adds, not giving the opportunity for anybody to say a word, her angry, whining voice turning even angrier, "you *know* that I would have wanted to be there! You *know* that I would have given anything to listen to *him!*"

"What are you talking about?" asks Doña Rosaura, looking at Gabriela, while Sol, now intrigued by what Gabriela has said, adds, "Who is that *him* you're referring to?"

Gabriela turns to face her older sister, sitting always *so* correctly next to her mother, and violently shakes her head. "Oh, Sol, you never know *anything!*" she says, totally exasperated, directing her anger at her sister, her voice loud and with more than a cutting edge.

"*Gabriela!*" her mother tells her. "Please, compose yourself. A lady never raises her—"

"But it is true, Mamá," Gabriela tells her mother, her voice now more than defensive. "Sol never knows *anything,*" Gabriela repeats, facing her mother, heavily underlining the *any* in anything, "and you know it," she adds, belligerently. "She's always lost in the clouds!" she says, then adds, her voice now sarcastic, "When she's not playing the piano or hiding in the gazebo by the river!" She then faces Sol again. "Haven't you heard me talk about that new Cuban teacher at school," she says to her older sister, "the one who was thrown out of Cuba because of his poems? Or are you deaf?" She doesn't give time for Sol to answer. She turns and faces the rest of her family. "Well, last night he gave a speech at *my* school," she says, angry, heavily underscoring the word *my*. "*My* school," she repeats. "And Daddy was there, and he didn't even tell me he was going to go there! Listen to *this!*" she says as she begins to read aloud the final paragraph of the review, her voice quivering with intense emotion.

> *The young exiled Cuban proudly wears the heavy toga of ostracism. From the moment he pronounces his opening words, one discovers beneath that toga the tunic of a brilliant orator—of a Demosthenes, of a Cicero. His words now imitate the soothing sounds of the murmuring brook, now roar like the wildest of torrents. He leaves the podium amid explosive applause, after having proved that he knows his history and his philosophy; that his erudition is encyclopedic, and that he knows how to call upon all the resources of eloquence. People of Guatemala, a powerful new orator has been revealed. Let's listen to him.*

Gabriela stops her reading, looks at her father, and slowly shakes her head from side to side, making her long banana-curls swing like soft pendulums around her pretty pink face. "Oh, Daddy, I cannot believe you did this to me! Why didn't you take me along? You know, you *know* I would have loved to be there!" she says, deeply hurt.

And then she begins to sob.

Doña Rosaura instantly throws her lace-hemmed napkin on the table, rushes to her daughter, embraces her tight, and then faces Don Manuel. "Now are you happy? Look what you've done!" She then turns to Gabriela, who goes on crying and crying, big tears sliding down her pretty pink cheeks. "Now, Gabriela," Doña Rosaura says, "hush, hush, my little love. Hush, hush," she says and keeps on saying as she holds her not-quite-fourteen-year-old daughter, the *only* one that gives her headaches, tight against her heart.

BY THE TIME Julián gets to school that morning—with a painfully throbbing hangover headache—it is extremely late, so late it is almost time for the noontime meal. Thank God I am not teaching today, he thinks as he enters Saavedra's office. Saavedra smiles at Julián as he sees him come in, and grins ear to ear when he surprises Julián by showing him the newspaper review.

After Julián reads it, he rushes elated to the center of town—the painfully throbbing headache now miraculously gone—and buys several copies of the paper. He carefully cuts the review out, and he encloses it within short, swiftly written letters that he sends to Señor Fermín and Lucía in Mexico City.

WHEN SEÑOR FERMÍN gets Julián's letter and a copy of the review, he reads the newspaper article over and over, again and again, and then shows it proudly to his friends, saying, "I told that boy he had a future in Guatemala, didn't I? Well, look at this, look at *this!*"

WHEN LUCÍA gets Julián's letter and a copy of the review, her first reaction is that of anger. In the entire letter there is not one personal word for her. Not a single one. Only the simple, *I send you my love.* And then a plain, *Yours, as always.*

Doesn't he know how much she needs to hear of his desperate need of her? Doesn't he know that it is only his words that give her the courage to face her friends and family, the very same friends and family who think that he is not the kind of a man who will keep his word? The very same friends and family who think that he will never come back and, least of all, marry her? Doesn't he know what the Cuban song says, that absence just brings oblivion? How long has he been away from her? Weeks? Months? Soon it will be over half a year. Does he remember that? Is he aware of how long it has been since they saw each other last? Doesn't he know that little by little she is beginning to forget what his face, the face of the man she is supposed to marry, looks like?

Time after time, when she is all alone on her bed and feels her long black hair caress her naked breasts, she closes her eyes and tries to imagine what it will be like to be with him, his skin next to her skin, his lips to her breasts, the weight of his body heavily pressing against her. But time after time, as she dreams of him, his face, that face she would love to press against her heart, begins to dissolve little by little, becoming at first flat—like the flat face on the fading sepia photograph of himself he gave her to keep—and then, slowly, it begins to evanesce, disappearing altogether as if into thin air, leaving her alone on her bed, her long black hair caressing her naked breasts, while her arms embrace nothing but broken dreams and unfulfilled promises.

And as if that were not bad enough, he tells now in this letter that he is doing all of this for the good of Cuba.

For the good of Cuba? she asks, incredulously, not believing the words in the letter. Did she just read, For the good of *Cuba?*

What about *us?* she asks, demands. What about, For the good of *us?*

Angrily, she crumples both letter and review in her hands and throws them on the floor. What about me? she says, speaking to the ball of crumpled paper on the floor as if those two crunched, badly mangled pieces of paper were him, lying right there, on the floor, at her feet, prostrate. When are you going to stop thinking of Cuba and start thinking of me?

Me!

Then, realizing what she has just done, angry at herself for having lost her temper, she picks up the crumpled papers off the floor, straightens them the best she can, and smooths out their partly torn corners. She goes to the office of her father, sits at his desk, and applies glue to the back of both letter and review—not too much, she doesn't want them to fall apart. Then, after delicately positioning letter and review on opposite pages of her album, she presses each down, gently passing the tips of her fingers over each, carefully taking the bubbles out, until she is happy with the way they look.

She leaves the album—open—right where it belongs, on top of her father's desk, where a public letter and a public review deserve to be: in a public album in a public place.

That will impress them—her friends and family—she thinks, those who think Julián will never amount to anything.

She is about to leave the room when she remembers something.

She comes back to her father's desk, and with her father's pen she gently underlines part of the text of the letter, where it says, *For the good of Cuba.* Yes, she thinks, if anything will impress them, that will. Then, as she looks at it, she grabs her father's pen again and, with a bold stroke of the pen, she swiftly underlines a second time one word, a single word, the last word in the sentence:

Cuba.

And as she forcefully underlines the word *Cuba* a second time, the sharp pen tears the thin paper, still partly wet from the glue.

CHAPTER X

A DISCREET KNOCK at the door interrupts Julián, who is in Saavedra's office, sitting in his chair and leaning wearily on the huge partners desk, barely lit by a kerosene lamp turned very low, as he writes in the tiny notebook he always carries with him—the notebook where he jots down his most intimate thoughts and ideas as they come, so later on he can include them in his diary, kept at home.

> *Don't you wish that before something important happens in your life, a sign of some kind, music of some kind—yes, music, anything musical, from the blaring, epic fanfare of a thousand trumpets to the delicate, lyric plucking of a single harp string—could be heard, letting you know in advance that something great is about to happen, that something great is about to—*

Julián does not complete the sentence he is writing.

He turns around and sees, framed by the heavy dark brown velvet portières, Professor Saavedra and his wife, in impeccable formal evening attire. The professor, in a tailored black frock coat with black silk faille lapels, holds a black beaver top hat in his white-gloved hands, and the buttons on his gloves—made of iridescent nacre—glitter like a rainbow even in the dim light of the room. His wife, a former Guatemalan beauty who still remains a beauty despite her years, is dressed in a dark purple velvet dress with long tight sleeves and a sizable bustle. The front of the skirt is heavily ornamented with a swagged fringe, while the tight bodice has a wide and low-cut square neckline outlined with pale cream Valenciennes lace that handsomely frames her still-beautiful breasts, which are, as the new fashion dictates, modestly shielded by a gauzy and almost transparent pale cream lace mantilla. Her hands—gloved, as married women's should be—hold an exquisite ivory fan trimmed with pale cream lace; and her silvering dark hair, piled in a chignon, is adorned with a single magnolia blossom whose silken pale cream color matches perfectly the color of her gloves, of her fan, and of the elegant lace that trims her bodice.

Upon seeing them, Julián instantly places his pen in the inkwell built into his side of the partners desk, closes his tiny notebook, puts it inside his coat pocket, and then rushes to Señora Saavedra. He bows in front of her, gently takes the hand she offers to him, gloved in the softest, thinnest kid, and brings it close to his lips as if he were about to kiss it, but being careful not to—as custom dictates.

"Señora," he says, in utmost sincerity, "the Guatemalan moon, beautiful as it is, pales in your presence."

Señora Saavedra gently smiles at him. No woman can ever be blind to Julián's quiet yet virile attractiveness, nor is Señora Saavedra. Then, delicately touching his shoulder with her lace fan, she says, coquettishly, "Julián, keep those compliments for the pretty girls at the party. As you can see"—she points at her husband with her fan—"pretty as you say I may be . . . I am already taken," she adds, smiling broadly at him, and making the three of them break into a chuckle.

"Ready?" asks Professor Saavedra, who seems eager to get going.

Julián runs the fingers of his right hand through his unruly long hair, trying to tame it. It has grown far too long, and early this morning he had thought of going to Cholito's barbershop in the afternoon to have it cut, but being so heavily involved in his thoughts, he simply forgot. When late in the afternoon Saavedra reminded him about the reception tonight at Don Manuel's house—to celebrate the coming of age of Don Manuel's oldest daughter—all he could do was to quickly set aside his books, rush back to his room, and beg the landlady to, please, *please*, let him use her bath, which the landlady let him do. This *one* time. Then, clean and shaven, having no frock coat, he donned his better black suit, neatly pressed by a Mayan woman working for the Ladino lady in whose house Julián is staying. It did have a couple of places where the black wool fabric was beginning to shine perhaps a bit too much, Julián thought, when he looked at his image in the small mirror in his room, but, in the darkness of the evening to come, and with so many other people there, who will be able to notice this? he thought, hoping to feel better, even though he knew that he was just trying to fool himself. Still, where there's a clean heart, nothing else matters, he reassured himself right before he started to walk back to the school. And his heart was clean. That, he knew to be true.

"Ready," Julián says, answering Saavedra's question, as he runs his fingers through his unruly long hair one more time, still failing to tame it.

Then he gallantly offers his arm to Señora Saavedra, giving Professor Saavedra a questioning look, which Saavedra answers by nodding at him, thus giving his consent for Julián to escort his wife. Señora Saavedra takes Julián's arm. And the two of them, side by side, start to walk slowly away from the office, followed closely by the professor, whose tight, heavily starched linen standing collar is already making him suffer.

Right before she enters the carriage that is waiting for them at the main entrance door of the school to take them to the reception, Señora Saavedra turns to Julián and, tapping his shoulder several times with her lace fan, she admonishes him. "Julián," she says, flirtatiously, "the minute we get to the reception, I want you to forget that my husband and I exist. Young people belong with young people. I will be very angry—and my husband will be too, let me warn you, Julián, very, *very* angry—if we don't see you waltz with every beautiful girl at the party." And with that she enters the carriage, followed by her husband—who sits nervously by her side, constantly fingering his offending collar—and by Julián, who sits quietly opposite the two of them.

As the horses begin to trot, bouncing the carriage noisily through the already-dark streets of Guatemala City, Saavedra's wife, who cannot believe this is truly happening to her, turns to her husband, sitting by her side, and cannot stop herself from babbling over and over again, "Isn't this exciting! Look at me! Accompanied by two of the handsomest men in all of Guatemala! Who would have believed it? I still don't understand how it was we were invited to this fancy reception! And invited by none other

than Don Manuel *himself!* To such an incredible party at his *very* own
house! And on *such* an occasion! Everybody who is anybody in Guatemala
is going to be there tonight! Isn't this incredibly exciting!" Her husband,
who has been looking out the side window, pretends to listen to her and
nods, once or twice, out of habit, though he hasn't heard a single word his
wife of thirty-one years has said.

Suddenly the carriage hits a very bad bump, shaking everybody inside,
and forces the old lady to look ahead. It is then she notices Julián sitting
there, seemingly lost in thought, as he is reminding himself why he is
going to this most fancy of receptions where everyone will be wearing
their very best formal attire while he is wearing his well-worn black suit. I
am going to this party that I really don't want to attend—Julián is thinking—for the very same reason I am not rereading Cicero tonight in prepa-
ration for tomorrow's lecture class.

For the good of Cuba.

The carriage arrives in front of a huge two-story stone mansion that
is magnificently lit, one of the very few buildings in the whole of Guatemala—other than the churches—that is two stories high, as if Don
Manuel, not satisfied with challenging his entire world, had also decided
to challenge earthquakes. Julián is the first one to step out of the carriage.
As he helps Señora Saavedra down the steps, he hears some wonderful
distant music, a slow, sensual Viennese waltz he doesn't remember ever
hearing.

"Oh, listen to that!" Señora Saavedra says as she steps out of the carriage. "Leave it to Don Manuel to play music written by a composer from
this side of the Atlantic."

Julián looks at her, intrigued. "A composer from the Americas wrote
that waltz?" he asks. "I'd swear that's a Viennese waltz."

"Well, yes. It *is* a Viennese waltz," answers Señora Saavedra, who
being in charge of the music concerts at the school, knows her music.
"But a Mexican wrote it. Juan de Dios Rosado. A Mexican *Indian*," she
adds, stressing the word Indian. Professor Saavedra steps out of the carriage, fingering his bothersome collar, and joins them. "He wrote it,"
Señora Saavedra continues, "when was it? Ten, twelve years ago, during
the time when the unfortunate Maximilian and his wife Carlota were
emperor and empress of Mexico. 'Song of the Danube,' that's how

Rosado called it, even though I'm sure the poor man probably does not even know where the Danube is. That is why to this day many people— not only in Europe but here in the Americas as well—still do not believe he wrote it. How could a Mexican, they say, and of all Mexicans, a Mexican *Indian*, have written anything so beautiful, so civilized—and so European—as that waltz? But he did! Have you really never heard it before, Julián?"

Julián shakes his head as he offers her his arm, again with Saavedra's tacit permission.

"Well then, Julián, you who love beauty so much, you should consider yourself a very lucky man tonight. To be able to hear such beautiful music for the first time in such a beautiful place as this. It's like an omen, isn't it? An omen of great beauty. Isn't this place incredibly beautiful?" Señora Saavedra adds, looking at the magnificent entrance, two-story-high double doors that are opened by two young Mayan men dressed in formal European livery as the three of them approach, causing Señora Saavedra to say "Oh . . . !" when she sees the splendor of the entrance hall to the palatial mansion.

As the doors open, the music, which up to then had been more felt than heard, suddenly becomes warm and rich, embracing the three of them with its dreamy sensuousness. An orchestra, made up of Mayan and Ladino men conducted by a white man, all of them wearing elegant frock coats, is on the veranda that runs around the entire second floor of the house, overlooking the immense patio where the reception is taking place. The patio, filled with huge magnolia trees that permeate the cool evening air of the sparkling night with their wonderful sweet scent, has been ornamented for the occasion with myriads of lighted candles set inside perforated tin lanterns that are everywhere—*everywhere*: placed on tables, on steps, on railings, on pedestals; hanging from the trees and from the balconies, and suspended from thin, invisible wires strung across the entire patio, all aglitter like stars softly flickering in the darkness of the night.

Servants, Mayan men and women dressed in black with white aprons, circulate about the patio, their white-gloved hands holding large silver trays that bear cut-crystal glasses filled with bubbling champagne. The various guests who have already arrived are all in full formal evening attire—the men in impeccable frock coats, the women glittering in silk and satin bustle dresses—and they are as sparkling as the sparkling lights illuminating the patio, and as the sparkling music the orchestra has been playing, which tempts everyone to dance. But no dancing is taking place. Not until after President Rubios arrives. Protocol demands it.

As Saavedra, his wife, and Julián begin to descend the three marble steps that lead down to the patio, a loud voice is heard from across it, and a man quickly steps from the shadows and moves toward them, his hand already extended in a warm, welcoming greeting. "Saavedra, how great of you to come!"

"Don Manuel!" Saavedra says, vigorously shaking hands with the general. "This is my wife," the professor adds. Don Manuel gallantly bows to her. "And this is Señor—" he starts to say, pointing at Julián. But he cannot finish his sentence.

"Julián!" Don Manuel interrupts Saavedra, his voice filled with both joy and admiration as he greets Julián intimately with his arms outstretched, smiling broadly as he roughly embraces Julián's shoulders with his large hands. "How great that *you* could come," he adds, warmly welcoming Julián to his home. "I had both the pleasure and the honor of hearing you speak the other night at Saavedra's school. A beautiful, heartfelt speech, beautifully delivered." Then, letting go of Julián, he turns to the rest of the guests. "Ladies and gentlemen! Ladies and gentlemen!" he shouts. The guests turn to look at Don Manuel, who faces Julián and with lowered voice confides, "Julián, do you know how the whole of Guatemala will be calling you after tomorrow?" Julián, puzzled, smiles at Don Manuel and shakes his head from side to side. Don Manuel goes on. "Well then, son, you will find out soon enough." He turns to the attentive crowd and shouts, "Ladies and gentlemen, we have the honor to have with us a young man who in addition to being a brilliant teacher . . ."—he lowers his voice, again addressing Julián in a confidential aside—"My daughter Gabriela has not stopped talking about you, Julián." Then, facing his guests again he continues, shouting, "This man is also a brilliant orator. And if anyone doubts it, let's ask Don Aurelio González Mendoza, the literary critic from our great conservative paper, *El Estandarte,* who in an article that will appear tomorrow calls him"—he looks at Julián, then at his guests again—"*Doctor Torrent!* Because of the endless rushing stream of brilliant thoughts that flows from his mouth when he speaks!" He offers his hand to Julián, who shakes it heartily while the entire party of guests applauds enthusiastically. "Doctor Torrent, son," Don Manuel says, a sincere smile lighting his face, "welcome to Guatemala."

Saavedra looks meaningfully at his wife, who answers by meaningfully looking back at her husband. All of a sudden each has realized that the reason they were invited to this reception was to bring Julián. But how could that be? they each wonder. When they received Don Manuel's invitation, Julián was an unknown. He had not yet delivered his magnificent oration at Saavedra's school. And yet, both Saavedra and his wife feel, with total certainty, that the only reason they were invited to this reception was to bring Julián.

"Rosaura," says Don Manuel, addressing his wife, who has just joined them and stands by her husband's side, "this is Señor and Señora Saav— Oh, but you already know each other from school, don't you?" Doña Rosaura nods her head. "And this," Don Manuel adds, proudly indicating Julián, "this is Julián, the wonderful teacher about whom our Gabriela has not stopped talking."

Julián bows politely to Don Manuel's wife.

"Señora," he says, taking the gloved hand she offers close to his lips, stopping short of kissing it, as custom demands.

Doña Rosaura looks at Julián and, like every other woman Julián meets, Doña Rosaura finds him immensely attractive, for reasons she cannot really understand. What makes him so? His candor? His warmth? His wonderful smile? "A great pleasure having all of you here," Doña Rosaura says, addressing her remarks to all three of her guests. "And, if I may say so," she adds, looking admiringly at Señora Saavedra, "what a stunning fan you have there, Señora Saavedra. Ceylon ivory?"

While the two women are getting acquainted, Don Manuel takes the opportunity to address the men. "Gentlemen," he says, "let's get out of here quickly, before the women realize we are gone!" He gestures Saavedra to follow him as he grabs Julián by the arm and, lowering his voice, confides, "I have some very important people here, Julián. Perhaps the two of us can entice them to part with some of their money so we can buy weapons to free Cuba and help you with your noble cause. My friends at El Ateneo have told me what you want to do. But the pen can only go so far, my boy, only so far. Come this way, Julián. And you too, Saavedra. This way." He leads them to an area in a remote corner of the huge patio, behind a luxuriantly leafy magnolia tree that shelters that area from the eyes of everyone else at the party. There, several elegantly dressed men are already gathered, animatedly talking in a loud, argumentative yet friendly manner as they gesture passionately with their fragrant cigars.

"Cuban cigars?" asks Julián, inhaling their deliciously pungent perfume.

"What else, son?" says Don Manuel.

He calls one of the servants, who comes in, carrying a mahogany-and-brass humidor in his hands. "Here, have one," says Don Manuel, opening the humidor and offering its contents to Julián. "And you too, Saavedra. Have one," Don Manuel immediately adds, apparently addressing Saavedra, but as he says it, his eyes remain fastened on Julián.

Don Manuel looks at Julián with a mixture of admiration and hope—admiration for what Julián has already achieved, and hope for what he knows Julián has yet to accomplish. He no longer sees Julián as the wonderful teacher his daughter Gabriela has been hailing, nor as the magnificent writer the newspapers have been commending, nor as the outstanding orator the whole of Guatemala has been praising. Instead, he sees Julián as a son: the son he does not have. The son he lost to malaria. The son he would have loved to have had by his side as he fought to free Guatemala.

Suddenly the waltz music the string musicians have been playing up to that time is interrupted abruptly, and after a moment of silence, the orchestra's brass section proudly begins to play the national anthem of Guatemala, the blaring trumpets singing heroically.

"Rubios must have arrived," Don Manuel tells Julián and Saavedra the moment he hears that call. "Please, excuse me," he tells them and the rest of his male guests, and, slowly, almost martially, he starts to walk toward the entrance steps, where he sees President Rubios and his wife already standing. The rest of the men who were meeting behind the huge magnolia tree cease their loud talking and their wild gesturing, and, cigars in hand, they follow Don Manuel, almost as a retinue, to meet and welcome Rubios.

At the same time, Doña Rosaura, who up to then had been patiently listening and listening to Señora Saavedra babble on and on about this new piece of music or that other piece of music, hears the blaring of the trumpets announcing the arrival of President Rubios. Doña Rosaura turns around and, almost frantically, begins to scan the guests, looking for someone in particular. "Where can that girl be?" she says aloud, shaking her head, "What can be keeping her?" She notices her two younger daughters rushing to meet Rubios, and grabbing Gabriela by the arm, Doña Rosaura asks her in a soft voice, "Gabriela, where is Sol?" Gabriela looks at her mother. "Last I saw her she was sitting at her dressing table putting even *more* flowers in her hair," Gabriela says as she escapes Doña Rosaura's grip and runs with her baby sister to the entrance steps. Doña Rosaura faces Señora Saavedra, "Please excuse me, Señora Saavedra. I'm sure you understand," she says, nodding politely at Señora Saavedra, who returns the cordial nod. Doña Rosaura, then, still scanning the crowd for her oldest daughter, begins to walk hurriedly toward the entrance steps to welcome Rubios and his wife.

Tonight Rubios is Rubios the president, not Rubios the citizen, and he is dressed as such. A white moiré silk band edged with blue—the colors of Guatemala—diagonally spans his double-breasted black silk frock coat, and medals and ribbons cover his proud chest. Servants remove a black silk cape that hangs from his shoulders, and take a black top hat from his white-gloved hands. His wife, dressed in a magnificent cobalt blue satin gown, proudly stands by his side, as they both are greeted by all the guests who have rushed to them.

Meanwhile, Julián has remained behind.

Standing by the side of the huge magnolia tree, he watches everyone—women as well as men—rush to the entrance steps to welcome President Rubios, their loud oohs and aahs now accompanied by the soothing sound of the string section of the orchestra, which has resumed playing lilting waltzes.

Julián watches Rubios shake hands with each of the men and bow to each of the beautiful women. And then, all of a sudden, something snaps inside of Julián, making him smile at himself. He has been so busy greeting Don Manuel's gentlemen friends, shaking this man's hand and that other man's hand, that he had not taken the time to look at—and appreciate in detail—all the alluring young women, the niñas, who all of a sudden have come into focus and seem to fill the entire patio with their beauty as they excitedly rush to meet Rubios and his wife.

From where he is, almost in hiding by the side of the huge magnolia tree, Julián surveys each and every one of these beautiful girls. He notices their slender bodies, which are corseted as tight as can be; and their beautiful breasts that seem about to burst out of those tight, imprisoning bodices; and their large bustles that sway gently when they walk, just like the palm trees of his native Cuba sway, sensuously, almost sinfully. And as he looks at them, Julián remembers Señora Saavedra's words. "Julián," the old lady said, "young people belong with young people. I will be very angry—and my husband will be too, let me warn you, Julián, very, *very* angry—if we don't see you waltz with every beautiful girl at the party." If the old lady said that, what else could he do but follow her advice? he thinks. The problem is going to be that in order to comply with the old lady's request he will have to dance with every single girl at the party, they are all so very beautiful! Every time he looks at one, she seems to be more beautiful than the one he looked at before. But then he looks at yet a third one, and the other two girls pale in comparison. Well, he tells himself, if waltzing is what Señora Saavedra told me to do . . . No, not told me, but *commanded* me to do. Well, what else can I do but to obey the old lady's command? He thinks of Lucía in Mexico, and mentally begs her to forgive him, which he knows she will, at least this once. What harm can there be in waltzing once or twice? Or even three or four times? Limping does not show too badly as one waltzes, he tells himself.

Besides, he thinks, what does the Cuban song say?

And then he hums to himself the bawdy Cuban song he heard Yubirio sing day and night while working on the deck of *El Futuro,* the small steamship that brought Julián here, to this magnificent land that is filled with bewitching women with eyes so dark and so intense that gypsy women would envy them!

> *The man who doesn't know how to drink*
> *and doesn't know how to make love,*
> *What good is a man like that?* Eh?
> *What good is a man like that?*

He smiles to himself as he looks at the glass of champagne in his hand. I've already been doing a little drinking tonight, he thinks, so what harm can there be in a little flirting?

No sooner does he think this than out of the corner of his eye he feels more than notices something, or someone, moving on the second floor of the house.

He raises his eyes and turns his head.

And there, at the top of the stairs, he sees a young woman, who, from where Julián stands, seems to be the most beautiful girl he has ever seen in his life.

She has the shiniest hair, golden hair that frames her head as if it were a resplendent halo that in the light of the myriads of flickering candles surrounding her, seems to glimmer, every so often sparkling of fire. Decorated with the tiniest of white flowers, her hair, pinned up in back, falls in long curls over her shoulders, which are as white as alabaster and are modestly covered with a delicate, almost transparent, white lace shawl that falls languidly over her magnificent white silk bustle dress.

Julián looks at her and then shakes his head, not believing his eyes.

On her shoulders, are those *wings?* White *wings?* Like the exquisite and beautifully carved white wings of the white marble angels he sees each day as he passes by the cemetery? He shakes his head again, rubs his eyes, and looks at the girl one more time, still at the top of the stairs. But the wings are now gone. Were they ever there? This champagne is getting to me, he thinks. He looks at her again. It is then he notices the shawl the girl is wearing, partially covering her naked shoulders. In the dim light of the night what I saw as wings must have been this shawl, he tells himself as he focuses his eyes on her again.

Julián is intrigued.

Who *is* this young woman? he asks himself. He thinks he has seen her before. But where? He feels that he knows her well, really well, almost intimately. And yet, he cannot place her. From where he is standing, Julián sees her only in silhouette. He moves to the other side of the magnolia tree to take a better look at her, and his movement causes the girl to turn and face him.

She looks at him, her eyes fastened on Julián's, leaning her head slightly to one side, scrutinizing Julián's face, intrigued by him. Who *is* this young man? she seems to be asking herself. She thinks she has seen him before. But where? She feels that she knows him well, really well, even intimately. And yet, she cannot quite place him.

She descends a couple of steps of the staircase, to take a closer look at him, just as Julián takes a couple of steps toward her, to take a closer look at her.

She pauses to face Julián, her eyes fastened to his.

He pauses to face her, his eyes fastened to hers.

And then, simultaneously, the inquiring smile they are giving each other transforms itself into a very different kind of smile: a smile of recognition that is immediately followed by a look of utter amazement.

Unaware that he is doing it, Julián shakes his head in disbelief.

Things like this do not happen, cannot happen in real life. Do they? Can they? For suddenly he realizes who she is. This young woman is the woman of his poems, the one to whom he has told the most intimate secrets of his heart, the one to whom he has dedicated every action he has ever taken, the one who appears to him in all of his most secret dreams and looks him in the eye, not only with the most heavenly of loves but with the most sensual of passions as well. A woman of whom he knows absolutely everything there is to know. And yet, a woman of whom he knows absolutely nothing.

Not even her name.

And as Julián shakes his head in disbelief, the young woman also shakes hers. For now she knows who he is. This young man is the man with the piercing dark blue eyes Santa Rita showed her in a wondrous vision, the man the gods mean for her to have always by her side, the one she has been writing about in her diary for as long as she can remember, pouring out the most intimate secrets of her heart, the one to whom she has dedicated every piece of music she has ever played on the piano, the one who appears to her in all of her most secret dreams and looks her in the eye, not only with the most sensual of passions but with the most heavenly of loves as well. A man of whom she knows absolutely everything there is to know. And yet, a man of whom she knows absolutely nothing.

Not even his name.

They are both looking in total amazement at each other when, all of a sudden, despite the loud noises of the excited crowd, they each hear a strange sound, like that of a delicate, lyric plucking of a single harp string.

Upon hearing that sound, they both raise their eyes to where the sound came from and see, on the second-floor veranda, where the orchestra is, one of the Mayan musicians, holding a Guatemalan harp, who is gesticulating extravagantly as he keeps apologizing for something he thinks has angered the conductor and ruined the piece of music.

"It is not my fault, maestro," the poor Mayan musician keeps repeating and repeating to the elegant white conductor with the impeccable white gloves. "I was just tuning my harp and one of its strings—this one, you see? The lowest one, the E string, the one with the most heart, burst. Just like that. What was I to do?" the poor Mayan musician keeps saying. "It isn't my fault, maestro. The gods made it happen," he says. "So don't blame me, maestro, please. Blame the gods, blame the gods."

When they hear this, the young woman and Julián look back at each other. And then, thoroughly embarrassed, not knowing what else to do, they both begin to laugh, gently at first, then louder, at the poor Mayan musician's utterly tragic predicament.

Suddenly, feeling a hearty slap on his back, Julián returns to consciousness as he hears his name uttered by Don Manuel. "Julián," the general says, pointing at the beautiful young woman on the stairs, "I'd like you to meet my oldest daughter, Sol. She graduated from your school last year." They move close to Sol, who is now at the foot of the stairs. "Her real name is Soledad," Don Manuel says, "but all of us, I mean, family and friends, call her Sol—the Spanish word for sun—because she looks like the sun, doesn't she? With all of that beautiful golden hair?" He then turns to his daughter. "Sol," Don Manuel says, "I would like you to meet a young man who honors us with his visit, the Cuban professor your sister Gabriela has not stopped talking about, someone who is not only a great teacher but also a great orator, and a—"

But Julián, impatient, eager to meet her, anxious to hold her hand in his, does not let—cannot let, will not let—Don Manuel complete his sentence. Impetuously, he rushes up to Sol, getting as close to her as decency allows, and bows to her, staring deeply into her eyes, just as he has been doing since their eyes first met each other. Then, though he finds himself shaking with excitement, still keeping his dark blue eyes deeply fastened to those magnificent dark eyes of hers, he tries to keep his voice as firm as he can as he says, "Please, call me Julián."

Sol doesn't know how she finds the strength to answer, "Please, call me Sol," as she offers her hand to him, ungloved, naked, as the hands of young unmarried women are.

He takes it in his. Her hand is as cold as ice; his, burning with fire, which seems to make the ice of her hand melt instantly as his hand and her hand silently caress each other for an eternity. Or is it just for the briefest of seconds? Then, still keeping his eyes deeply fastened into hers, Julián raises her hand to his lips as the gallant gentleman in him is supposed to do.

But the impudent man inside him suddenly takes over, and boldly doing away with what society allows, defiantly, audaciously, that brash young man Julián has become dares to brush the back of her hand with a delicate, tender kiss of his lips, a mere brushing of a kiss that touches his entire soul—and hers—in a way neither of their souls have ever been touched before. And then, before either of them realizes it, while their eyes are still deeply fastened to each other's, in a movement so swift Julián himself does not notice it until after he has done it, that man inside Julián who had so delicately brushed the back of her hand with such a tender, delicate kiss, turns her hand around in his hand, and defiantly brands the palm of her hand with another kiss, a scorching kiss from his lips, a fiery kiss that this time shakes his entire body—and hers—in a way neither of their bodies have ever been shaken.

They are so oblivious to everything surrounding them that they fail to realize that Don Manuel is still standing there, by their side, looking at them, a broad grin on his face.

Sol, as if in a daze, is still trying to make sense of what those two kisses of Julián's, or was it only one long one? have done to her—brushing her soul with tenderness and branding her body with fire at the very same time—when, before she even realizes it, she finds his hand caressing her waist. And then, while he holds her quivering body tight against his exhilarated body, she finds herself dauntlessly swirling away into a world where nothing else exists, where nothing else matters but the two of them—the two of them *and* the music, the inebriating, whirling waltz music that intoxicates her. Him.

Them.

If he can boldly do away with conventions, Sol tells herself, by kissing her

hand and branding her soul and her body forever, so can she, by boldly tearing her dance card in half and giving it to him, the way engaged women do.

Nobody sees her do this—but Julián.

And her mother.

Doña Rosaura rushes to her, her face twisted almost in anguish.

"Sol," she says quietly, almost whispering, "What are you thinking?"
and hands Sol her own dance card.

But Don Manuel comes promptly to his daughter's aid.

"Let her be, Rosaura," he says, taking his wife's card from Sol's hand and
tearing it in half. "From tonight on Sol is old enough to do as she pleases."

Doña Rosaura looks at her husband, disconcerted. "But, but . . ." she
starts to say, running out of words.

"But nothing," Don Manuel says, completing his wife's sentence as he
takes Rosaura by the waist and forces her to join the crowd of exhilarated
couples dancing faster and faster in tighter and tighter circles around the
patio. "Don't you remember when you were her age?" Don Manuel whispers in his wife's ear. "Can twenty-seven years erase what you and I felt
that first night I held you in my arms?"

"Sshhh," Rosaura says softly, blushing head to toe, "our guests are
going to hear you!"

"Let them hear me," Don Manuel answers. And as he and Doña
Rosaura take one more turn to the enrapturing music, he shouts the same
words he shouted twenty-seven years ago, "I love this woman, and even if
you all were to mind it, I'm going to kiss her and make her mine." Then,
despite Doña Rosaura's apparent opposition, Don Manuel bends over,
pulls her tight to him, and shamelessly kisses his wife, the woman he loves
without limits.

"Manuel!" Doña Rosaura says, deeply embarrassed, though her heart
is brimming with joy at her husband's passionate kiss. "Are you drunk?"
Nervously, she looks around. But the dancing couples are too busy with
each other to notice what one couple on the dance floor is doing, even if
that couple is Don Manuel and his beautiful wife.

"Yes, my love, tonight I am drunk with life!" Don Manuel answers as
he sees Julián and Sol swirl past him and his wife, the sparkling eyes of the
two young people filled with an infectious excitement.

CHAPTER XI

BACK IN HIS ROOM, Julián lies on his bed, still fully dressed, staring up into space, unable to fall asleep.

He has not lighted the candle by the side of his bed, and his tiny room is lit only by the gas street lamp located one corner away, a gas lamp that flickers softly, casting a distorted rectangle that constantly moves on the whitewashed wall opposite Julián as the flickering light enters his room through the small, high window above his bed.

The Saavedras dropped him at his rooming house on their way back home. Unbelievably, Señora Saavedra had been very quiet during the entire trip back. The champagne, Julián thought, must have gotten to her.

It had been Professor Saavedra who said the very few words that were spoken during the ride back.

"She is beautiful, isn't she?"

That was all he said. Julián just looked at him and nodded, not saying a word. What *could* he say?

How does one describe the sun?

SOL IS IN HER BEDROOM, still entranced by the magic of what had happened to her just minutes ago.

Xenufla, the old Indian woman who takes loving care of her, has just left the room, after helping Sol unlace the back of her ball gown and after placing it back on the dummy by the tall oval mirror at the other end of the bedroom. Sol has taken off her shoes and stockings, and now barefoot, she is wearing only her petticoat and camisole.

She goes to her bed, and from under the mattress, where she keeps it secretly hidden, she pulls her diary—her dearest friend—the friend who knows everything there is to know about her, the friend who knows every one of her most intimate thoughts. She kisses it, thanking it with her kiss for bringing Julián to her—Julián who is just as she dreamed: a poet, a *real* poet. And so virile! And so attractive! And with such piercing eyes! The piercing eyes that have been following her to her bed and into her dreams ever since she went to visit Saint Rita in the little church atop the hill of Jocotenango; the piercing eyes that made her tremble and shake as badly tonight as they did then; the piercing eyes that made her feel as if she were living through an earthquake every time she looked into them. She sits at her dressing table, places the diary on top—after kissing it again—and opens it to the next blank page. Her pen in her hand, she pauses as she looks out the tall window opposite her bed. The window is fully open, letting the moon, which finally decided to make an appearance after all, bathe her room with its pale blue light. How could she ever attempt to explain to her diary what it was like to have Julián look into her eyes, speak to her, touch her, that very first time?

Sol had been forewarned. Last Saturday, after her sister Gabriela confessed to Sol that she had manipulated their father, Don Manuel, into inviting Julián to Sol's coming-of-age party, and after Gabriela made Sol read the poems she had ripped from the bound copies of *La Revista Universal* in her father's library, Gabriela added, jokingly, "Sol, I'm sure *you* will fall head over heels over him, because, after all, they say he is half crazy— And so are *you!* So the two of you should make a perfect match!" Sol had not believed her sister's descriptions at the time about how smart this professor of hers was, and about how passionate, and how sensual, and how incredibly attractive. Now she knows better.

Sol looks at herself in the mirror above her dressing table and realizes that her hair is still up, still covered with tiny white flowers. She puts her pen down, raises her bare arms, and delicately begins to unpin her hair, which falls loosely on her shoulders. She gives her head several shakes, letting her hair swirl wildly around her face, and as she does, she unbuttons the top three buttons of her white cotton camisole, partly exposing her breasts. Some of her fine, long golden hair finds its point of repose lying right in the space between her now bare breasts, as do some of the tiny flowers. She closes her eyes and imagines him there, his head between her breasts, covered by her hair, resting among those flowers.

With her eyes still closed, she remembers one of Julián's poems, one of those poems that Gabriela had ripped from an old yellowing journal in their father's library, a poem Gabriela told her Julián had dedicated to the mysterious woman of his dreams, a poem Sol fell in love with the moment she first read it. A poem she now knows Julián dedicated to no one but her.

> *Do you want to love me? Do you want to welcome*
> *this most weary of travelers? Do you want to kiss him?*
> *Do you want to embrace him, and against your throbbing heart,*
> *shelter his head, filled with lifelong yearnings and desires?*

Oh, yes! She answers to the dark melodious voice that whispers in her ear. Oh, yes!

She opens her eyes and looks at herself closely in the mirror, staring deeply into her eyes—her receptive eyes that are so dark they are almost black—and she sees, on the other side of the mirror, his eyes—his penetrating eyes that are so blue and so deep—staring back intently into hers.

And then she feels the penetrating blueness of his eyes enter the receptive darkness of hers.

She closes her eyes again and, suddenly, she feels a delirious current go up and down her entire body, simultaneously bringing wave after wave of an indescribable pain intricately interwoven with an immensely incredible pleasure.

It is only after the last of the earth-shattering waves has been released from her body that she can return to her diary.

She stares at it for a long while and then closes it, after having written nothing in it.

What has happened, what *is* happening, between Julián and her is so incredibly intimate that—even if she could describe it—she does not think she could ever share it, not even with her best, her only true friend. Her dear friend, her diary.

UNABLE TO SLEEP, unable to think, Julián stands up and leaves his room, not really knowing what to do, where to go. He steps out of his rooming house into the darkness of the street and begins to walk, slowly, in silence, his legs propelling him as if of their own accord. The cool night air seems to aggravate his limp, but he does not notice it. He turns up the lapels of his suit coat and looks up at the corner gas lamp flickering gold and seeming to send sparks of fire into the night, reminding him again of Sol's golden hair that sparkles with fire. It is then he remembers Saavedra's words to him.

She is beautiful, isn't she?

The very same words Julián has been repeating to himself since he first saw her, at the top of the stairs, and for the briefest of seconds thought he had seen alabaster wings on her shoulders.

Up to the time that Saavedra said those words inside the carriage, Julián felt as if he had been half asleep—he tells himself. Or in a daze. But isn't it just the opposite? he asks himself now. Isn't tonight the first time in my life that I am awake, truly awake? That I can see clearly all there is to see? That I understand everything there is to understand? That the questions I had been asking myself all of my life until the moment I met Sol, have, all of a sudden, been answered in my mind by her glowing radiance?

He nods silently to himself.

Yes, he tells himself. For the very first time in my entire life, I know what it is like to be really awake. To be really alive.

It is then he remembers Lucía, the woman to whom he has given his most sacred word, promising marriage. But no sooner does Lucía come into his mind, than two questions that were awakened in his mind by Saavedra's words begin to circle inside his head, like carrion birds slowly circling around a wounded animal.

What have you done, you fool? What have you done? asks and asks the first bird. What are you going to do now? asks the other.

Julián shakes his head.

How could I have done as I did? How could I have acted as I did when, ignoring what custom demanded of me, I dared to kiss Sol's hand? What impelled me to do it? he asks himself.

He shakes his head.

How could I *not* have done it?

A rooster crows daringly in the distance, breaking the silence. Another one, farther away, answers the first one's dare. Moments ago, the moon, which had been intermittently hiding all night long, finally had decided to reveal itself in full, and no sooner did it appear from behind the clouds than the thin line outlining the mountain peaks along the entire horizon began to turn the color of embers. Now the sky itself seems to have caught fire. The white stucco houses, seconds ago pale blue in the dying light of the night, are now tinged with the red orange of the early rising sun, as Mayan men and women, their heads and shoulders covered with black shawls under their black hats, begin to exit their homes. The streets of Guatemala have just begun to come alive.

Julián looks around, disconcerted. He doesn't know exactly where he is. He has been walking aimlessly, his feet guiding him while the carrion birds in his head keep asking and asking the same two questions.

He turns one more corner, and there, backlit by the amber light of the rising sun, he sees a beautiful woman, with wings on her shoulders. He rubs his eyes and looks at her again. She is still there, but her eyes do not look back at him. Instead, they look up toward heaven. It takes him a second before he realizes that this woman is made of marble, white and cold.

How different are the eyes of this marble angel from Sol's eyes, he thinks.

"Still riding high on the wave of the gods?" he hears somebody say, the words breaking the silence of the almost empty street. Then he feels a hand on his shoulder. "Hey, Ginebrita, are you all right?" He turns and sees a man he does not recognize. "What brings you here so early in the morning?" the man says.

"Panoplo!" he exhales, after a short while, finally recognizing the man, the word escaping from his lips and sounding almost as if the old Mayan man had just fallen from heaven as an answer to a prayer Julián had yet to make. Julián looks around, the streets surrounding him suddenly familiar. It is only then that he realizes where he is.

"Panoplo," he says, "the most wonderful, the most incredible thing that can ever happen to a man happened to me last night." Then, not letting the old Mayan man say a word, he adds, "I met her, Panoplo. I met her. The woman of my dreams. The woman of my poems. The one to whom I have been dedicating all of my verses, all of my work, all of my life."

And then, suddenly, unexpectedly, Julián begins to cry, to weep, clinging desperately to the old Mayan man as if his life depended on it, while he keeps repeating and repeating.

"I met her, I met her, I met her," his words almost incomprehensible.

Julián has never cried.

He didn't cry when a vile Spanish man dressed as a judge accused him, a young man of seventeen, of treason; nor when his gray-haired mother was forcibly escorted by vile men from the courtroom as she screamed, "My son, My son"; nor when his head was shaved and a vile iron ball was shackled around his ankle; nor when he was forced away from his home, and from his friends, and from his country. He thought crying was something beneath the godlike men and women he admired. He didn't know that gods cry too. But only at the joy of it all. It had taken Sol—angel, woman, goddess that she is—to teach that to him; to have him experience the incredible joy that it is to cry at being awake, at being alive. To cry, to weep, at the beauty of it all.

Panoplo embraces him, brother to brother. "Ginebrita, Ginebrita," the old man says, "whatever you've been drinking, you've been drinking too much of it. It's never wise to drink too much of anything. Unless, of course, you're riding high on the wave of the gods. Are you?"

Panoplo looks at Julián, whose teary eyes seem exultant with the most indescribable joy, and, at the same time, with the most unimaginable pain. For, as Julián cries, as he weeps for joy, the two carrion birds inside his head circle and circle, again and again, the first one calling and calling with anguish, What have you done, you fool? What have you done? What have you done? while the other one keeps desperately asking, What are you going to do now? What are you going to do now? What are you going to do now?

And as Julián weeps for joy, he finds himself also weeping at the devastating realization that, as close as he has been to the woman of his dreams, the woman of his poems, he must learn to forget her, he must not—ever—see her again.

His most sacred word of honor has been given to Lucía.

And once a Cuban criollo man gives his word of honor, it is never to be broken.

Never.

CHAPTER XII

LATER THAT AFTERNOON, Julián, who has only had a couple of hours of sleep, is in the middle of the Roman forum, defending the Roman Republic. He has already crushed the conspiracy of Catiline and he is now urgently asking his fellow senators to help him drive Mark Antony—and his dreams of becoming emperor—out of Rome.

"Rome does not want another Caesar," Julián's Cicero is saying to the girls that surround him, all of them now senators enraptured by Julián. "Let Rome be a republic, the kind of a republic that will light the world for eternity, a republic for all people, and for the good of all people."

Cicero's enemies are about to come out of the dark and slay him, when Professor Saavedra suddenly bursts into Julián's class, interrupting the dramatic scene and making the girls giggle nervously.

Saavedra asks Julián to join him outside the classroom.

"Julián," he says, his voice extremely concerned, "this note just came in, from the Ministry of Public Instruction. The messenger said it was urgent that it be opened right away, and I did, not realizing that it was addressed to you. I'm sorry. The minister wants to see you. At once," he adds, handing the note to Julián.

Julián, not knowing what this urgent call is all about, afraid he may be asked to stop teaching at the school, or worse, leave Guatemala, asks Saavedra to go with him. And as soon as Saavedra gets a substitute teacher to cover Julián's class, he and Julián grab a carriage and less than a half hour after receiving the minister's urgent note, both Julián and Saavedra appear at Minister Andrújal's office.

The minister himself welcomes them inside and asks them to sit on the cordovan leather chairs by the side of his desk while he sits behind his desk, obviously nervous.

"I was not expecting you to come so soon," he says, apologetically, as he looks at the door that separates him from the adjoining room. "This, as you can understand . . ." the minister says, his voice unsure, "this is most irregular. I myself have barely had the time to prepare the—"

A knock is heard at the door, which opens, revealing an older man, a Ladino, wearing a plain black suit and spectacles on the top of his head, holding what appears to be a piece of parchment in his hand. "I'm sorry to bother you, Señor Ministro," the man says, "but I could not find the seal in my office. Do you, by any chance, have it? Last time I saw it—"He suddenly realizes that Julián and Saavedra are in the minister's office. "Oh, I'm sorry, Señor Ministro, I didn't know you—"

"Here, here," the minister says, pulling out a large brass seal from the top drawer of his desk and handing it to the old man. "Take it, and let me know the minute you are done."

After the man hurriedly leaves the room and shuts the door behind him, the minister sits again behind his desk.

Minister Andrújal is a tall, skinny man, balding and cleanly shaven, with long, thin delicate hands that have long, elegant fingers, the hands of a man who has never labored with them. He makes a steeple out of those elongated hands of his, as if he were praying, and lets his bony forearms rest on his mahogany desk.

Then, after a long, embarrassing pause, he addresses both Saavedra and Julián.

"Gentlemen, I am extremely sorry that I was not able to—"

A knock is heard at the door, and the door opens again.

"Are they finished already?" the minister inquires.

The Ladino man nods as he steps over to the minister's desk and hands the minister two parchments, each with a red wax seal at the bottom. The minister reads them slowly. Then, after nodding to the Ladino man, he grabs his pen, and signs them. The Ladino man exits silently and closes the door behind him, his body that of a servant in the presence of a lord, making Julián ask himself, Is this what a republic becomes? Is this the kind of republic of equality Cicero devoted his life to and died for?

The minister looks at Saavedra first, then at Julián, his face difficult to decipher.

"As I was saying, I am extremely sorry that I was not able to meet with either of you at Don Manuel's party last night," the minister says, "but"—he makes a sweeping gesture with his right hand indicating the top of his desk, covered with papers—"I am sure you both understand, affairs of state kept me away from the party."

Saavedra nods, while Julián remains impassively looking at the minister's long hands, which are now drumming nervously on the documents the Ladino man just gave him.

"Now, to this," the minister adds, and again makes his elongated hands into a steeple as if he were praying.

"As you know," he says, "there are many people in Guatemala, important people, who think that a school as prestigious as yours, Professor Saavedra"—he pauses, looking at the professor, who nods slightly, accepting the compliment—"should not be run by a Cuban man, but by a Guatemalan."

Saavedra suddenly stops his nodding.

"But I am not one of them," the minister promptly adds. "You have transformed our school into the kind of establishment that exists only in the land of our strong neighbor, the rapacious eagle to the north, which is exactly what our consul in New York asked you to do. How else can we defend ourselves from that eagle unless our students are at the same level as that eagle's students? That's what the consul himself asked me when he came to me with the proposal to hire you, which I immediately accepted, as you well know. The consul himself—and I, of course—have only high praises for your school, which, the consul tells me, reminds him of a New York City school, because of the way you have organized it, and because of the caliber of the education our students are getting, which, we know, is due to you, and to your excellent teachers." He pauses, as if waiting for applause.

Saavedra takes his cue. "Thank you, Señor Ministro. Please extend my thanks to the consul when you see him again."

"However," the minister continues, "there are still people who think that such a school should not be headed by someone who is not a Guatemalan, as you well know. And now, those same people are in total and complete disagreement with your nominating another non-Guatemalan for a full-time post of such responsibility as you have requested."

He pauses for a brief moment and sighs. "I believe that the proper teaching of philosophy and the history of civilization can and will change the future of our country, of our entire world, as we all know it. As you yourself said recently," he adds, looking at Julián, "the sword must be tempered by the pen, or else our countries will be covered by seas of blood, as countries were in Roman times."

He pauses, then places his elegant hands on the desk and feels the parchment the Ladino man had placed there earlier. "That is why our office has prepared these documents," he says, "at the express and urgent request of President Rubios himself, who thinks exactly as I do." He stands up and hands the two documents to Julián. "It is the pleasure of Guatemala to grant you the status of full professor of philosophy and the history of civilization *not only* at Saavedra's school, the Escuela Central, for the benefit of the very few; but, *in addition,* at the oldest university of all Central America, our great Universidad de Guatemala, for the benefit of all. Congratulations, my dear Julián, you have earned this," he adds, extending his hand to Julián. "President Rubios and I thank you for your magnificent labor and accomplishments, which we know is nothing compared to what you are surely destined to accomplish in the future."

Saavedra, at first shocked by the news, turns and faces Julián, beaming with pride and joy, while Julián, after shaking hands with the minister, does nothing but stare at the parchment documents in his hands.

This was an honor he did not expect, an honor past his wildest dreams.

He is still in the state of shock when he and Saavedra get back into the carriage Saavedra had kept waiting for them at the entrance to the ministry. He sits by Saavedra's side, the neatly rolled parchments in his hands, still not believing it possible.

Saavedra places his arm over Julián's shoulders. "For a moment I thought the worst was going to happen. I thought he was going to ask *both* of us to leave Guatemala."

Julián looks at him and smiles. "I did too."

"Well, my friend," Saavedra adds, patting Julián's shoulder, "now that you have not *one* but *two* well-paid jobs, you will finally be able to accomplish what you came to Guatemala for."

Julián gives the professor a puzzled look.

Saavedra smiles at him. "You don't remember? What you told me the first time we met?"

Julián shakes his head.

"You told me that you had come to Guatemala to get a job so you could marry and start a family, don't you remember? Well, my friend," he continues, again patting Julián's shoulder, "now you have *two* jobs! So now you can finally get married to that girl who's been waiting for you for so long and start your own family. Isn't it about time?"

He smiles at Julián, who evades Saavedra's eyes and looks at the rolled parchments in his hands. Then, raising his eyes, he stares emptily into space.

"Yes," Julián answers, after a long, long pause. "It's about time."

THE MINUTE JULIÁN gets back to school, he goes to Saavedra's office and starts to write a note to Lucía, the Cuban woman who has been patiently waiting for him in Mexico City for how long? For how many months now? Five? Six? How long have we been engaged? he asks himself. How long ago did I give her my word of honor that I would marry her? Soon it will be two years. Can that be true? *Two* years?

My beloved Lucía, he starts to write. Then, violently, crumples the sheet of paper and throws it on the floor.

My dearest Lucía, he begins again on a new sheet of paper, only to crumple it again and throw it again on the floor.

My faithful Lucía . . . My beautiful Lucía . . . My Lucía . . .

He sighs a deep, long sigh.

Then, needing to be sure that his handwriting conveys the impression that he is totally under control and that, despite the constant circling and circling of the carrion birds inside his head, he is not under duress of any kind, he slows down his usually turbulent handwriting, and writes,

Lucía,

I have just been appointed Professor of Philosophy and the History of Civilization at the University of Guatemala by the Ministry of Public Instruction, starting with the new school year. As soon as I receive my first pay I will send you money so you can start putting the finishing touches on your wedding trousseau. I know how long you have been waiting for this moment, and I, like you, cannot wait for the time in which we will be able to be together again. Professor Saavedra has agreed to let me have a month's leave so I can go to Mexico and bring you to this wonderful land—

He pauses as his mind suddenly changes course.

Where the most wonderful thing has happened to me, he wishes he could write. Where I have met the woman of my dreams, a woman with white wings on her shoulders. Where I experienced what it is like to be totally awake, totally alive for the first time in my life. Where I have been face to face with the sun.

That's what he wishes he could write. But that is *not* what he writes.

He writes,

—where we will be able to live the life of your dreams.

He reads the letter again, signs it, folds it, and seals it, not realizing that he wrote, the life of *your* dreams, not, the life of *our* dreams.

He steps outside Saavedra's office and calls the son of the old Mayan gardener, a boy who is trimming the huge magnolia trees in the patio of the school.

"Here, Pancracio," he says, giving the boy the letter, "take this letter to the large Correos building on the main street and post it right away. Here's two reales. One to post it and the other for you."

Julián stays at the door, watching the boy rush into the street with the letter.

Go quickly, he thinks as he sees the boy disappear past the entrance door. Quickly! Before I weaken and change my mind.

He walks back into Saavedra's office, and after he picks up all the crumpled pieces of paper from the floor, he places them on the large porcelain cigar ashtray on Saavedra's desk. Taking a match out of Saavedra's silver matchbox, he strikes it against the pumice stone on top of the desk and sets the papers on fire. He stands there, by the side of Saavedra's desk, seeing the papers slowly turn into ash.

Then, feeling an urgent need to tell his diary of his despair, he searches inside his coat and finds in his pocket the tiny notebook where he always writes his most intimate thoughts. He sits on his chair and opens the notebook to the last written page. There, he is startled by what he finds, something he wrote, something he does not remember ever writing.

Don't you wish that before something important happens in your life, a sign of some kind, music of some kind—yes, music, anything musical, from the blaring, epic fanfare of a thousand trumpets to the delicate, lyric plucking of a single harp string—could be heard, letting you know in advance that something great is about to happen, that something great is about to—

Reading this makes him remember Sol again, and the way that they, embarrassed, laughed together at the poor Mayan musician and his broken harp string. And, suddenly, Julián's body is pierced by a new kind of pain, an intense pain he has never felt before, not even when he was forced to wear the slave chains around his ankles.

Because he knows that after what he's done—after what he, a man of honor, had no choice but to do, sending Lucía that letter—now he knows that he will never be able to hear again the wonderful music he heard the moment he first looked deeply into Sol's eyes. For he must never—*ever*—see her again. If he dares to see Sol just one more time, he is afraid he might weaken and break his word to Lucía.

But he is not that kind of a man. He is not—he will never be—the kind of a man who weakens and breaks his word.

Or is he?

He shakes his head. He does not want to find out. No. It is better never to see Sol again. He gives his word of honor to himself.

I will *never* see her again.

Except in your mind, he hears a warning voice say within himself.

And in your dreams, the voice adds.

He sighs a deep, deep sigh, coming from the bottom of his soul. Then, not knowing what else to do, he just sits there, by Saavedra's desk, looking at the tiny notebook in his hands, lit by the fading afternoon sun. And as he peruses, once and again, the words he wrote not even twenty-four hours ago, he hears one of the two carrion birds that have been circling inside his head asking him, once and again, What have you done? What have you done?

Yet, the other carrion bird, the one that used to ask, What are you going to do now? That carrion bird is already silent, standing close to the lonely young man with unruly hair, a thick mustache, and with the saddest of eyes, who is quietly sitting on a borrowed leather chair at a fancy partners desk that doesn't belong to him.

A young man who just stares emptily into space.

And as that carrion bird looks at the almost frozen eyes of that young man at the desk, the bird wonders if there is any life left in those eyes.

THAT NIGHT, on the way back to his rooming house, when he stops at Panoplo's cantina, Julián asks Panoplo for a bottle of gin.

Panoplo, surprised by Julián's request—a request Julián has never made before—stares at his only white friend for a second, and then, asking no questions, hands Julián the bottle he asked for. Julián takes it, sits quietly all by himself at a tiny table in a lost corner of the bar and, not saying a word, begins to drink directly from the bottle.

Never has he felt so alone in his entire life. Never. He knows what loneliness is. Oh, yes, he knows. He has lived with an almost unbearable loneliness ever since he left Cuba. Even before that, since the day his Spaniard-to-the-core father, ashamed of his son's dreams of freeing Cuba from Spain, had stopped talking to Julián. His own father had disowned him! Oh, yes, Julián tells himself as he takes another long swallow from the bottle, I know—*I know*—about loneliness. But it has never been like this. No. Never like this. Never.

Later on, after Panoplo has gotten rid of most of his customers, he comes to Julián's table, bringing his own unlabeled bottle of mescal. The old Mayan man sits by Julián's side and takes a long sip of his mescal as he looks at Julián, who, avoiding Panoplo's eyes, is staring into his now almost empty bottle of gin.

Julián sees Panoplo's old, wrinkled face reflected in the bottle. He raises his eyes to Panoplo and finally manages to speak. After he starts his sentence twice, his speech blurred, his words barely intelligible, he says, "Remember what I told you this morning?" and no sooner does he say that—he shakes his head.

Can it be possible that my life has so totally and so abruptly changed course in less than twenty-four hours? he asks himself. This morning feels like such a long time ago, a lifetime ago. Last night I held her tight in my arms, he thinks, and tonight . . . He shakes his head again in disbelief and stares at Panoplo, not looking into his old Indian friend's kind eyes, but staring through him. Past him. Deep into tomorrow's empty nights. Into tomorrow's long, lonely, sleepless nights yet to come. *El futuro.* The future.

His future.

"Remember what I told you this morning . . . ?" Julián repeats, after a long, long pause. "About my finding her, the woman of my dreams?" he adds, lowering his eyes and staring silently at the bottle in his hands.

Panoplo takes another long swallow from his bottle, keeping his eyes on Julián, listens, and says nothing.

"Well," Julián says, "last night I found her. And this afternoon . . . This afternoon I lost her, Panoplo. This afternoon I lost her." He pauses. Then adds, "Forever."

Panoplo smiles at Julián. "Then, Ginebrita," the old Mayan man says, looking at Julián with the kind eyes of a loving father, "you never really found her. Because if you found her, if you really found the woman the gods mean for you to have, then she will always be by your side, no matter what," he says. "Because souls that have been woven together by the gods can never be unraveled," he adds, quoting an ancient Mayan Cakchiquel saying, and then takes another long swallow of his mescal.

Julián looks at him, his blurry eyes hopeful. "Are you sure?" he asks.

Panoplo wipes his mouth with the back of his long sleeve and silently begins to nod his head up and down several times as he stares at Julián, who has a puzzled look on his face. "Of course I'm sure," Panoplo answers with total certainty, after a while, placing the bottle on the wood tabletop and looking deeply into Julián's eyes.

"*If* you did find her," Panoplo adds after another pause.

"But I *did* find her," Julián says, looking back at Panoplo. "I know I did, Panoplo," Julián repeats, more intensely this time, "I *know* I did."

"Well then, Ginebrita," Panoplo says, jovially, "if you really did, then you have nothing to worry about. Because if you *truly* found her, no matter what you do, no matter what may happen, she will always be by your side."

Panoplo looks deeply into Julián's eyes and smiles at him.

"*Always!*" Panoplo repeats.

And then, bringing his bottle to his lips, the old Mayan takes another long swallow of mescal.

Julián's eyes, now beaming with hope, no longer stare through the old Mayan man, nor at the empty bottle on the table, but at one of those beautiful white marble women with silent wings on their shoulders across the street.

PART THREE

THE WAVE OF THE GODS

CHAPTER XIII

T HE MONDAY AFTER he mails his letter to Lucía, early in the morning, Julián—who holds no classes on Mondays—goes to the exclusive library of El Ateneo, to start researching the play he was asked to write by Francisco Tresbán, the minister of fine arts, who is a charter member of El Ateneo, and who has offered the use of the club's outstanding library to Julián.

Minister Tresbán found out that *Alcibíades,* a play written by Julián in classical alexandrine meter—about a Greek general who chooses to die for the freedom of Athens rather than to forsake his honor—had been performed in Mexico City two years ago to great critical success, and, now that Julián is here in Guatemala, he thought of asking Julián to write a play to celebrate Guatemala's Independence Day—next September 15—which is less than four months away.

What better way can there be to celebrate Independence Day, Minister Tresbán told himself, than by performing a new play dealing with the struggle of Latin American nations to achieve their freedom, written by a brilliant new dramatist who has experienced prison first hand and who is now experiencing exile from his homeland precisely because of his love of freedom? When Minister Tresbán approached Julián last week and asked Julián what he thought of the idea, Julián, who knew that he would have extra time on his hands as soon as the current school year ended, was immediately ignited by it and instantly accepted the challenging commission, despite the short time before rehearsals were to start.

While Julián is assiduously working at a desk, studying the voluminous annals of the Guatemalan Revolution neatly kept at the huge library of El Ateneo, and looking for an idea to inspire his play, Don Manuel passes through the library. Recognizing him, the general invites Julián to join him and his friends for the noontime meal, the largest daily meal in Guatemala. When he sees Julián begin to shake his head, the old man interrupts. "Don't say no, Julián," he says, and then lowers his voice as he confides, "every one of these men has enough money to provide you with weapons to arm a full expedition to go to Cuba, and then some. All they need is someone with ideas to organize it and with balls big enough to set it in motion. Believe me, my boy, it will not hurt you to meet them." Still seeing hesitation in Julián's eyes, the general continues, "It seems to me that the possibility of giving Cuba weapons to fight for her freedom is more important than any play you may be writing about us—old-timers, who are already free—isn't it?" He pauses. "Besides," he adds, jovially, "even playwrights have to eat, don't they?"

The chef of El Ateneo, Panchuelo, an old Ladino man who years ago fought bravely against the Spaniards under Don Manuel's own command, is delighted by this rare opportunity to prepare a meal for his former commander in chief—since the general, who prefers to have his meals at home with his family, rarely eats at El Ateneo—and the noontime meal he prepares for the general and all of his guests for this occasion is truly sumptuous, including several of the general's favorite dishes. An appetizer made of squash and vegetables, Fiambre—served with an excellent Gràves, a dark-red French wine that is the perfect complement to the dish—is followed by Chojín, a hearty dish Julián is warned in advance by the general and the rest of the men at the table is "hot as hell," because it is made with the hottest of Mexican chiles. And it is. Julián—as well as every other man at the finely set table—keeps begging, demanding, glass after glass of a beer brewed right in the basement of El Ateneo, a delicious beer that manages to soothe with its sparkling coolness the scorching throats of all at the table.

"And now," Don Manuel says, "to conclude this magnificent repast—since we are at the end of May, what could be a better dessert than just-

picked jocotillos?" All at the table squirm with delight at the idea, except
for Julián, who does not know what those are.

Don Manuel turns to Julián. "They are tiny plums that melt in your
mouth, son. They come from the nearby Indian village of Jocotenango,"
he says, "where the annual cattle fair will take place at the end of summer.
They are worth trying, Julián," the old man adds. "Believe me, my boy,
they are even worth writing about. They may even inspire your playwrit-
ing!"

Exceedingly pleased with the succulent meal, the general asks
Panchuelo, the chef, to come to the table, and after the two men shake
hands and the general praises and thanks the old soldier for the splendid
feast he prepared, the general invites the old Ladino man to sit by his side
and enjoy some of those exquisite jocotillos with him and the rest of the
men sitting at the table. But Panchuelo, embarrassed, shakes his head. He
knows a Ladino man does not belong at that table, and though he knows
that the general does not think that, a lot of the other men at the table—
his regular customers—would be infuriated by his joining them. "Oh, no,
Don Manuel," he says, politely refusing the general's request. "I am honored, but I still have a lot of work to do. Thanks so much, so very much,"
he adds, and rushes back to the kitchen and orders one of his assistants, a
Mayan boy all dressed in black with a long white apron, to bring another
large silver tray overflowing with more of those sinfully sweet little
jocotillos to the general's table.

While everybody, including Julián, is having a second serving of those
wonderful dessert delicacies, the conversation centers around how great
generals have traditionally been great chess players.

It is then Julián mentions that he loves chess.

"Oh, you do?" Don Manuel says, a smirk in his voice. "Well, it so happens I do too. Would you care to try your hand at a game?"

The other gentlemen excuse themselves, and Don Manuel and Julián
move to the game room, where an ivory and ebony chess set sits on a
mahogany and ebony board. Julián suggests a draw to see who starts the
game, but Don Manuel shakes his head.

"No, son," the general says, pointing to the ivory men, "You go ahead.
You start."

The game becomes a serious match, watched closely by the members of El Ateneo who are there that afternoon. They all know Don Manuel to be both a great military strategist and a brilliant chess player. But so it seems is Julián.

Suddenly Julián makes an unexpected move, putting his queen at risk.

Don Manuel shakes his head as he takes her. "Julián, my boy, watch what you are doing," he says, and then leans back in his chair.

Julián immediately moves his last knight and then looks up at Don Manuel with an engaging grin on his face.

"Checkmate," he says.

Don Manuel, who was leaning back in his chair, does not believe what he just heard. He leans over and looks at the board, studying it carefully for a long while. Then he leans back in his chair again, and after a short laugh, he elegantly accepts defeat.

"Well done, son, well done!" he says, and turning to the astounded gallery, exclaims, "I don't remember the last time I was defeated, do you gentlemen?" The men around him shake their heads. "You're a much better player than I thought you were," Don Manuel says to Julián. Then, facing the men surrounding them, he tells them, jovially, "Maybe that is why I lost this game." And, offering an explanation nobody is demanding, he adds, "I certainly underestimated my opponent, and that, as we all know, is the surest way to lose a battle."

He turns to Julián. "We must do this again, Julián. Why don't you come to my house, let's say, this coming Friday afternoon, right after school, and let us face each other again?" He sees Julián starting to shake his head. "I would rather challenge you there than here, Julián, just in case you should win again. What would my friends think of me then? If I am going to be embarrassed by you, Julián—or by anyone—I would rather be embarrassed at home than here, don't you think that's best?" He smiles as he faces the rest of his crowd, all of whom agree with him. There is a short pause. "My honor demands it, Julián," the general insists, seeing that Julián is still shaking his head. "I will not take no for an answer." Don Manuel still sees hesitation in Julián's eyes. "It is the least you can do for me, Julián," he adds, suppliantly, "after you have humiliated me in front of all my closest friends."

What else can Julián do?

He feigns a smile and agrees to the follow-up match next Friday afternoon at Don Manuel's house, even though he does not want to go there at
all, for he is afraid of what might happen if he were to see Sol again, if
only for the briefest of seconds.

THAT NIGHT, while having supper, Don Manuel mentions in passing
that Julián beat him at chess that same afternoon at El Ateneo, and that he
invited the "young man," as he called Julián, to come play chess with him
next Friday afternoon, right after school. Then Don Manuel looks at Sol
and adds, "He's not a bad dancer, that young man, is he? I saw the two of
you swirling and swirling all night long during your party. The two of you
seemed to be having such a good time. Did you like him?"

Did she *like* him? For a moment Sol does not know what to say. She
feels the blood rush to her cheeks. Thank God for Gabriela, who answers
for her.

"Oh, Daddy, what a *stupid* question. *Every*body likes Professor Julián!"
she says.

"Gabriela!" interjects Doña Rosaura. "Watch your language! Young
ladies *never* use words like 'stupid.' And least of all when referring to their
fathers!"

"But, Mamá, it *was* a stupid question! Everybody likes Professor Julián.
Don't *you*?"

The question takes Doña Rosaura by surprise. "Well, yes, I do, but—"

"Well, mother," Gabriela continues, "if *you* like him, then *everybody*
does!" she says and starts to laugh, making everybody at the table laugh,
even Doña Rosaura herself, who has no choice but to admit that, yes,
Gabriela is perhaps right for once, after all.

THE DAYS FOLLOWING seem interminable to Sol. She does not know
what to do with herself. She sits at the piano. Plays a few notes. Stands up.
Nervously walks out. To the gazebo overlooking the river. Only to return
to the music room, where she sits again at the piano and plays again a few
notes. Only to stand up, nervously, once again.

Xenufla, the old Mayan woman who looks after her, stares at her, studying her carefully, and shakes her head. "What is wrong with you, niña?" she keeps saying. "Something must be very wrong with you, when even playing the piano can not calm you down!"

But Sol keeps ignoring her questions. If she cannot tell her best friend—her diary—how she feels, how can she tell Xenufla? Or her mother? Oh, how she wishes her Aunt Soledad, her mentor, the woman Sol was named after, were still around, so she could go to her and ask her, "What am I supposed to do, to say, next time I see him?"

So little was said while we were dancing with each other, Sol tells herself. But then, so little needed to be said! Certainly Aunt Soledad would not be frightened of seeing a man a second time. But I certainly am, Sol tells herself. Frightened and incredibly excited at the same time. Oh, how slow the hours move since her father gave her the fantastic news that the young man with the piercing eyes she loves so much would be coming! How unbelievably slow! How much longer do I have to wait to see him again? she keeps asking herself.

But even the longest hours come to an end.

By the time the grandfather's clock in the elegant entrance hall to Don Manuel's house strikes noon on Friday, Sol has already changed dresses three times since morning, which is driving Xenufla crazy. "Niña," the old Indian woman keeps saying, "what is wrong with you? I'm tired of lacing dress after dress after dress. First the pink one. 'Makes me look sick,' you say. Then the white one. 'Makes me look too pale.' Then the cream one. 'It doesn't bring out the color of my hair.' Tell me, niña, what are you hiding from me? Have you been bitten by something I don't know of?"

And Sol smiles at her and answers, "Oh, Xenufla, Xenufla, don't you see it's summer, and it's gorgeous outside, and the sun is out, and the river has been singing all day long, and—"

"Yes, yes, and the flies are teeming and they are driving all of us crazy, you most of all! That must be what it is. The flies and those damn mosquitoes by the river. Sometimes I tell myself, 'What a great thing it is to be an Indian woman! And, do you know when I think that? Whenever I see you run down to that old gazebo of your aunt's and jump into the river to swim as naked as the day on which you were born! Just like your dear Aunt Soledad, may she rest in peace—if peace is what would have made

her happy. One day some man is going to come along and see you swim-
ming naked like that down by the gazebo, and then, God forbid! What
might happen?"

"He will take me into his arms, and possess me, and make eternal love
to me. Oh, Xenufla, wouldn't that be just wonderful?"

Xenufla instantly crosses herself. "Niña, niña," she says, as she shakes
her head violently, "don't you ever joke about things like that. Don't you
know the gods are always listening to everything we mortals say?"

"But I am not joking, Xenufla," Sol says, as she tries on a pale turquoise
dress, that brings up the fire in her hair, and looks approvingly at herself in
the tall oval mirror in a corner of her room.

Xenufla shakes her head once again as she stands behind her niña and
laces the back of her dress. "That's what I am afraid of," she says, almost to
herself. "That is exactly what I am afraid of."

AS THE BELLS of Guatemala announce the hour of the Angelus and the
end of the last school day of this week—which Julián thinks has gone by
like a flash of lightning—Julián is still debating with himself whether or
not to go to Don Manuel's house; a debate that has been going on in his
mind since last Monday afternoon, when Don Manuel invited him to play
chess at his home.

Julián does not want to see Sol again. He gave himself his own word of
honor he would never see her ever again. That is why he rushed that letter
to Lucía. Because he felt—he knew—that if he ever saw Sol again, he
might break his word of marriage to Lucía. And once a man has given his
word, he can never break it. Ever. Life is difficult enough as it is, seeing
Sol's face everywhere he looks, for he thinks of her day and night, from
the moment he wakes up till the moment he falls asleep. And even then,
even while he is asleep, he thinks of her. How could he ever dare to face
the *real* Sol, in the flesh? No, he tells himself, I cannot go to Don Manuel's
house.

And yet, he wants to go to Don Manuel's house.

Desperately.

He wants to see Sol again, needs to, has to. If there is anything in the
world he wants, he wants to subject himself again to her glowing radi-

ance, be branded by her incandescent light, feel her soothing, fiery eyes burn again through his skin, hear again her melody of a voice, experience her touch, and let her hand again melt in his.

But no! he tells himself, I won't do it. I can't do it.

No, he tells himself, as he climbs on a horse—a horse he can now afford. No, he tells himself, as he spurs his horse, and as he rides his horse at a gallop, and as he hitches his sweat-covered horse to a cast-iron pole in front of the huge two-story-high stone mansion atop a mountain. No, he tells himself, as he knocks at the huge entrance doors, and as the doors open to let him in, and as the doors close silently behind him. No, he tells himself, as Don Manuel greets him, and as Don Manuel takes him to his own personal library, and as Don Manuel places the chessmen on the board. No, he keeps telling himself, as he sits across the board from Don Manuel, and as he moves first one man and then another, and as he forces himself to concentrate for what seems to him hours and hours, and as some wonderful piano music begins to be heard, and as Don Manuel catches himself beginning to nod off, and as Don Manuel shouts, "Sol, please, come here and keep Julián company for a short while," and as Don Manuel tells him, "Julián, you won't mind, will you? I feel like taking a short siesta to recoup my strength before we continue this intense match." No, no, please, do not do this to me, he silently begs as he watches Don Manuel go, and as the piano music ceases to be heard, and as a door begins to open.

And then . . .

Then, Oh, yes, he tells himself, Yes! as he sees her, Sol, his sun, illuminating the room, illuminating his body, illuminating his soul with her radiance, embracing him with her eyes and lifting him from his lonely world into another world, a magical world of exaltation and glory, where all his sorrows seem to end.

It never occurred to Julián to ask any questions, such as: Who told Minister Tresbán about Julián's play in Mexico City? Why did Don Manuel go to El Ateneo last Monday, the very same day Julián started using the club's library, and stay there long enough to have his noontime meal at the club, when he rarely did? Why did the conversation turn to chess? And the most important question of them all: How could the general, who is both one of the greatest military strategists ever in all Latin America and a brilliant chess player, how could he lose to Julián? No, it never occurred to Julián—or to anyone else—that Don Manuel had planned this second meeting of Julián with Sol in the same manner Don Manuel had planned his campaign to liberate Guatemala, which resulted in the general achieving his goals swiftly, without ever losing a single battle, exactly as he had planned it.

Now that Julián is here, embraced by the glowing radiance of Sol, his sun, what difference does it make how or why they are together again?

As he stands facing her, Julián realizes that only one thing matters.

And that is that he must ride the wave of the gods as high and for as long as the gods will let him.

CHAPTER XIV

EXHAUSTED FROM THE CHESS GAME, and yet exhilarated at the same time, Julián returns that night to the place he calls home, the room he rents in the house of the Ladino widow, and falls into his bed, still fully dressed, hoping that this night he will be able to sleep peacefully. For the last nine nights, ever since he met Sol, he has tried to sleep, but to no avail. For the last nine nights he has been haunted by the thoughts circling in his head. But tonight is different, because today he saw her. Today he broke his promise to himself and he dared to look into her eyes again.

Yes, I did it. I broke my *word*, the word of honor I had given to my own *self,* he thinks as he lies in bed and looks up at the wood ceiling of his tiny room. I threw caution to the wind and decided to let the cards fall where they may. Let Panoplo's gods punish me for what I've done, breaking my own word to myself. But I would do it again, a thousand times again, if I had to, just to look at her, just to see her one more time.

He sighs a deeply felt sigh. I know I should have told Sol about Lucía and me, he tells himself, accusingly. I know I should have told her the truth. As I rode on the horse to Don Manuel's house, wishing to see Sol again, and at the same time hoping I wouldn't, I told myself: All right, Julián, when you first saw her at the party, you dared to act as you did because you had been drinking champagne, and you had told yourself that a little flirting could do you no harm, and there had been all of that enrapturing music surrounding the two of you when you held her tight in your arms. You can blame what you did that night on all of the trappings of the party. When you see her again, if you do, tell her just that, and act the way a man should—must. Apologize to her for what you had no right whatsoever to do and tell her the whole truth. That's what you must do, he had repeatedly told himself as he rode to her father's house for a game of chess. That's what an honorable man must do.

But when he saw her, when Sol, the woman of his dreams, appeared in front of him in her pale turquoise dress, her golden hair flashing with fire in the light of the dying sun, he just stood there, in front of her, unable to move, unable to say a word, unable to tell her how he felt, not daring to open his mouth for fear that he would blurt out his truth.

What excuse can he use now?

His mind travels from Sol to Lucía, the woman to whom he is promised. Maybe then, he thinks, when Lucía comes to Guatemala and I finally have a woman to sleep with, maybe then this woman of my dreams, will evanesce, disappear, vanish totally out of my life. Maybe then. But now this woman of my dreams has come alive, become real, he tells himself. Just as I begged her to do in my poems. Oh, how he wishes she could be here, with him, in his bed, right now!

Frantically, almost in despair, he stands up from his bed, rushes to the tiny table he uses as a desk, opens his diary lying on top of his table, flips through it, finds the last empty page, and by the pale blue light of the moon, he writes down with a hurried hand words that gallop through his head.

There's nothing I wouldn't give to spread on your naked shoulders
that hair of yours, long, untamed; that hair of yours, made of gold:
Very slowly, more than slowly,
strand after strand I would part it.

There's nothing I wouldn't give to free the knot of your hair
and spread on your naked shoulders that hair of yours, made of fire:
Very slowly, more than slowly,
thread after thread I would kiss it.

But then, knowing he can never do this, violently, he covers those lines with swift, angry strokes of his pen until they can no longer be read, totally obliterating them.

As if he had never written those lines.

As if those lines had never existed.

A UNIVERSITY PROFESSOR! Lucía says to herself, not believing what she has just read.

She reads Julián's letter again. Then shakes her head from side to side.

"Julián . . . ?" she says aloud. "A university professor . . . ?"

She still cannot believe it. If there is one job that sounds like stability to her, this is it! And stability is what she needs and has wanted ever since she and her family were forced to leave their comfortable, stable life back in Cuba, years ago, just because of what her father had dared to say in a public meeting.

With Julián's letter still in her hands, Lucía remembers what she and her father and her aunts had to go through when they first arrived in Mexico City, how afraid they were escaping from Cuba, bringing with them nothing but a few pieces of luggage. How hard life had been then, how ugly the places where she and her family had been forced to live, how much she dreamed then, as all young girls dream, of a beautiful place to live, of beautiful clothes to wear, of beautiful parties to attend, where she would meet a man who would make her his wife and give her the home and the family that she always wanted. She was barely eighteen at the time. But whenever she looked at herself in the mirror then, the person she saw there, the woman she was becoming, seemed to be much older and uglier than she thought possible, a woman who seemed to grow even older and uglier by the day, with a sad empty look in her eyes—eyes that no longer dared to dream.

It was then that her hatred for anything connected with the Cuban revolutionary war began. It had been because of that "damned war" that she had been forced to leave her home and come to a foreign city in a foreign land, where she and her family lived worse than the poorest people she knew ever did back in Cuba: in an ugly place in the noisiest and dirtiest part of town, wearing repeatedly mended out-of-fashion clothes, and feeling totally alone, with no friends—only her two old-maid aunts.

But that was many years ago. Eleven. Almost twelve now.

Since then, her father, who had been a lawyer in Cuba and was forced to wait three long years to get his law degree validated in Mexico, had started his own practice and, working long hours, had finally managed to provide her with the home, the clothes, and the parties she once dreamed of. But by then she thought it was too late. Neither the home, nor the clothes, nor the parties had made her feel young. And certainly not beautiful. In an attempt to give her the friends he thought she needed, her father began taking her to many of his wealthy clients' homes, where she met many young women her age who over the years had gotten married and had child after child, until all of them were happy wives and proud mothers.

All of them—but her.

Since the moment Julián proposed to her and she instantly accepted him, since that very moment, she worried that her life with him, as his wife, might be a going back to that frightening, harsh period of her life when she didn't know where the next meal was coming from. What other kind of life could there be for the wife of a graduate lawyer who was not allowed to practice law in Mexico because of his ultraliberal political thinking and who was forced to eke out a living by writing and by teaching part-time when he could? And she was willing to accept that, if that was what it took to be a wife and a mother, like all of her lady friends.

But now . . .

Now that Julián is a *university professor,* she thinks as she looks at Julián's letter in her hands, now things are totally different. No more wondering what her future will bring. Now she knows she will be able to have what she never thought was possible as Julián's wife: a beautiful, elegant home. With plenty of room for the children—lots of children.

With a large family, Julián will have to think twice before he does anything rash and stupid, like going to fight for Cuba, or something idiotic like that. The way he has been talking! If he wants to do something on behalf of the freedom of Cuba, let him write all he wants about it—what harm can there be in writing? But fighting? Risking his life? For Cuba? *Certainly not!* What about *her*? And *her* children to come? Let the fighting be done by the military men, she thinks. Let the men with the swords do what they know how to do. *Her* husband, the man with the pen, will do what *he* knows how to do.

Julián is a writer. What does he know about guns?

SHE MAKES A POINT of showing Julián's letter to all of her friends and family, the same friends and family who until now have doubted him and pitied her, but now, she thinks, must envy her, because she is happy, oh, so happy, *so* happy that she has begun to play the piano that had sat forgotten in the music room for such a long time. And at times, enraptured by the music, she even sings, astonishing her dear old aunts, who keep praising the Lord for the good fortune that has befallen Lucía, something the old ladies have been praying for day after day for such a long time.

If anybody ever doubted that prayers work, her aunts tell each other, well, here is the answer, for Lucía has all of a sudden become a different person. "The dear thing," the aunts keep telling each other, "she surely deserves it. She has waited for that boy for so long! Who would have told us that boy would turn out to be so successful?" they keep asking each other. "Who?"

Lucía has already decided when the wedding will take place: during the Christmas holidays, so all her family and friends will be there to see her as she walks triumphantly down the aisle in a beautiful bridal gown; a gown she has yet to select but whose grandeur she can already foresee in her heart. And where: La Gran Catedral de Mexico. Where else can a graduate lawyer—by the time of their wedding a university professor— and his bride get married?

And for a honeymoon, Chilpancingo first, to get away from it all for a couple of days, and then Acapulco, of course, where *everything* happens and where she has been told the weather is perfect at that time of year, the early part of January. And then, from there to her brand-new home in Guatemala. Some beginning for a new year! she thinks.

Oh, 1878 is going to be such a spectacular year for her!

What with her new gowns, and her new hats, and her new everything, including her new husband, by then a fully employed and well-paid university professor, and no longer an out-of-work poet, a poor-as-a-rat poet who used to write all of those overheated verses her lady friends still keep telling her are just this side of being obscene.

"Will he be that obscene in bed?" her lady friends tease her, and giggle, just as Lucía does, when she answers, "I hope so!" and laughs—or pretends to.

That is the only thing about which she is apprehensive: his passion, which she is not sure she will be able to match.

There has never been that much passion between the two of them. When he said, "Lucía, would you marry me?" he was almost a stranger to her, as much as she was a stranger to him. Why did he ask her? *That*, she doesn't know. Why did she accept? What else could a woman her age have done? Oh, sure, she knows he is likable and his conversation entertaining—when he talks about something other than Cuba's liberation—and his way of looking at her is intriguing: always as if he were studying her. And he is handsome, even *really* good looking—her lady friends tell her this, so it must be true. But she has never felt for him what she thinks he expects of her. A delirious passion. The delirious passion the woman in his poems is able to give—to return, to share—with him. Lucía wants to have that passion. Deep inside of her, she feels there lies a passionate woman waiting to be awakened. But . . . can the passion of that woman inside her ever match the passion of the woman in his poems?

But then—Lucía tells herself, dismissing those doubts of hers—Julián is no longer the same man he was. He has changed so much, she tells herself, every time she reads this latest letter of his, a letter she has read and reread hundreds of times. He has matured. He has become much more adult. He has already lost some of that impetuousness and wildness she had been so frightened of in the past. She can see all that in his letter.

She loves everything about this letter.

She loves the way he began the letter. *Lucía*, he wrote. Just that, *Lucía*. She likes that. That sounds the way a married man would address a letter to his wife. She loves the way his handwriting now seems so even, so calm, so much less passionate, the handwriting of a man totally in control of himself. She loves the way he is even beginning to sound like a university professor—his prose now curt and to the point.

And she particularly loves the way the word Cuba does not appear in this letter, not even once.

But what she loves the most about the letter is the last line, a line she loves to read and reread, though she has long ago memorized it and knows it by heart, a line that tells her how much Julián has changed:

—where we will be able to live the life of your dreams.

She loves that line because for the first time in any of his letters, in that line he shows that he is concerned with *her* dreams, not with *his*.

And because with that line she realizes that, after all this time, he has finally begun to think, first and above all, of *her*.

CHAPTER XV

"CHECKMATE AGAIN, Julián!" Don Manuel says as he raises his eyes to Julián's face.

Then, after realizing that Julián seems to be lost in the piano music that Sol is playing in the music room at the other end of the patio, the general adds, in his usual jovial way, "Julián, if I didn't know you are a man of honor, I would say you keep letting me win so you can get something out of me!"

Don Manuel and Julián have been playing on a tiny table with a black-and-white onyx chessboard top that stands in a shady corner of the immense patio of Don Manuel's house, right under one of those exuberantly leafy magnolia trees with its huge waxy leaves, which has been shading them from the afternoon sun on this beautiful mid-June day.

"Two games in a row!" the general continues. "Where is the challenging opponent who beat me a couple of weeks ago in front of all of my best friends? They still have not stopped talking about it at the club. I wonder how much longer I will have to live through their bad jokes!" Not giving Julián a chance to say a word, he shouts, "Sol, stop playing that piano and come keep Julián company for a while." He turns and faces Julián. "You won't mind, will you, Julián? These afternoon tournaments of ours always get the best of me. Besides," he adds, chuckling, "I can see your thoughts are not on chess today." Then, after landing a friendly slap on

Julián's shoulder, he stands up and starts for the house, where he enters the library, leaving Julián alone.

The afternoon light is pristine, as pristine as the clear cobalt blue sky above, and a soft, delicate breeze is blowing from the mountains, cooling the patio, which is paved with terra-cotta tiles laid in a checkerboard pattern.

Julián looks at the other end of the patio, where the doors leading to the music room have just opened and where Sol now stands, like a distant vision.

Never has he seen her looking so beautiful, he thinks. The gauzy white summer dress she is wearing makes her seem ethereal, almost not real.

As he looks at her, all he can think about are the words he wrote early this morning, when the rising sun caught him at his little table again, his pen in his hand.

> *What a pleasure it is, and what a fortune it is,*
> *to be able to yearn, to crave. To be able to dream.*
> *How many dawns have surprised me*
> *with your lips sealing mine in an everlasting kiss.*

WHILE JULIÁN STANDS THERE, silently staring at Sol in the distance, Doña Rosaura rushes into the library.

"Manuel, you're leaving them alone *again!*" she says, her voice sharp. "You know how people like to talk. You know what they would say. They made your sister Soledad into a black sheep, shunning her, ousting her from their company. I will not allow them to do that to Sol," she adds as she starts for the patio.

Don Manuel grabs her by the wrist and stops her. She violently pulls her wrist away from his hand.

"Rosaura, please," Don Manuel says, a concealed warning in his voice, "do not start over again, I beg you. You know that we have no sons and that I am *determined* to have, if not a son, at least a son-in-law of my *own* choosing. And, tell me, Rosaura, in all truth, who better than Julián?"

Doña Rosaura looks at her husband with pleading eyes. "But Manuel, you do not seem to understand. He *is* a foreigner," she says, her voice deeply concerned. "Sooner or later he may go back to Cuba to fight, maybe even get killed there." She turns and looks through the open slats of a shutter at her daughter, still at the far end of the patio. "What then of Sol?" she demands. "Don't you care about her?"

Don Manuel smiles at his wife. "Does it occur to you that he may succeed? We succeeded, didn't we? Our country is free. Why not his?"

Doña Rosaura faces him. "Then he'll steal her away from us and take her to his own country. I may never get to see my own daughter again." She fastens her angry eyes on his eyes. "Don't you care about me?" she says, and again begins to hurry to where Sol is, only to be stopped by Don Manuel again, who grabs her by the arm and pulls her to him.

Then, staring at his wife with loving eyes, he says, his voice soft and gentle, "Rosaura, you know your mother never liked me when I met you because she thought I was just a soldier with wild dreams." He pauses. Takes his wife's face in his hands, lifts it, and makes her look at him. "Did that stop you from loving me?"

Doña Rosaura looks at Don Manuel and, unable to say a word, she just shakes her head. Don Manuel smiles at her. "Do you really think anyone can stop them?" he adds, looking through the shutters at Julián, who has remained silently standing by the onyx chess table in the patio, looking at Sol, who, step by step, has been coming to him.

Rosaura looks at them and has no choice but to shake her head again.

Don Manuel places his arm around her shoulders, embraces her tight to him, and, gently, guides her back into the library.

"YOU WERE PLAYING beautifully," Julián says as he moves closer to Sol. "I wish you had not stopped. Was that the piece you were telling me about last week? The one Señora Saavedra thinks is too passionate?"

"Yes. Didn't you just love it?" she says as she starts for a nearby marble bench, gently leading him there. "It's the love theme from *Tristan and Isolde,* the opera by Wagner. Señora Saavedra thinks it's far too dissonant and claims that she doesn't like it, but I'm sure she does. Who wouldn't?" She looks at him and smiles. "It's so filled with longing, isn't it?" She sits at one end of the bench. "It's my favorite piece of music," she adds.

"Well, then . . ." Julián answers, standing by her side, "then it is mine too."

There is a short embarrassing pause, during which time Julián looks at

Sol, unable to speak. What am I doing? he asks himself. Just to hear himself answer, Tell her, Julián. Tell her! You have got to tell her that your life isn't yours anymore. "Sol," he finally manages to say after a long while, his voice nervous, apologetic, fumbling for words, "when I am with you, I don't know, I . . . I find it difficult to find the words to say what I want to say, what needs to be said."

"Sometimes words are not needed, Julián," she answers, her voice, calm, soothing. "I understand."

"No, Sol, you don't understand. How could you?" he says as he sits by her side and passionately grabs one of her hands. "How could you understand what this . . ."

Suddenly he realizes what he has done and lets her hand go.

"What this . . ." He searches nervously for the right word, a word to describe, and at the same time, mask, what he feels. He would like to say, What this incredible *love* of mine. But he cannot say that. He has to settle for the only thing he can offer her. " . . . what this *friendship* of ours," he says, and immediately corrects himself, "I mean, what the friendship of your family means to a man like me," he says. "Coming here, sharing a few minutes of my life with you—with *all* of you—how could you understand what this really means to me?" he adds, words now pouring from the mouth that moments ago could not speak. "Being with you, talking with you, feeling so much at home when I am by your side. And yet . . ." he looks deep into her sparkling dark eyes, "what right do I have to talk to you?" He stands, embarrassed. "I," he says, placing his right hand over his heart, "a man with no country. I," he says, tapping his chest again with his hand, "a man whose hands are tied behind his back. Tied by a promise, a promise I've made to—"

He pauses abruptly.

"I'm sorry. Sometimes I don't know what I am saying," he says and moves away from her as he realizes that he had almost told her. The truth had almost spilled from his lips. But telling that truth would condemn him never to see her again, and that . . . That, he could not bear. He looks away from Sol, who is looking at him with understanding eyes, for she thinks she knows what is going through his mind, what is going through his heart. For she thinks she knows what this promise is he cannot talk about.

For the last few weeks, Sol has been asking her father question after question about Julián, and Don Manuel has been happy to answer the questions, eager to encourage the interest Sol has begun to show in the young man whom Don Manuel already sees as a potential son-in-law.

When Don Manuel lost his firstborn, Manuelito, a three-year-old boy he doted on, to malaria, in his grief he turned all of his affection toward Sol, the only daughter he had at the time. It did not take long for him to begin seeing in his bright, intelligent girl the son he had lost. It was then he decided he would educate her just as he would have educated his lost boy; and consequently he taught Sol everything about his campaign to liberate Guatemala—and in full detail. Using sets of toy lead soldiers, he demonstrated to Sol, then still a young girl, the brilliant strategies he used to achieve victory over Spain in barely a month, when other Latin American countries had to fight years for their freedom. "But we had trump cards in our hands," Don Manuel explained to her, "because we, the people of Guatemala, are like our national bird, the quetzal, an incredibly beautiful bird that dies when in captivity. And just as the quetzal loves freedom, so do we, my child, so do we. That is why the quetzal is on our seal, on our flag, and on our money. Always remember that, Sol, and, like the quetzal, always let the love of freedom guide your life."

It was Don Manuel himself who gave Sol a copy of Julián's booklet *Life of a Political Prisoner in Cuba,* a booklet Julián dared to publish right in Spain when he was deported from Cuba. In its pages, Julián narrated not the horrors he had to live through as a prisoner, but the horrible things he saw done to others, things that made Sol weep as she read of them. "It took a lot of guts for anyone to dare to write something like that, anywhere," the general told Sol. "But to write it—and publish it—in Spain of all places!" Don Manuel added, his voice filled with admiration, an admiration he has passed on to Sol.

That is how Sol knows of the promise Julián has made to himself to free Cuba, just as her father had once promised himself he would free Guatemala. And that is also how Sol understands that Julián's dreams to free Cuba are more important than she herself is—and she admires that.

Like her father, Julián is a dreamer.

And like her father, Julián is also a fighter.

Sol knows Julián will have to do what he has to do: go to Cuba and fight. And she wouldn't want it any other way. If he were to die for his country while fighting for freedom, well then, that is the way gods die. And that only increases her love for him. She knows that after he's achieved his dream of freeing Cuba, he will come back to her. She knows that, with absolute certainty. Just as she knows she will willingly wait for him for as long as it takes, just as her mother waited for her father. She loves the warrior she knows Julián has inside, as much as the poet who just seconds ago had started to pour out his passionate heart to her. And if friendship is all this poet-warrior can offer her right now, well then, friendship is what she will accept and what she will settle for. A glorious friendship she will always cherish.

Thinking this gives her an idea. She smiles to herself.

"Julián," she says, aiming her smile at him, her voice still gentle, though with a touch of excitement and daring, "if you cannot say what you feel," she pauses, enjoying the expectancy she reads in his eyes, "perhaps you could write it down." She pauses again, for a tiny second. "I mean," she adds, "would you be so kind to write me a poem, Julián?"

She realizes what she has just said and though she blushes, she keeps her eyes steadily fastened to his. "I mean," she corrects herself, "to our . . . *friendship?*"

Julián answers her daring smile with a daring smile of his own.

"I'd be honored, Sol."

Seeing that smile in his eyes, Sol immediately stands up and rushes toward the house, becoming again the girl she is at heart. But then, realizing that a young woman her age is not ever supposed to rush—or so both her mother and Xenufla keep reminding her—she pauses, regains her composure, and faces Julián. "I'll be right back, Julián," she says, and then she forces herself to walk slowly into the house. But no sooner is she inside than she rushes upstairs, climbing the steps two at a time.

Julián, left alone, sitting on the bench, catches himself smiling at her as he sees her leave, and immediately shakes his head. *What* am I doing? Julián asks himself. What am *I* doing? Why don't I just stand up and go, get out, leave? He shakes his head and begins to stand up, decisively, ready to walk away from it all, when Sol, forgetting how well-bred young ladies are supposed to move, rushes back to the patio, carrying her diary in her hands, a beaming smile on her face. She hands the diary to Julián, who sits again on the bench, opens the handsome leather-bound book without looking at it, and begins to leaf quickly through it, looking for an empty page. It is only when he glances at the book, and, not really meaning to, reads part of the last entry, which begins, *Dear Diary,* that he realizes what he has in his hands. Embarrassed, and thinking Sol must have made a mistake and brought him the wrong book, he immediately closes it and hands it back to her.

"Sol, I think you made a mistake. You brought me your diary, not your poetry album. Surely you must have a poetry album where all your thousands of admirers have written poems dedicated to you, don't you? Or isn't this done here in Guatemala? Back in Cuba, each of my sisters has a—"

Sol smiles at him. "Oh, yes, I have one of those poetry albums. But I could not let your beautiful words share space with the words of those other men, Julián. Theirs are banal, trite. Meaningless. Repeating what somebody else said—and repeating it badly. Yours, on the other hand . . ." she pauses. "Your wonderful words do not belong next to theirs, Julián. Yours deserve a special place. That is why I brought you my diary, which is my best friend. I want you to get to know my diary, Julián, just as much as I want my diary to get to know you. I keep no secrets from my diary, Julián. None whatsoever."

Julián smiles at her, a mischievous smile. "You don't mean to tell me that if I were to read through all of these pages I would get to know everything there is to know about you, do you?"

Sol nods at him, echoing the mischief in his eyes and in his tone of voice.

"Every little secret?" he adds.

Sol nods again.

"Even the most intimate things in your life?"

Sol looks at him, catching his playful eyes, and after nodding once again, she says, "But you wouldn't need to read through all of those pages to know my most intimate secrets, Julián." Julián looks at her, puzzled. Sol tilts her head to one side and fastens her eyes on his. "All you would have to do is ask me, and I would tell you," she says, and pauses—a long deliberate pause—enjoying herself thoroughly, looking at Julián, who, embarrassed by her bluntness, has begun to blush.

Men look so handsome when they blush, Sol tells herself.

Then, after she thinks she has made him suffer enough, she adds, "Isn't that what . . . *friends* do?"

Julián realizes that he has been caught in his own trap and begins to laugh, a loud belly laugh, the kind he has never before enjoyed in the presence of a woman. And his loud laughter makes her laugh equally as loudly and freely, the kind of laughter she has never before enjoyed in the presence of a man.

LATER ON, after Don Manuel shouts, "Julián, chess calls!" and after Julián obediently joins her father for another game of chess, Sol rushes to her favorite place on the whole Earth, a small white gazebo by the river, a tiny pavilion the family calls El Mirador—The Lookout—because the views from it are outstanding.

Located at the end of the long serpentine path that leads from the house to the river, the gazebo is a tall, slender, hexagonal structure of classic Greek pillars, made of wood painted white and roofed with a dome. And because the mosquitoes and flies that occasionally teem at the edge of the river can be extremely annoying, the gazebo has gauzy sheer drapes that can be left opened—tied back to the Greek pillars, as they usually are—or closed, as needed. This gazebo is Sol's "place of power," her *Katok,* a Mayan word Xenufla taught her, the word Cakchiquel Indians use to refer to magical places that allow the soul "to travel ahead and move forward."

There, sitting on the steps, enjoying the cool breezes, and listening to the dreamy song of the river as it rushes from the mountaintops down to the valley, she eagerly turns the pages of her diary until she finds the page she is looking for, where just minutes ago Julián wrote her a poem, the ink barely dry.

She didn't want to read his poem anywhere else.

She feels that, somehow, the gazebo is the only place in the world that can properly frame Julián's beautiful words.

The gazebo. And the river.

It was difficult waiting all the time it took for her to reach the gazebo to read Julián's words. But now that she is there, she knows she was right.

Julián, the gazebo, and the river belong together.

Just as she belongs with them.

She reads the poem to herself. And as she reads it, she imagines him there, close to her, by her side, his dark melodious voice whispering in her ear, daring to tell her now, through the pages of her diary, what he did not dare tell her then, when he stood tongue-tied in the patio, staring at her.

> *You ask me for verses to friendship like ours,*
> *and to you I'm sending my brotherly love.*
> *How different my song would sound*
> *should I dare use a harp made of your hair!*

"I understand, Julián!" she says aloud, as if speaking to him when she finishes reading his poem.

"I understand."

CHAPTER XVI

TWO WEEKS LATER, Sol and Julián are strolling by the bank of the river, talking quietly to each other and looking every so often across the distant mountains at what promises to be a magnificent sunset as Xenufla—the old Mayan woman, Sol's chaperone—follows them, discreetly keeping quite a few steps behind them.

"Oh, no! We were never allowed to read Whitman in school," Sol says, answering Julián's question. "They claimed that his poetry was immoral and obscene. But my Aunt Soledad loved his poems and introduced them to me." Sol stops walking and looks in the far distance, remembering. "I miss her so much! She was not only my mentor but my closest friend, always guiding me and teaching me. Except for us, the family, nobody really understood her. She was so outspoken. And so funny too!" Sol turns and faces Julián again. "No wonder people called her a black sheep. She used to smoke cigars and ride horses at full speed, sitting astride, wearing men's trousers. Rumor has it that she had a lover, a young Mayan man half her age, and that they used to meet in the middle of the night at a tiny gazebo she had designed. As a matter of fact . . ."

Sol turns around and, realizing that Xenufla, pretending to be out of breath, has indeed stayed quite a distance behind them and is not in sight—as Sol herself had suggested that Xenufla should do—Sol decides to take advantage of the rare moment of privacy, just as she had planned it, like one of those military maneuvers she had learned from her father.

She turns back to Julián and, facing him, smiles her most mischievous smile as she lowers her voice to a bare whisper.

"Julián," she says, with urgency in her voice, "there is something I would like to show you. Here, come with me. Follow me." She starts to walk hurriedly ahead of him, leading him up a small hill until they reach an area from where the rushing rapids of the river can be heard close by, but no longer be seen. "Now, close your eyes," she adds, "and do not open them until I tell you. I will lead you."

Obediently, Julián closes his eyes as he was asked to, and as he does, he remembers the opening lines of a poem he wrote to Sol, years before he ever met her.

I close my eyes and there, in front of me, I see her . . .

"Keep your eyes closed. Here is my hand, give me yours," Sol adds, and he places his hand in hers.

Never has he felt so safe as when she begins to lead him up the path— he, now blind, submerged in a totally different world, a world of shadows and darkness where only her voice is alive, her warm gentle voice filled with a sense of adventure and excitement.

"Stay right here," he hears her say, after a short while, as she lets his hand go. "And don't you dare open your eyes until I tell you!"

I extend my hand, and within the dark shadows
of my dreams she hides away . . .

His eyes still closed, for a few seconds Julián hears nothing but the rustle of Sol's long skirt as she rushes away from him. And for those few precious seconds he gives himself permission to dream.

But soon, within the world of shadows, we will make love
with a light so immense it will surpass all the stars . . .

Still in his dream world, he suddenly realizes what a magical thing it is to hear the rustling of a woman's skirt. Especially when it is followed by a luminous, melodious voice, Sol's smiling voice, saying, "Now!"

He opens his eyes and can barely believe what he sees.

He is standing in front of a gazebo, a tall, slender, white Greek temple, on the side of a mountain, from where he can see the entire world, he thinks. Down at his feet is the magnificent City of Guatemala, dotted by dozens, hundreds, of bell towers, proudly standing erect, their bronze bells singing softly in the faraway distance, scintillating like sparkling bronze stars whenever they catch and reflect the light of the setting sun as they sing. By his side, the river, a ribbon of copper glittering and shimmering as if illuminated from within, rushes turbulently by. Beyond the river, the magical volcanoes that encircle the city stand proudly, their high peaks catching the fire of the sun. And in front of him, backlit by the sun and framed by the mystical temple, a goddess—an incredibly beautiful goddess—has unpinned her hair, has shaken her head, and has let her hair fall loose, her beautiful long golden hair that has never been cut and that reaches down to her waist, and is now surrounding her, enveloping her, like a golden mantle. All of a sudden, the distant bells begin to peal, loudly announcing the time of vespers and giving their farewell to the sun. And as if answering them, the sun begins to glow brilliant red behind this goddess, leaving her body in silhouette, while her golden hair, lighted by the brilliant light of the last rays of the sunset, begins to glow as blinding red as the sun itself.

Julián feels as if his soul has left his body.

Is this what death is? he asks himself. Is this the feeling one has when one encounters one's final destiny? He has never felt closer to God, whatever God there may be, than now, as he stands there, staring at this portentous vision of a loving goddess whose divine voice has both the power to soothe him and to call him to action at the same time. He faces away from her. He has to. To survive. To avoid rushing to her and grabbing her in his arms, then kissing her feet, her hands, her entire body, every single strand of her glorious hair, her eyes, her mouth.

"This is my favorite place in the whole world," he hears his goddess say. "A place where I come for answers. Here you can always find me." And then he hears his goddess ask, "Isn't it wonderful?"

Speechless, afraid to open his mouth, all Julián can do is to nod.

· · ·

THE FOLLOWING MORNING, after breakfast, an Indian boy delivers to Don Manuel's house a letter addressed to Sol in Julián's handwriting.

Sol takes the unopened missive to the white gazebo, and there, by the river, she opens it and begins to read it to herself. And as she reads it, she feels him there, standing by her side, speaking to her.

At first it is Julián, the man, who addresses her:

"Sol,

"Yesterday, when you asked me what gift you could bestow on me in return for the poem I wrote in your diary weeks ago, I was left without words, for you have already given me, and repeatedly, the greatest gifts I have ever received: the rippling gaiety of your laughter and the soothing melody of your voice—sounds I shall always carry with me; sounds I shall always cherish."

But then Julián, the poet, speaks:

> *Others may not hear in the echoes of your laughter*
> *and in the music of your voice what I hear: promises, pain, joy.*
> *Everything that hides beneath the deepest lake,*
> *everything that lies atop the highest cloud.*
>
> *Those sounds, your gift, may be all I can take with me;*
> *they may be all I will ever be able to have of you.*
> *Those sounds, your gift, shall always bring solace and peace*
> *to my broken soul wherever I go, wherever I am.*

Sol presses the letter against her heart, as her eyes sparkle with infinite bliss. For Julián's words make her feel no longer like a girl, but like a woman. A beautiful woman. Beautiful inside, beautiful outside.

Just that, a woman. But a woman like no other.

The happiest woman in the entire universe.

And the proudest.

"LUCÍA, PLEASE," Aunt Ifigenia says, beginning to sound irate, "I told you *not* to move. As soon as I am finished with this blessed hem you'll be able to move all you want, but until then, child, *please,* I beg you, stay put," the gray-haired old lady adds, her voice now much less harsh. "Now, where's that pin box? What did I do with it? Celestina, do you happen to know where I— Oh, there it is."

For the last hour and a half—an hour and a half that to Lucía has seemed like an unbearable eternity—Lucía, trying hard not to move, has been standing on a small wooden platform in front of an oval cheval mirror in the sewing room on the second floor of her house, by a tall, slender window. Her Aunt Ifigenia, who is now kneeling by her side, has been basting the hem of the first fitting of the muslin mock-up of Lucía's wedding gown as fast as she can, while her other aunt, Celestina, is working on the fitting of the complex twelve-panel bodice.

Both of Lucía's aunts, Ifigenia and Celestina, have spent the last two weeks drawing, cutting, and fitting: paper patterns first, then muslin patterns. The two old maids have been trying hard to decipher the complex design Lucía selected for her wedding gown, a magnificent dress Lucía saw in an engraving in a French fashion magazine. This dress was designed by the head of the House of Worth himself, Charles Worth, the famous British couturier who revolutionized Paris by expurgating with one single stroke of his pen the very wide hoopskirts that were in vogue when Lucía's aunts were young women, and who single-handedly created the bustle dress, now all the rage.

The bustle dress made a lot of sense. Many young women were burned to death by those dangerous hoopskirts that constantly managed to bump into lighted candles or gaslights and catch on fire. Aunt Ifigenia herself almost died once when her eleven-yard skirt caught on fire, and she will always thank God she suffered no disfiguring scars on her face, just on her legs. The new bustle dresses Charles Worth has been designing use as many yards as the old hoopskirt dresses did, or even more—after all, someone has to keep the fabric factories that Worth's family owns in England in operation. But since the bustle skirts are tight in front and all the extra yardage goes on the bustled back, a woman can walk not only with much more ease but with much less fear of hitting something dangerous unawares. It was Eugenia de Montijo, the wife of Napoleon III, who dared to wear the first of Charles Worth's bustle dresses, astonishing all of Paris. And Lucía badly wants her wedding dress to be a copy of that very same dress, the one worn by the dark Spanish beauty who became the empress of France. Even if it has to be homemade.

"Please, Lucía, stop fidgeting!" Aunt Ifigenia begs once again. "I almost cut myself with the scissors! Just hold still a little longer, child. A couple more panels and I'll be done with this blessed hem."

The dress has a very tight-fitting bodice, with a narrow waistline; long, tight sleeves; and a very low-cut square neckline that reveals a lot of Lucía's bust—which at first her aunts found most objectionable. In addition, Worth's drawing shows a considerable bustle, which Lucía asked her aunts to elongate into a highly ornate train—the kind of train the wedding dress of the bride of a university professor must have. Except for the ivory satin ruching that will trim the neckline, the hem, and the cuffs, and for the shirred front panel, the dress itself will have almost no ornamentation at all. It does not need it because of the richness of the fabric, an ivory shot silk taffeta Lucía ordered from Paris five weeks ago, just a few days after she received Julián's letter telling her of his becoming a university professor. But so far, as of this fitting, the fabric has yet to arrive in Mexico City. In fact, the delay in getting the fabric is the main reason her aunts decided to do a complete mock-up of the dress in muslin, because, as they said, "Once the real fabric is cut, it is cut. And since we didn't order any extra fabric, it'd better be right." The only truly ornamented parts of the dress, the bustle and the train, are to be trimmed with hand-tatted Spanish lace, ordered directly from Sevilla—an outrageously expensive lace that, in addition to their making of the dress, will be the wedding present from both her aunts.

To Aunts Ifigenia and Celestina, Lucía's wedding is a dream come true. Since they themselves never got married, they are living through Lucía's wedding as if it were their own. Nothing seems to be too much for their "child," as they still call Lucía—something Lucía has always liked, for it makes her feel wanted and loved.

"Done at last!" loudly sighs Aunt Ifigenia, as she completes the hem she has been working on for so long and begins to stand up, something she does with a great deal of difficulty, due both to her abundant years and to her fire-scarred legs. "How are you coming along with that sleeve, Celestina?" she asks. "Do you need any help?"

"No, thanks, I'm almost done," answers Celestina, who then faces Lucía. "One last stitch and we're done, child," the old lady tells her niece as she finishes basting the long, narrow right sleeve of the dress to the shoulder line, which seems to fit perfectly.

"Now, child," the old lady adds as she moves back, "what do you think?"

Lucía has been facing away from the mirror on purpose. She didn't want to look at herself until the tentative fitting had been completed. She wanted to see what kind of a first impression the dress would give, what the dress would look like to someone who had never seen it before. Keeping her eyes on the floor, and with the help of her aunts, who delicately hold the long train in their hands, Lucía turns around slowly, so as not to disturb the pieces making up the dress, some of which are barely basted together. Then, when she sees the feet of the cheval mirror directly in front of her, she slowly raises her eyes and looks at herself. And she can barely believe her own eyes.

Though the mock-up of her wedding dress is made of inexpensive unbleached muslin, it is spectacularly beautiful in its elegant, tailored cut and in its austere simplicity. Just as she hoped, the dress brings out the best of her: her trim waist, her elegant arms, her long, thin neck.

But the dress does much more than just that.

It transforms her.

Lucía looks at herself in the mirror, and the person she sees there does not look at all like her old self, the ugly woman she remembers seeing in that very same mirror every time she looked into it, but like a totally different person. A person she does not remember ever seeing before.

Her aunts have been looking at Lucía in the mirror, smiling apprehensively and wondering whether Lucía will like the dress as interpreted by them, when they see the look on Lucía's face—a look they have never seen before. Then, unwillingly, almost unaware that they are doing it, they both begin to cry at the same time, for suddenly they both have realized that their little niece—their child—is no longer little, nor a child. In this dress Lucía has somehow matured. Grown up. Bloomed.

"Lucía . . . !" that's all the two aunts can manage to say, the word a long admiring sigh.

When she hears this appreciative exclamation coming from both her aunts, Lucía, who has not stopped looking at herself in the mirror, smiles at herself, agreeing with her aunts, as her eyes, which all of a sudden have lost the sad, empty look they have had for years, now sparkle with infinite bliss. For the woman Lucía sees in the mirror, wearing a muslin mock-up of her wedding dress, is a beautiful woman. Beautiful inside, beautiful outside.

Just that, a woman. But a woman like no other.

The happiest woman in the entire universe.

And the proudest.

CHAPTER XVII

THREE FRIDAYS LATER, the first Friday in August, no sooner does the general beat Julián again at their weekly chess game than he says, "Julián, I ran into Minister Tresbán yesterday at the club, El Ateneo, and he was very concerned about your play. He has already ordered the invitations to the opening to be engraved, and so far, Tresbán tells me, there *is* no play. I certainly don't want to be blamed if you have no play," the general continues, a smile on his face. "So, my dear Doctor Torrent, from now on, our game is postponed. Go back to your room, stay there, write your play, and then, after the play opens, you may come back to us. Maybe by then you'll pay more attention to your chess game," he adds, laughing, as he calls Sol, who is in the music room.

"Sol," he says to her as she joins them on the patio. "I just told Julián I don't want to see him again until his play is finished. So"—he smiles at her—"I want you to show him to the door! This may be your last chance to talk to this boy before he goes into seclusion."

He turns to Julián.

"Next time we see you will be on opening night, Julián. Until then." Don Manuel smiles broadly at Julián and goes into the library, closing the louvered door behind him as he walks inside.

Julián and Sol begin to walk slowly across the patio toward the entrance doors. Julián, as nervous as he always is whenever he is in Sol's company, keeps his hands behind his back.

The afternoon has begun to die, and another wonderful Guatemalan sunset is being announced, the sky already beginning to change colors from a deep cobalt blue to a soft turquoise, while a tinge of pale amber begins to outline the distant mountains.

Julián takes a deep breath, looks up at the sky, and sighs.

"You know, Sol," he says, still looking up at the sky, "beautiful as sunsets are, I prefer sunrises. Every sunset reminds me of another day gone by with little if anything accomplished. That is why I love sunrises, because they are filled with hope. I love it when the sun rises and catches me sitting at my table, thinking, and calls me to work—a bugle calling me to action. Maybe today, I say to myself, maybe today I'll come up with an answer, a solution, a way to move my dreams closer to reality." He faces her. "But when the sun hides and another day goes by, I find myself thinking that maybe I'm just wasting my life away. Too much thinking and not enough doing. Writing about freedom when I should be joining the men in Cuba who are fighting for it. But what can a single person do? And a single person like me, who has nothing but a pen in his hand."

"Oh, no, Julián, no," Sol immediately interjects, her voice urgent, impetuous, "you have everything, because you have the urge, the need. The passion. Without that passion, nothing can ever be accomplished. But with that passion, Julián, *nothing* can ever get in your way." Sol smiles at him. "Besides, Julián," she adds, insistently, "don't you remember what you yourself said? The sword is nothing without the pen. Dreams make the world change, Julián, they are the sparks. And words are the means to communicate those sparks to others. You have the dreams, Julián. And you also have the words. Don't let anything get in the way of those dreams of yours, Julián. Bringing the joy of freedom to your homeland is what you must do, what God placed you on Earth for. Like the quetzal," she says, fervently echoing her father's words, "always let the love of freedom guide your life, Julián. Nothing else is important. That is why God has given you the power of words, those wonderful words of yours."

Julián turns to Sol, desperately wanting to grab her hand in his, but forces himself to keep his distance from her, while his thankful eyes sketch a small smile echoing hers. "Sometimes words are very stubborn, Sol," he responds. "Sometimes they don't want to come. At all. Like this play of mine . . . I *know* what needs to be said, and yet, somehow, I cannot find the words to say it." They are now by the entrance door to the house. Julián's horse, held by the reins by a young Mayan man, is whinnying, ready to go. "There is *so much* I want to say with this play, Sol," Julián says, vehemently, almost in despair. "But the verses . . ." He pauses as he climbs on his horse. "The verses simply do not want to come," he adds, despondently.

"They will, Julián," Sol says, smiling broadly at him as she waves him good-bye. "Just let your soul soar, Julián, and they will come. I know they will."

Julián nods to her, and after looking at her one more time, he spurs his horse into a gentle trot, while his mind begins to swirl as he asks himself, How can I write verses about truth, and about bravery, and about freedom, when I am neither truthful, nor brave, nor free every time I am around Sol? When I lack the courage to tell her the truth?

THE MOMENT he gets back to the house of the Ladino widow and enters his room, Julián looks at the calendar he keeps on his table, a calendar in which he has circled important dates in red, one of which dates is coming *far* too fast.

Saturday, December 20, the calendar reads.

And underneath it, one word, one single word written in small capital letters:

WEDDING

He flips through the calendar, stares again at that red-circled date, December 20, thinks of Sol and tells himself, Tomorrow I *will* tell her. But then he shakes his head. How many times has he said those very same words before?

He flips again through the calendar, and finds another red-circled date.

September 15
PLAY OPENS

If the rehearsal period is only two weeks long, that means that the parts must be copied and handed to the actors by the first day of September, he thinks, and that is less than three weeks away. I can't leave this room until the play is finished, he tells himself. As Don Manuel said, I have to go into seclusion, forget about everything else, and think exclusively of how this play might help Cuba.

He shakes his head. How will I ever be able to put Sol out of my mind and concentrate on writing the play?

Again he flips through the calendar and sees other red-circled dates.

September 24
SCHOOL BEGINS

December 19
CHRISTMAS BREAK

December 10 is the latest date I can leave for Mexico and make it in time for the wedding on the 20th, he tells himself, since he has found out that it takes a minimum of eight days to reach Mexico City via the Pacific coast, and once there he will probably need at least two days to get ready for the wedding.

He has decided that, by then, he will have the money to afford a first-class trip going to Mexico, and that rather than travel by mule, the way he had to do when he came to Guatemala City via the Caribbean, he will take the stagecoach, first to Adjuintla, at the foot of the mountains, and then to Chirimacotengo on the Pacific coast, where Panoplo is from. There he will get on a passenger steamship to Acapulco, and once there, he will take the railroad to Mexico City. But that means he will have to miss classes for at least nine days before the Christmas break.

Tell Saavedra, he writes in his notebook.

Notify University.

Then, as he is looking at the calendar again, he realizes that there is one more date that needs to be circled. He sits at his table and looks for a long while at that date.

December 9, the day before he is to leave for Mexico.

Then, he sighs as he circles it and writes underneath.

SOL

It is only then that he puts the calendar aside and begins to work once more on the play. And to crumple piece after piece of paper, letting them fall to the floor, working assiduously until, at one point, angry, unable to produce anything he likes, he pulls his flask of gin from his coat and begins to take at first one small sip after another, then a longer swallow after another, hoping the gin will help him write something good. But soon he finds that he has drained the flask totally empty. He tries to stand up, but is hardly able to do it. Holding on to the table, he manages to get to the door, and there, barely able to hold on to the door frame, he calls the son of his Ladino landlady, who runs to him.

"Panchito," he says, his speech blurred, "could you do me a favor?"

The boy nods.

Julián smiles at him. "Could you go to Panoplo's cantina"—he pauses. "Do you know which one is Panoplo's cantina?"

Panchito shakes his head from side to side.

"It has a big sign on top that says El *Último*—" Julián begins to say, and then he remembers that though Panchito is almost ten he probably does not know how to read. "Do you know the cantina that is across from the entrance of the cemetery, right on the Street of the Angels, do you know the one?"

Panchito nods.

"Well, go there and ask Panoplo—Panoplo is the cantina man—ask Panoplo to fill this flask." He smiles at the young boy with the huge black eyes who is looking intently at him. Never has he seen Señor Julián like this, never. "Just tell him this is for Ginebrita," Julián adds. "Panoplo will know," and gives the boy a few reales.

He goes back to his table, sits at it, and then he has a wondrous vision: A larger-than-life tall and handsome white woman wearing a torn classic Greek robe that lets her beautiful bare breasts show—the statue in El Parque de la Victoria, The Spirit of Guatemala—appears to him in his dreams. Proudly looking up at heaven, she is breaking the infamous chains of slavery as she steps, defiantly, over the Spanish Crown, which lies crushed at her feet. Except that this woman is no longer The Spirit of Guatemala, a statue made of cold white marble, but Sol, made of warm real flesh and blood. Sol, who has appeared to him in his dreams, her beautiful breasts exposed, her nipples hard and erect, as her robe, white and blue—the colors of Guatemala—made of a thin, vaporous, virtually transparent material that barely hides her naked body underneath, seems to encircle him, filling him with an indescribable warmth. Sol, telling him, "Just let your soul soar, Julián."

Suddenly he finds himself awakening, surprised that he had fallen asleep at the table he was using as his desk. He opens his blurry eyes and sees the open gin flask on the table—drained totally empty—and does not remember Panchito returning with it. How long have I been asleep? he asks himself. Hoping to make up for the lost time, he grabs the pen and this time the verses flow. Free. Uninterrupted. Filling page after page, until the very last scene, where a man debating between two immense loves has to make a decision: Shall he choose the love of his country? Or choose the love of his wife, who, holding their son in her arms, demands that her husband not put his life at risk in his fight for freedom but stay behind and care for her and their son?

By the time Julián finishes the rough draft of the play he is thoroughly exhausted. Totally drained. He feels as if each line came from the bottom of his heart and was drawn with his own blood. And yet, he also feels jubilant, exalted, for in this play, virtue manages to win without sacrificing love.

FIVE WEEKS LATER, after innumerable revisions and rewrites, Julián is standing in the wings of the stage, now a nervous author silently repeating his own words in his mind as the actors on stage are saying them.

The scene is lighted both by closely spaced gas footlights bordering the front of the stage and by a number of gaslights that are located in the fly gallery above the stage, where several large painted drops—scenery from the previous acts of Julián's play—are hanging. Because the fly gallery is several stories high, it creates a chimneylike effect that makes the hot air at stage level rise, and because the stage floor was just swept during the previous interval, the dust floating in the air creates almost imperceptible currents of dust that, lighted by the footlights and by the lights located above, seem to dance up the fly gallery, just to drift down and settle, just to dance up again as the actors move on the stage.

But Julián does not notice any of that.

He just listens carefully to his lines being spoken by the actors; lines that not that long ago were nothing but abstract words on paper, but which all of a sudden, in the knowledgeable voices of the actors saying them, have become meaningful sentences that will forever alter the lives of the characters saying them. And those characters, who not long ago were simply names on a piece of paper, have now become fully fleshed human beings whose lives are guided by their dreams—much as horse-drawn carriages are guided by their drivers—but dreams that are often controlled by precariously insecure reins that are filled with flaws.

Julián knows about those dreams.

He also knows about those flaws.

And now he is presenting those same dreams and flaws to the people of Guatemala, who, bejeweled and handsomely dressed, have flocked to the theater to see this new play by this exiled Cuban writer about whom they have heard so much.

September 15 has finally arrived, and all of Guatemala is indeed present at El Teatro Nacional, watching an actor playing a man dressed in a plain black suit who is desperately pacing back and forth inside a full-stage set of an elegant parlor. At stage left, an actress playing his wife—a dark-haired woman costumed in a dark burgundy hoopskirt dress—crouches on the floor, protectively embracing their young son. At stage right, an actress playing The Spirit of Guatemala—wearing a torn white-and-blue classic Greek robe, her long golden hair loose and free, her arms bare, her hands fastened with chains and shackles—stands, begging the man to leave everything behind and fight for her freedom. It is a painful struggle. Each of the two women appeals to different parts of the man, and they present him with opposite arguments, both of which are irrefutable, since both points of view are right.

The audience, caught in the dilemma, is totally silent.

Even the musicians in the pit, who have lived through an entire week of rehearsals and who by now know most of the lines by heart, are carefully listening to the words the characters on stage—who are no longer characters but persons caught in a real conflict—are saying.

Torn between two such opposite forces, and knowing that he must come to a final decision, the man on the stage presses his hands to his temples, as if in immense pain. And then, suddenly, as if triggered by that gesture, the walls of the room encircling him unexpectedly become transparent, which makes the entire audience gasp aloud, for behind those transparent walls the audience sees, surrounding the people onstage, lines of full-sized marble heroes of the past standing proudly on pedestals: silent white marble statues with marble swords by their sides.

Each of the statues is lit by a single gas footlight, while the rest of the stage is now almost totally dark, except for the man in the black suit at the center of the stage, who is in the flickering pool of a limelight.

The man kneels down by his wife.

Then, gently lifting her face in his hands he makes his wife look at him, and while embracing her, he gestures in a wide circle with his right arm, including the whole of the audience in his embrace, as he tells her:

> *I dream of cloisters of marble where in a deep frozen silence*
> *heroes of marble are standing. At night, lighted by my soul,*
> *I speak to them all. Proud soldiers, in rank and file they all stand*
> *as I walk amongst their lines. I kiss their cold hands of stone.*
> *They open their eyes of stone. Their frozen beards of stone tremble*
> *as they try to move their lips. Their hands of stone tightly grip*
> *their throbbing swords, which pulsate in their sheaths. And as they do,*
> *the heroes of marble weep. In silence I kiss their hands.*

The man stands up, his eyes as if illuminated from within.

> *I speak to them through the night. They all are in lines. I walk*
> *amongst their lines and, in tears, I embrace one of the statues.*
> *"O Marble Hero," I say, "your children crave to be freed*
> *from their masters, who enslave them. Unwilling to act, they starve,*
> *eating the crumbs of their honor at a table stained with want.*
> *In meaningless worlds they lose the last of their fire. They say,*
> *O Statue that stands asleep, that none are left of your race!"*

He addresses his wife, who is holding her son tight to her breast.

> *The hero I am embracing lifts me from the dirt. He grabs me*
> *by the shoulder, lifts my chin up to the sky and then raises*
> *his arm of stone—a stone arm that shines as bright as the sun!*
> *Grabs his sword with glowing hand, and places it within mine,*
> *entrusting me with his sword. Trembling, I hold it aloft*
> *and point it toward the sky. Loud and bright resounds the sword!*
> *And suddenly, in my soul, come alive the men of marble!*

The heroic men on pedestals behind the transparent wall, all at once, raise their swords high in the air just as the man in the black suit pantomimes holding a sword aloft and freezes in this position, his body seemingly surrounded by an aura of light.

The man's wife, still crouching on the floor, has been looking up at her husband as she silently listened to his dream. Then, not saying a single word, she stands, and letting go of her son, in an act of great courage, she urges the boy toward her husband so the two of them, father and son, can go and fight for freedom, side by side. The son slowly moves to his father, who awaits him with open arms. While son and father embrace each other, the orchestra builds up to a gigantic climax, as The Spirit of Guatemala little by little raises her chained hands high in the air and then pulls them apart, breaking open the humiliating shackles, the symbol of her enslavement and that of all people, as the curtain begins to fall to thunderous applause.

THE HEADLINE OF *El Progreso's* review of Julián's play the morning following the opening, reads: FOR A NEW KIND OF WORLD, A NEW KIND OF DRAMA, AND A NEW KIND OF VERSE.

"'For a free world,' says the author, 'let the verse be free,'" continues the review. "And the author has certainly fulfilled his promise. The gallant and brave actions of the heroic characters in his play are ignited by his fiery words delivered in verses totally free of rhyme, totally free of rhythmic conventions, and yet, filled with an honestly heartfelt emotion one can only praise."

A WEEK AND TWO DAYS after the play opens, school begins.

Claiming that he needs more time to prepare for his full schedule of lectures at both the school and the university, Julián continues to distance himself from Don Manuel and their chess games—and therefore, from Sol. He tells Don Manuel that he can only play chess with him every other week. But it is very difficult. He cannot wait two weeks between visits, two long weeks without seeing Sol.

I need her now, he tells himself. Now more than ever.

Awhile after, he resumes the weekly chess game at Don Manuel's house. And, as had happened in the past, no sooner has their game ended than Don Manuel excuses himself and asks Sol to keep Julián company for a while.

Sol, obediently, keeps company with Julián, sitting in the parlor. Or in the patio. Or playing the passionate music she loves so much on the piano for Julián. Or accompanying him on long walks by the river, ending up at the white gazebo, where under the vigilant eyes of Xenufla, who pretends to knit, Sol sits enraptured, listening to Julián talk of poetry, and of slavery, and of social injustice. And, especially, of the plans Julián has begun to make: plans to unify all criollo Cubans into a single party—"the Cuban Revolutionary Party," he calls it—and plans to raise the huge amounts of money needed to buy the weapons revolutionary Cubans must have to free Cuba.

All the while looking at Julián with eyes that are filled with admiration. And with understanding.

CHAPTER XVIII

ONE MONTH AFTER school begins, Julián receives his first pay, in gold quetzales.

The amount seems staggering.

He didn't realize that he was earning a salary from the moment he was appointed full professor at the beginning of the summer, three months ago, even though classes had not begun until recently. So, when all of that money falls, as a huge lump sum, in his hands, he can barely believe what he sees. He has made more money doing nothing for two, almost three months than during the two previous years of his life!

Early the next morning, Julián goes to the Correos building, where the new telegraph services have just been installed, and there, with the kind assistance of Señor Patricio Melández, a gentleman Julián met at El Ateneo, he wires Lucía a large portion of the money, which by the portentous magic of Progress she manages to receive the very same day, with a note included that reads, succinctly:

Leaving for Mexico December 10.

Scheduled to arrive December 18.

WITHIN TWO AND A HALF WEEKS, Lucía has already spent all of that money. There's just so much a woman must buy to get married!

The Tuesday after Lucía completes her purchases, the day she is officially "at home," her friends arrive to see her trousseau on exhibition. All the things she has bought: dresses, fans, hats, shoes—along with the linens she and her aunts have patiently cut, sewn, and embroidered over the last two *long* years—are proudly displayed on her bed, and on all of the chairs in the parlor, even spilling onto the piano in the music room.

"Oh, Lucía, how lucky you are!" says one of her lady friends who is holding a three-year-old child by the hand, just to add, "How much more lucky can you get?" and laughs. To which another of her lady friends, who brought along her eleven-year-old daughter to look at Lucía's trousseau, says, "Just when we all thought that time was running out!" And then they all giggle.

Lucía says nothing. She just nods at the truth in those words. And feigns a smile.

After her friends leave her alone, she sighs. Only three more weeks until he leaves Guatemala, she thinks. I wonder what he'll think of me after so long?

She goes to her room, grabs her wedding veil—made of the same lace that trims the bustle and the long train of her wedding dress, a sheer, almost transparent, ivory Spanish lace—puts it on, and, for the hundredth time, she looks at herself in the mirror. And as she does she wonders, for the hundredth time, about the wedding night.

Will I be able to be as passionate as that woman Julián has portrayed in his poems—his dream lover? Will I be able to equal her in reality?

She looks at herself again in the mirror.

The woman she sees there has glossy black hair, sparkling hazel eyes, a distinguished nose, and elegant thin lips. Her body is trim, and her breasts, though not as large as she would have liked them to be, are still firm. Not bad for a woman her age, she thinks. She is twenty-nine now. She has never told him, but she is three, almost four years older than he is. Already nearing thirty. I wonder, she asks herself, does it show?

She looks again at herself in the mirror, carefully scrutinizing her face. Seeing no wrinkles around her mouth, she starts to look for wrinkles around her eyes. Seeing none, she smiles at herself. She likes what she sees. She finds herself beautiful. But . . . She stares deeply into her eyes again and asks herself the same question she has been asking herself over and over.

Will he like me?

That question triggers another set of questions in her mind, questions she has never been able to answer. Do I love him? The way women love the men they marry? The way I have heard my lady friends talk so much about?

She shakes her head in doubt.

She would like to love him. She wants to. She *needs* to love him. She needs to let the passionate woman she hides inside come out and fully experience that kind of love, the kind she has heard so much about, whatever that kind of love is like. All she knows about that kind of love is through her lady friends. Every time she asks them, "How do you know you are in love?" or, "When did you find out you were in love?" her lady friends either shrug their shoulders or simply shake their heads at her. "Oh, Lucía," they answer, "you just know." And then they add, "If you don't know it yet, you will soon. On your wedding night," and then they all giggle. All of them—but her.

She fears that wedding night. And yet she cannot wait for it to happen.

She has often fantasized about it, lying naked on her bed, pretending she is holding him, naked, close to her, pressing down on her. She wonders what the moment will be like when she finally becomes his wife.

Her lady friends have told her about that moment: a magical moment in which all thought ceases, in which time suddenly stops, in which she will see, hear, smell, taste, feel nothing else but the exhilarating feeling that will envelop her and will make her erupt into shattering wave after shattering wave of incredible power, the violent outbursts of forces she didn't even know—could not even suspect—were hidden inside her body, her body, which will finally come alive on that night. That is what her lady friends have told her. And that moment that she has been told about so often is the moment she both yearns for—and fears—at the same time.

She wants, she needs—so much—for that moment to be magical. A moment that will fill the emptiness, the void, she feels inside. A moment that will make her feel complete. Satisfied. Fulfilled. A truly magical moment that will finally—and once and for all—eradicate all her fears and make her feel at peace with herself.

She feels like a woman now. The day she tried on the mock-up of her wedding dress she felt it for the first time and has been feeling it since then.

But feeling like a woman is no longer enough for her. Now she wants to become a woman. A true woman.

A woman who has experienced life at its fullest.

For years she feared she might be left an old maid, like her two elderly aunts. For years she thought she might die childless, a virgin. For years she prayed day and night for a man to ask her to marry him. When, totally unexpectedly, Julián did, she was elated beyond belief, for her prayers had been miraculously answered. When Julián had no choice but to leave Mexico—and her—she felt miserable and dejected. For a while, for a long while, she abandoned all hope he would ever come back. And so did her aunts, and her friends, and her family. Again she prayed day and night for another miracle to happen. And when it happened, when she got that letter of Julián's she so much adores, she felt exhilarated beyond description. He is coming back, she kept telling and telling herself, pinching herself, still unable to believe it. Coming back! For me.

For *me!*

And now that she knows he is coming back, now that she knows that soon she will be by his side, lying naked on *their* bed, allowing him to possess her, bringing out the woman in her . . . Now that she knows all that, all she can do is pray again. A silent prayer, not of thanks. No, not of thanks.

But a prayer asking for assistance.

A prayer asking for help.

CHAPTER XIX

J ULIÁN STANDS, waiting in the middle of the huge entrance hall of Don Manuel's house, as if frozen, looking toward the top of the stairs, his forehead covered with thick drops of perspiration.

Though it is December 9, Guatemala City is going through a strange heat wave, which some people think is an omen foreshadowing either a strong earthquake or a huge volcanic eruption, while other people hope it is not. It is mid-afternoon and the heat is almost unbearable, even inside this two-story-high hall, which is almost totally dark except for the few sharply slanted beams of sunlight that manage to enter the room through the slender, tall, shuttered windows, which have been closed to keep the heat out.

Sol appears at the top of the stairs, in a pale cream dress, wearing a pale cream ribbon in her hair, her beautiful golden hair that even in the dim light of the room seems to glow.

Julián has decided to be blunt about it. The faster the better, he has been repeating to himself. So the minute he sees Sol at the top of the stairs, he blurts out, "Sol, I have to go away. I must leave Guatemala. On a trip. To Mexico."

Sol looks at him and interrupts.

"Wait there, Julián," she says. "I have something for you." She disappears into the long hallway that leads to the rest of the house.

This, Sol thinks, is the trip he has been planning since the day they first met. His trip to Cuba. To fight for his dream. Perhaps even to die. She certainly doesn't want him to see her show fear, or cry. One thing she has told herself she would never do is to cry. She has been preparing for this trip of his since that very first time he disclosed to her that he would someday return to his native Cuba, to fight for freedom. She will be courageous, like the woman in Julián's play who offered her son in sacrifice to her country. She will be strong. And brave. Like her mother was when Don Manuel left Doña Rosaura behind to fight for freedom.

She also wants Julián to know that no matter where he is, she will always be there, with him, right by his side.

Downstairs, Julián begins to pace nervously across the entrance hall, intermittently glancing toward the top of the stairs. No sounds are heard, except the sounds of Julián's riding boots against the hard marble floor, which echo in the enclosed and stifling space. Suddenly Julián catches sight of her at the top of the stairs. Sol is there, holding something in her hands. She comes down the steps very slowly, her nervousness apparent. She reaches the bottom of the stairs and stands by his side, the two of them very, very close to each other now; the two of them still in silence. Sol takes a miniature photograph of herself that she is carrying and places it in his hand, closing his hand around it with her own. Then she takes a white rose from between her breasts and offers it to him, breaking the long silence with her speech. "For your trip, Julián," she says, her voice gentle, soft.

"Sol, I—" Julián begins to say, but he is stopped by her as she raises her fingers in front of his mouth.

"Please, don't forget me," she adds.

Julián stares deeply into her eyes, and after taking a deep breath, he blurts out, "Sol, for months I've been gathering the strength to tell you what I must. And yet . . . Now . . . I find no words to tell you that—"

Sol interrupts his words by gently touching his lips with the tips of her fingers. "There are times when words are not needed, Julián. I understand." She smiles at him. "When you come back, when you do . . . we shall talk then."

Julián gets closer to her. "Sol," he says, ardently, "you do not understand. What I must tell you is . . . That I . . . and you—"

But he cannot complete his speech.

Sol has closed her eyes that have been looking imploringly at Julián. He is now very close to her, closer than he has ever been.

His hands are telling him: Hold her. His lips are telling him: Kiss her. But his will . . . His will is telling him: Step back, you fool. Step back!

Damn my will! Julián tells himself.

He reaches for her, passionately, and brings her close to him, so close to him that he can feel the heat of her body, and smell the perfume of her hair, and even hear the violent beating of her heart, matching the violent beating of his. He brings her even closer to him, wishing, dreaming, dying to kiss those lips that are being offered to him.

But his will keeps telling him, Step back, you fool. Step back. *Step back!*

Damn my will, Julián tells himself again and again. Damn my will, damn my will!

But this time Julián's will wins.

Realizing what he cannot do, what he must not ever do, Julián pushes her away from him and, refusing to taste the passion her mouth is promising, he kisses her forehead instead, which seems to be burning, almost feverishly.

Sol, suddenly embarrassed by this kiss, moves slowly away from Julián, her eyes fixed on him. Little by little she begins to walk upstairs, always keeping her eyes fastened on Julián, until she reaches the uppermost step, her slow, graceful movements failing to reveal the incredible turmoil of emotions that this kiss has created in her heart.

When she reaches the top step, she pauses for a second, uselessly trying to bring under control the way her body is shaking, trembling, as she stares at Julián. She remembers the way her body trembled and shook when she went to beg the Saint of Jocotenango to show her the man the gods had assigned to her, and the Saint let her have a vision of this very same man, this wondrous man with the piercing blue eyes who just kissed her, branding her forehead forever with the fire of his lips. She stares at him, her eyes avidly scrutinizing his face, desperately trying to capture this image of him forever and engrave it deeply inside her mind, trying to memorize the way he is, the way he looks as he stands there at the foot of the stairs, with his chiseled face, and his unruly dark hair, and with his dark eyebrows that are slanting so sadly, framing those dark blue eyes of his she loves so much. Eyes that always seem to sparkle. She smiles at the way he hides his hands nervously behind his back, and at the way his bow tie is always at a crooked angle. Oh, how much she would like to run back to him and straighten that tie! And while doing it, to be close to him, so close that she could smell the incredibly delicious fragrance that emanates from his body that lets her know—that has always let her know—that he desires her with the same desperate intensity that she desires him. Her soul is telling her: Run back to him. Her heart is telling her: Run back to him. Her entire body is telling her: Run back to him. *Run back to him!* But her will . . . Her will is telling her: Step back, you fool. Step back before he sees you being weak, before he sees you cry.

"Good-bye, Julián!" she says. And then, before tears spill from her eyes, she rushes into the safety of her room, leaving Julián alone, holding the white rose and the small photograph in his hands.

He calls her as she disappears, shouting at her, his despairing voice echoing all through the marble hall.

"Sol! Sol! You don't understand! You do *not* understand!"

He stands there, at the foot of the stairs, awkwardly toying with the rose and the small photograph in his hands, when, unexpectedly, the entrance doors suddenly open, and a shaft of blinding light instantly bathes the dim entrance hall. The doors are held open by two Mayan Indian servants as Don Manuel and his wife enter their home. Don Manuel, pleasantly surprised at finding Julián there, rushes to him, his arms already extended to embrace him. "Why, Julián! What a pleasure! We weren't expecting you today."

Julián, hiding the photograph and the rose in his left hand, refuses the embrace and offers Don Manuel his right hand instead, which the old man shakes vigorously.

Doña Rosaura offers her hand to Julián. "Aren't you teaching today?"

Julián takes her hand to his lips, stopping short of kissing it, as custom demands, and immediately says, his voice curt, "Señora. Señor General. I just came to say good-bye."

Don Manuel looks at him, puzzled. "Good-bye? You leave us?" while his wife, also puzzled, asks at the same time, "To say good-bye?"

Julián, still hiding the rose and Sol's photograph in his left hand behind his back, adds, "I must depart immediately. Tomorrow morning. To Mexico. Where I have to keep a promise. To someone I gave my word. My word—"

He pauses. Then adds, his voice barely audible.

"—in marriage."

There's a brief moment of silence, suddenly broken by Don Manuel, who, evidently shocked by the news, and still not believing what he has just heard, asks with urgency in his voice, "Are *you* getting married?" At the very same time, and almost to herself, Doña Rosaura says, "Your word . . . in marriage?"

Don Manuel then moves to Julián, feigning an enthusiasm he doesn't feel, and taking Julián by the shoulders, says, "Congratulations, my boy. Congratulations!"

Doña Rosaura cannot manage to feign a smile.

"But, but . . . And your bride?" she asks, almost pleadingly.

Julián looks first at Doña Rosaura, then at Don Manuel. Then, nervously, looks away from both of them as he answers. "It's been a long time since I saw her last. Almost a full year." He pauses. "Almost one *entire* very long year." He pauses again. "She's far from Cuba," he says after a while. "Just as I am," he adds, despondently, almost to himself. "It is very hard and very lonesome to be this far from our dear homeland. To be this far away, and to suspect that"—he pauses for a long while, trying hard to avoid showing too much emotion—"that unless something happens . . . That unless *we* make something happen, we may never be able to go back there ever again!" he finally manages to say.

Julián's words can only be answered by a long silence, during which time Julián, embarrassed, avoids looking at Sol's parents, who avoid looking at him.

Then, after an interminable pause, Julián adds, "Please, say good-bye to . . ."

He's about to say Sol, but realizes he cannot say her name. He glances once more to the top of the stairs and tightens his grip around the rose and Sol's photograph, which he has been hiding behind his back. "Say good-bye . . . to the girls," he says, and after a brief pause, he starts to move toward the entrance door.

Don Manuel stops him. "But . . . will you come back to Guatemala?"

Julián faces him. "Yes," he says, looking the general in the eye, "at the start of the new year."

"Then . . ." Don Manuel says and glances at his wife, "then you must bring us your bride."

As Julián hears this he seems to bow his head in compliance.

"If that is your wish," he answers quietly, accepting his fate.

WHEN HE GETS BACK to his room, Julián kisses the rose Sol has given him and pressing it, he places it gently inside one of his books. Then, he looks at the small photograph of herself that Sol has given him. He brings the photograph to his lips and kisses it feverishly, fervently, as if he were kissing her, as if he were giving her finally the kisses he has always wanted to give her and never dared to.

He is about to place the photo inside his diary for safekeeping when he notices there is something written on the back of the photograph. He reads it.

It says, *Always.* That is all it says.

Always.

CHAPTER XX

THE SUN HAS NOT YET BEGUN to tinge the outline of the distant volcanoes with fire. The sky has not yet changed from the vibrant dark blue it has been all night long. In the distance, the river, moving ever so gently, ever so quietly, has not yet begun to shimmer and glitter. There is a pervading silence in the night. No birds are yet singing, no dogs are yet barking, no people are yet rushing about. The city has not yet awakened. There seems to be a tranquil stillness everywhere.

Everywhere except in Sol's heart, where a torrent of conflicting emotions has been rushing and storming.

Sol is in her bedroom, looking out the window. She is barefoot, wearing nothing but her semitransparent nightgown. She has not been able to sleep all night long. How can she sleep, after what everyone—her mother, even her father—has told her after Julián left this afternoon? How can she ever sleep after she has been told something she refuses to believe? It all must be a mistake, she's been telling herself. If there is one thing she is certain of, it is that she knows how Julián feels toward her. His hands, his eyes, his entire body have said it many times since they first met. He never told her he loved her, no, not with words he didn't. But then, words never needed to be spoken between the two of them. And if words were ever needed, she has his poems, doesn't she?

She rushes to her bed, grabs her diary, which has been lying there, open, and turns the pages, searching avidly for his poems. Aren't these words his? she asks herself, flipping through the pages. And these? And these? All of these poems! Can every one of these poems be nothing but lies?

She begins to read aloud the last poem Julián wrote in her diary, less than a week ago, and as she reads it, she imagines his voice whispering the verses in her ear.

> *Today I have a need of singing. But, though I try, my voice fails me.*
> *Mine is a voice that longs to tell you*
> *of nights that are painful, of nights that are silent,*
> *of nights that are empty, yet filled with the thought of your laughter.*
> *And with that memory my voice begins to strengthen,*
> *becoming brighter and brighter, and then begins to soar.*
> *And there's fever in my singing. My voice rushes,*
> *then quivers and stutters, till it suddenly breaks,*
> *ending my singing before I could tell you what needs to be said.*
> *Today I have a need of singing, but . . . I cannot finish my song.*

"You don't have to, Julián. I know, I know," she says, speaking to her diary as if that small volume in her hands next to her breasts were him. She presses her diary—him—against her body and feels him there, the way she has imagined him so many times before. Then, closing her eyes, she relives once again in her mind Julián's farewell kiss.

As in a dream, she sees herself descending the stairs, placing the small photograph of herself within Julián's hands, removing a white rose from between her breasts and handing it to Julián, who is standing close to her, so close to her that she can feel the heat from his body. She offers her lips to Julián, and then, after the longest of moments, Julián kisses her forehead. That kiss triggers memories, and in her dream world she relives the first time Julián held her hand in his and passionately kissed it, not once, but twice. Or was it just one long kiss?

Julián's kisses brings her back to reality. Holding her diary close to her heart with her left hand, she takes her right hand—the hand he branded with his lips—to her forehead, still burning from Julián's ardent kiss.

And those kisses, she asks herself, were they not *true*?

Pressing her diary even tighter against her heart, she looks out at the distant river and sees it gently beginning to glitter in the nascent morning light.

The sunrise! she tells herself. If there is one day she does not want to miss the sunrise, the herald of hope, that day is today.

Still pressing the diary tight against her heart, she desperately rushes out of the house, hoping to get to her place of power, the white gazebo, before the sun breaks through the dark blue night sky. Maybe there she will be able to find peace, she tells herself. Maybe there she will find the answers to her myriad questions, she thinks.

Maybe there she will be able to understand.

SOL IS NOT the only one who has spent a sleepless night. Julián has been lying on his bed since he got back to his tiny room, staring up at nothing, hearing in his mind Sol's voice saying, "Please, don't forget me."

How could he ever forget her? Might as well ask him to stop breathing. Or to stop thinking of a free Cuba.

When he sees that the walls of his tiny room are beginning to glow with the fire of the rising sun, he stands up and, decisively, goes to the table and sits. He picks up a piece of paper and, impetuously, writes,

Lucía,

Please forgive me for what I am about to tell you, but I cannot marry you. I have found the woman of my dreams, the woman of my poems, and I have fallen madly, desperately in love with her. That is why I can no longer keep the word I gave you, a word given in haste. I—

He stops writing and shakes his head. No, he tells himself. I cannot do this. I cannot just write her a note and dismiss the whole thing as simply as this. It would not be fair to her. It would not be manly of me. I must face her when I tell her this. I must go to her, tell her the truth, and beg of her to forgive me and give me back my word of honor.

He pauses when he hears himself say that. Then he shakes his head.

"My word. Of honor," he slowly repeats aloud to himself.

I can't break my word to Lucía. I just can't do this to her. I can't embar-

rass and humiliate her in front of all of her friends and family. I would lose
not only her respect but the respect of all her friends and family. I would
lose *everyone*'s respect. Even my *own* self-respect. And self-respect is the
only thing a man in exile can call his own—the only thing he can be proud
of. If I were to lose it, then I would lose the only thing I still have left. No, I
cannot do this, he tells himself, staring at the letter in his hand as he keeps
shaking and shaking his head. If I were to do this, everyone would say that
I am a dishonorable man, a man whose word cannot be trusted! And they
would be right! How could I then ever go to people and ask them to help
me in my fight for Cuba, how could I ask them to place their trust in me, if
they know that I am not a man of my word? Why would people trust me
with their help, and with their confidence, and with their money—the
money we so badly need to buy weapons to free Cuba, *my* Cuba, the love
of my life, if they know I am a dishonorable man? "No," he says aloud,
and repeats it again. "No! I am *not* a dishonorable man! *No!*" he repeats,
this time shouting it emphatically, as if to give himself confidence, his
loud words angrily ricocheting like bullets all over the hard stucco surfaces
of the tiny room he calls home, while, resolutely, he tears the unfinished
letter to Lucía into myriad pieces.

But then he remembers Sol.

His sun.

Isn't she also the love of his life? Does he have to sacrifice her for the
good of Cuba? Does he have to sacrifice his *own* happiness for the good of
Cuba? Is this what he prayed for when he promised himself that he was *not*
going to end his life sitting behind a fancy desk and enjoying a Cuban cigar
while somebody else is fighting to free Cuba? He asked the Lord to let him
feed people's dreams, even if that meant that he'd have to become a martyr. Is this the price he has to pay?

Is this what it all comes down to?

Not knowing what to do, what decision to make, he shakes his head
again and again in utter frustration. And then, mustering all the strength
and violence that he is capable of, he furiously hits the table with his
closed fist, as he shouts, *"Goddammit!* Why did I ever have to come to this
godforsaken country!"

As if sparked by this self-destructive curse, his eyes focus on the flask of
gin, lying atop the table. He begins to grab it, when suddenly, realizing that

the answer does not lie inside that flask, he violently swipes it off the surface of the table, and as the pewter flask hits the tiled floor, it makes a loud clattering noise.

Enraged, he stands up. And as he does, he remembers Sol's voice, urgent, impetuous, as she said to him: *Don't let anything get in the way of those dreams of yours, Julián. Bringing the joy of freedom to your homeland is what you must do, what God placed you on Earth for. Like the quetzal, always let the love of freedom guide your life, Julián. Nothing else is important.*

Remembering Sol's impassioned words, words he knows she absolutely meant, brings him a soothing calm. He looks out his little window at the sun, already risen, and takes a deep breath.

"Bringing the joy of freedom to your homeland is what you must do," he says to himself, repeating Sol's words aloud. "Like the quetzal, always let the love of freedom guide your life, Julián. Nothing . . . *Nothing* else is important."

He nods his head in agreement several times.

And then he forces himself to smile as he faces the sun.

PART FOUR

ERUPTION

CHAPTER XXI

LUCÍA LOOKS OUT the window of the beautiful room where she and Julián have spent the last several nights of their wedding trip.

She can not only see but hear the rough surf of the violent Pacific Ocean breaking against the tall cliffs. The sky above, totally free of clouds, is a deep, vibrant blue, the exact color of the ocean, which at the horizon seems to become one with the sky. Acapulco at this time of year is just as her friends had described it, she thinks. Neither too hot, nor too cold. Perfect, on this gloriously beautiful morning of January 1, 1878.

What a great beginning for a new year, she thinks. This year will be wonderful!

Her bags and trunks are packed and stand next to the door, as she awaits the boys who will transport the luggage to the fancy steamship that is going to take them to their new home in Guatemala. Her husband, *the university professor,* is downstairs, settling the bill for their stay in this, the most expensive hotel in all of Acapulco.

How proud she was when she wrote to all of her friends and family— the very same friends and family who for the longest time kept telling her that her husband-to-be had no future! She wrote to them using the fancy embossed stationery provided by the hotel. Such exquisite paper! With such a silken texture! How she would love to see their faces when they get the beautifully engraved envelope and open it to find her letter inside, perfumed with petals from the roses decorating the hotel room, describing her blissful happiness.

She turns around and surveys the interior of the hotel room one last time.

This room is so elegant, she thinks.

When she gets to Guatemala she is going to have her bedroom done exactly like this one, she tells herself. She will cover the walls with the same pale blue silk moiré fabric that covers these walls, a fabric that matches the fabric on the furniture. She will have a high ceiling like the one in this room, and she will have it adorned with beautifully ornate plaster crown mouldings, like this ceiling has. And hanging from the heavy medallion right in the center of the room, she will have a huge crystal chandelier, just like this one, a chandelier that seems to be singing as the breezes coming from the ocean make the tiny dangling crystal pieces move and tinkle gently against each other.

Her eyes focus on the large four-poster bed that dominates the room.

It is covered with a dark blue brocade bedspread that she thinks is a perfect counterpoint to the pale blue color of the walls and to the deeply vibrant blue of the sky and ocean just outside the window.

She smiles to herself when she looks at the bed.

After all that she feared; after the long days, weeks, months of torment she lived through, wondering if she would be able to satisfy the ardent demands of that man she can now finally call husband, wondering if she would be able to quench his passionately fiery embrace, fearing that she would never be able to match that woman in his poems; after all her worrying, when the time came for her to have him in her arms that first time, it all had happened so . . .

So easily.

True, it felt awkward to lie in bed next to a man who seemed like a total stranger to her. The Julián she knew, the Julián to whom she had become engaged two years ago, that Julián no longer existed. When he arrived in Mexico City for the wedding, she barely was able to recognize him, after not having seen him for so long. This new Julián, who now wore a thick mustache, was far from the ebullient, clean-shaven young man who left her almost a whole year ago to seek his fortune. There was something about his eyes, about his body, about his whole being that had changed. Matured, she thought. Aged. But they barely had time to greet each other, let alone get reacquainted, before they were married and standing alone by a four-poster bed, two total strangers facing each other.

She remembers undoing her hair with tremulous hands, not knowing what to expect from him, her heart beating so fast she thought she was going to pass out. He took her hands and kissed them gently, and then, quietly led her to their bed, where she became his wife. How easy all of it was, she thinks. How very different from what she thought it was going to be! One moment he was shaking with intense agitation, the next moment he had already fallen asleep over her naked breasts, her long black hair draping gently over his face. She thought she had married a lion, when in fact, she had married a lamb.

She smiles to herself. How easy it is to tame a man, she thinks. How easy it is to have him do exactly as she wants. All she has to do is undo her hair, throw herself naked on the bed, close her eyes, and bear the weight of his body on top of hers for whatever little time it takes until his body bursts in silent spasms. Why had she been so apprehensive about all of it? she wonders. There was no reason at all, she tells herself, no reason at all.

Still, she has yet to experience that incredible moment of bodily joy her married friends have told her she would experience.

Or has she?

When after a few moments of turmoil he finally collapses and lies asleep on her, his body sweaty and hot, but hers cold, and she feels that she has him totally in her control, is that the feeling her married lady friends have been telling her about? The feeling that she is, for once, on top of the world? That the entire world is bowing to her, as he is bowing to her? Is that what she is supposed to feel? Because if that is what she is supposed to feel, that much she has felt. And yet, how come she has still to feel complete, as her married lady friends have told her they felt? Or satisfied? Or fulfilled? How come she always feels somehow defrauded, deceived, cheated, every time he collapses on top of her? It doesn't make sense, does it? she thinks and chuckles to herself. So much ado about nothing!

A delicate knock is heard at the door.

"Come in," she says.

Two Indian bellboys, dressed in dark blue uniforms trimmed with gold, enter the room quietly, and, almost in total silence, they begin to take all the pieces of luggage with them. She faces away from them and again stares out the tall window, looking at the ocean, now a deeply vibrant indigo blue, almost purple, and listens to its rough surf. She loves to hear how the ocean crashes loudly against the cliffs, in counterpoint to the delicate tinkling of the crystal chandelier.

The bellboys remove the last trunk just as Julián comes in.

Seeing Lucía by the window, he goes near her and stands silently behind her, not touching her, not saying a word, just looking—like her—out the window. Listening—like her—to the violent crashing of the surf and the delicate clinking of the myriad pieces of the crystal chandelier.

Time goes by, two strangers side by side, each of them in their own separate world. As if an invisible wall of glass has already been built between the two newlyweds. She is thinking about tomorrow, a tomorrow she sees as vibrant and as clear as the vibrantly clear sky in front of her. He is also thinking about tomorrow, but a tomorrow he sees as violent and as dark as the violently dark ocean in front of him.

After a while Julián says, softly, gently, "Lucía."

Surprised by his voice, she turns to him. "Oh," she says. "You startled me. I didn't even hear you come in."

He smiles at her with a sincerely heartfelt smile, the same way he has been smiling at her since he arrived for the wedding.

When he left Guatemala to get married he told himself that whatever he had felt for Sol, Lucía would never know. Lucía would never have to suffer because of him.

Never.

This is what he promised to himself when he took the stagecoach to Adjuintla, when he took the steamship to Acapulco, when he waited by the aisle for her to come to him. That is what he promised to himself when the priest asked him if he would take Lucía as his lawful wedded wife, when he placed his ring on her finger, when he removed the veil from her face. That is what he promised to himself when he signed his name on the wedding certificate, and when he toasted her, and when he embraced her that first night, and placed his head on her naked breasts.

Let Panoplo's gods punish me all they want, he said then, and many a time since. Let them make me suffer all I deserve. But not her. Let Lucía never suffer for what I've done, he prays every night as he falls asleep by her side. For the lie I'm living. For the lie I have condemned myself to live from now until, yes, until death does us part.

He kept his word to Lucía.

He married her, and he has taught himself to smile at her with a sincerely heartfelt smile, the same way he has been smiling at her since he arrived for the wedding—a sincerely heartfelt smile he will smile at her for the rest of his life.

"Are we ready to go?" Lucía asks, smiling back at him.

"Yes," he answers. "Guatemala awaits you."

Then, chivalrously, he opens the door to the hotel room, allowing her to go by.

Holding on to the elegant Brazilian rosewood handrail with her left hand, Lucía begins to descend the elegant Carrara marble stairs to the lobby, her eyes focusing on the golden band on her ring finger, as she walks slowly, almost regally, toward the elegant carriage that will take her to the elegant passenger steamship that will take her to her elegant future.

It is only when she reaches the foot of the steps that she turns around and realizes that Julián is not by her side. She looks up and finds him there, still at the top of the stairs, looking down at her, his eyes filled with a look Lucía cannot understand.

For as he realizes that he will always have Lucía by his side, Julián also realizes that he has never felt lonelier in his entire life.

A WEEK AND FOUR DAYS LATER, Professor Saavedra and his wife are at the station in Guatemala City, eagerly awaiting the arrival of the stagecoach that will bring Julián and Lucía, his wife. Señora Saavedra herself has made arrangements for the newlyweds to stay in a hotel in the center of town until they find a house to their liking. She has already located several suitable houses, one of them, the one she likes the most is within a short walking distance of the Escuela Central, near the house where the Saavedras live.

As soon as they arrive and basic pleasantries are exchanged, Professor Saavedra takes Julián aside, while his wife welcomes Lucía. "Julián," Saavedra says, lowering his voice, "I didn't want to say this in front of the women, I didn't want to scare them, but I have just heard something awful." He turns around and makes sure the women are still talking. Then he faces Julián again.

"You probably know, as everybody in Guatemala does," Saavedra says, speaking as softly as he can so as not to be overheard, "that there are a lot of people in Guatemala, the religious fanatics, the members of the Clerical Party, who have been dreaming for a long while of getting rid of President Rubios so they might regain the properties that they claim President Rubios stole from Catholic priests to make into schools and hospitals." Julián nods again. "Well, yesterday afternoon, Doña Lucrecia Suárez-Villegas—you know the woman I'm talking about, don't you? She always sits in the first row at our lectures and concerts and falls asleep." Julián nods silently. "Well, when she heard that those men were meeting last night, she went to Rubios and told him that some of those men were secretly conspiring to assassinate him. And then she told Rubios where it was that they were meeting."

Julián smiles. "Oh, Saavedra," he says, "Rubios didn't believe that malicious old lady, did he? Everybody knows she's always gossiping about every—"

"I know, I know," Saavedra interrupts. "That's just what I thought when I first heard the story, but, apparently, it was true. At least, some of it was." He gets closer to Julián. "Last night President Rubios rode, all by himself, to where Doña Lucrecia told him those men were meeting, and when he surprised them by throwing the door open and walking in, one of them pulled a gun on him. Rubios disarmed him at once with his whip, and later on sent the police to the men's homes. Now the entire group is in prison, accused of high treason."

He moves even closer to Julián, who is shaking his head in disbelief. "It's true. Julián. Rabbi Mordecai . . . You remember him, don't you? From the debate? He came to see me early this morning and told me that there was no secret meeting of any kind. That it was just a dinner party, and that he, who is not even a Catholic, had been invited to attend. Now he is happy he couldn't make it, he told me. And then he asked me if there was anything I, or you—he even mentioned you by name—if there was anything either of us could do to help those poor innocent men. I'm so glad you arrived today, Julián, I don't know what to do. What do you think?"

CHAPTER XXII

EARLY THE NEXT MORNING, Julián sits at the desk in the parlor of the hotel suite that the Saavedras had reserved for them. Lucía remains in bed, after waking up with morning sickness. Julián, in the parlor, starts to write a note to Don Manuel, asking him if it is all right for Julián and his wife to call on the general and his family that same afternoon.

Writing this note is not easy. The thought of Sol fills his mind as he writes the note, just as the thought of Sol fills his mind each day, from the moment he wakes up until the moment he falls asleep next to the woman he calls wife. And even then, even when asleep, his mind is filled with Sol.

Especially when he is asleep.

Less than a month ago, during that first night he spent alone with Lucía, he thought that perhaps he could close his eyes and pretend it was Sol there, next to him, in his bed, in his arms; wishing, hoping, that by doing that he could feel something for Lucía. But he could not do it. He was revolted by the idea of pretense. It would not be fair to either Lucía, *his* wife—or to Sol, *his* sun. It would not be fair to anybody, including himself. He could not spend the rest of his days living a life of self-deception.

Or the rest of his nights.

So that first night he spent alone with Lucía, less than a month ago, he did not close his eyes when he saw Lucía undo her hair, nor when he led her to the bed, nor when he held her in his arms. Nor when Lucía's body opened up to him, nor when his body convulsed with intense spasms, nor when the next moment, empty, exhausted, he laid his head on Lucía's naked breasts, her long black hair gently caressing his face. He did not close his eyes all night long, that first night he spent alone with Lucía, because he felt that if he were to close his eyes, he might see Sol again. And he could not cope with that.

Julián finishes writing his note, signs it, and seals it. Then he stands up, goes to the door, and gently pulls the bell cord hanging by the door frame. Within a couple of minutes a Mayan boy dressed in a plain brown uniform comes up to his room. Julián gives the boy the note, asks him to take it right away to Don Manuel's house, and to wait there for a reply.

By mid-morning, Lucía has finally risen, has eaten a bite of breakfast, and has finally managed to keep something in her stomach, when the Mayan boy rings the doorbell and hands Julián a note, in Don Manuel's own handwriting.

It reads,

My dear Julián,

Welcome back to Guatemala! I hear your young wife is very beautiful. Lucky you! Rosaura and I eagerly wait to meet the two of you around three o'clock.

Manuel

After Julián reads the note, he passes it to Lucía, who is sitting across from him at a small table by the window of this hotel room. She glances at the note, nods her head yes, and then, turning her face away from the window, looks at the hotel room.

This room is nothing in comparison with the one in Acapulco, Lucía thinks. Though the ceiling is almost as high, it lacks any ornamentation, except for the few rough-cut beams spanning the room, and a simple board trimming the top edge of the walls. The walls are not covered in fabric, but are roughly plastered and painted a chalky pale ocher, a color Lucía finds abhorrent. The floor is not carpeted wall to wall, like the one in Acapulco, but simply covered with plain terra-cotta tiles, some of which have lost their glaze. And the view is not of the rushing ocean and of a limpid sky but of the other rooms on the other side of the large central patio of the hotel.

As far as Lucía has been able to see, the level of living in Guatemala is certainly nowhere near that of Mexico. After their endless voyage to the port of Chirimacotengo, on the Pacific coast of Guatemala, they journeyed to Adjuintla, which she mistakenly thought was Guatemala City and the end of her long trip. Then they still had to travel four or five more of the longest days imaginable on roads that were almost impassable. It had been raining a lot, and what the Guatemalans called roads looked to her more like torrents of mud. Finally, after arriving in La Ciudad, as everybody calls Guatemala City, the trip from the stagecoach terminal to the hotel was, to say the least, very disappointing. To her, all the houses looked extremely poor, not a single one of them more than one story high, and the streets were not even paved with cobblestones, as they were in Mexico City, but were made of compacted dirt and seemed as noisy and dirty as the places she and her family had to live when they first arrived in Mexico.

And then, *this* hotel!

She looks around the room she is in. To call *this* a hotel! she thinks, and shakes her head. I sure hope the house Señora Saavedra has found for us and thinks is elegant doesn't resemble this place, she thinks.

Suddenly she feels another attack of nausea and she rushes to the chamber pot hidden behind a screen in a corner of the back room, where she vomits all she had eaten. Disgusted, she pours water in the washbowl and wipes the acidic taste from her mouth. And as she does, she looks at herself in the oval mirror placed above the bowl. How pallid I look, she tells herself. And then she holds her belly. Nobody told me it was going to be like this, she thinks. Do I have to live through eight more months of this? she asks herself, and shakes her head. Why didn't anybody tell me? Then she looks at herself in the mirror once again.

Why do I feel so cheated? she thinks.

"Lucía, are you all right?" she hears Julián ask, from the other side of the screen. "Lucía?" She hears him repeat, concern in his voice.

"Yes, yes," she finally answers, still looking at herself in the mirror. "I'm all right, I am perfectly fine."

She steps out from behind the screen.

"Do you see what you are putting me through?" she says. "One day I'm going to make you pay for this, Julián. Believe me. One day you're going to pay dearly for all of this," she adds jokingly, and feigns a smile.

. . .

A FEW HOURS LATER, that same afternoon, Lucía, feeling a little better, wearing her dark burgundy visiting suit and matching hat that she knows become her, and daring to wear a touch of rouge on her cheeks to brighten her pallid complexion, leaves the hotel room with Julián, dressed in his plain black suit, and climbs in the carriage that is to take them to Don Manuel's house.

She has heard Julián talk so much about Don Manuel, and about Don Manuel's house, and about Don Manuel's library, and about Don Manuel's books, that she feels she already knows the general well and is looking forward to being in the home of the man who liberated Guatemala from Spain, and to meeting his wife, whom Julián has told Lucía is a very handsome woman, even at her age. Lucía feels that, as the wife of a university professor, she needs to develop some friendships with the finer ladies of Guatemala.

"How do I look?" she asks Julián, nervously, as he helps her out of the carriage in front of the imposing entrance to Don Manuel's house, the first two-story house Lucía has seen in all of Guatemala City.

Julián looks at her, and he himself has to realize that, indeed, what the gossip of Guatemala has been saying is true, because today—and maybe perhaps always—Lucía does look beautiful; a beauty he had never noticed before. Her black hair, so black it is almost navy blue, sparkles, as do her hazel eyes, which glitter and shimmer with excitement, just as her black jet jewelry glitters and shimmers. If only my heart were not filled with someone else's radiance, Julián thinks. How much easier would everything be then, he tells himself, How much easier. But how can one change the beating of one's heart?

"You look beautiful," Julián answers her, which makes Lucía blush.

She does not ever remember Julián calling her beautiful. And the way he said it! The way he was looking at her now! When was the last time she saw him looking at her that way? She cannot remember if she ever did.

She knows he did not look at her that way when she approached him slowly, walking by her father's side, down the long aisle of the huge Catedral de Mexico. She had felt that she looked radiant in her ivory silk gown with its bustle and train of ivory Spanish lace. Her lady friends did not have to tell her. She knew. But when she looked at him, at the end of the aisle, she did not see the Julián to whom she had been engaged but a man totally strange to her, a man who was not looking at her but looking past her, through her, as if she had been transparent.

At the time she thought that maybe he was too nervous, too excited, too tired, to see her. And that his distant, formal manner would change. But it hasn't. Since that time, he has looked at her, but in a peculiar way, as if from a distance, making her feel as if she were being evaluated, compared, rated. Making her feel as if, somehow, she did not measure up to his standards. And yet, a second ago, for the briefest of moments, when he told her she was beautiful, he became again the Julián she used to know. The shy boy who had asked her to marry him when she thought that time had passed her by.

She looks at him warmly, a smile brightening her face, still pallid, despite the bit of rouge on her cheeks. And then, she grabs hold of his arm and is escorted by her husband toward the entrance of Don Manuel's mansion.

"SO *THIS* IS YOUR PRETTY BRIDE," says Don Manuel, at the entrance door, where the general and his wife, Doña Rosaura, are waiting to welcome the newlyweds into their home. Don Manuel takes both of Lucía's hands into his and, bowing to Lucía, raises them both to his lips, stopping short of kissing them, as custom demands.

Then he raises his admiring eyes to Lucía.

"For once the gossip of Guatemala is right," he tells her, smiling, and then, turning to Julián, he adds, "your wife is even more beautiful than I expected, Julián." Then, lowering his voice, he faces Lucía again and says confidentially, "And knowing Julián's tastes, I was expecting quite a lot," which makes Lucía blush delightedly as she smiles back at the general. Don Manuel offers his arm to Lucía and leads her into the rest of the house, followed by Julián and Doña Rosaura, who, after politely nodding to each other, have not yet said a word.

This house is truly elegant, Lucía thinks, as they go first through the large entrance hall and then, bypassing the huge patio, enter the parlor.

Though Lucía's father is a very successful lawyer in Mexico City and Lucía has often visited the homes of his wealthy clients, she has never been inside a place as beautiful, as simple, and as magnificently appointed as Don Manuel's mansion, she thinks. It is not that Don Manuel's house is filled with objects and curios of every kind, Lucía notices, as are most of the houses of the very wealthy she has visited. On the contrary, in this house the objects are very few, even scarce. And yet, each of them seems to have been chosen with the eye of an artist who has selected them for their simplicity and for their beauty—a simplicity and beauty that to Lucía's eyes clearly indicates quality. Every single object. From the specimen areca palms in huge Chinese blue-and-white porcelain planters that frame the imposing marble stair in the entrance hall, to the exquisite Oriental rug, of the palest of colors and the most intricate of designs, that covers the floor of the intimate parlor.

It is there the four of them are now seated, on large, comfortable Viennese armchairs made of ebonized wood and upholstered in a perfumed cordovan leather, the softest leather Lucía has ever touched. These chairs are placed around a low onyx table whose top is so shiny it mirrors, hanging above, a gas chandelier constructed of bronze leaves and stems growing into crystal tulips that glimmer in the soft afternoon light that peeks in through the tall shuttered windows. Lucía does not fail to notice that here and there throughout the parlor, whose tall walls are covered in a pale ivory-colored silk damask, there are several small tabourets, also upholstered in cordovan leather, placed in pleasant disarray. This room, Lucía thinks, is obviously a room where people actually live, not just a room to display expensive objects to astound visitors, as were many in the wealthy homes Lucía had visited in Mexico.

As Lucía and Doña Rosaura begin to get acquainted, their conversation turns to the latest dress styles and whether olive green, which they both have read is the color that is fashionable this season in Paris, suits their complexions or not.

Julián leans over to the general. "Don Manuel," Julián says, quietly, "could you give me a few minutes of your time?" He pauses. "In private," he adds. "There's something awfully important I must discuss with you."

"Sure, my boy, sure," says Don Manuel as he stands up. "If you ladies would be so kind as to excuse us," Don Manuel says, "I would like Julián to taste one of those new Cuban cigars I just received." He turns to Julián. "Right from Vuelta-Abajo, Julián. The best there is!"

The women nod politely to them, excusing them, and return to their animated conversation about this or that fabric, or this or that color, or this or that style of bustle, while Don Manuel leads Julián from the parlor and across the huge patio toward his library, where the two of them can be alone and talk without interruption.

CROSSING THE PATIO triggers memories in Julián's mind of wonderful moments spent there—memories that must be eradicated, now that he is married. Halfway across the patio, it seems to Julián that he still can hear the wonderful waltz he heard the first time he stepped into this house, when he looked up at the top of the stairs and saw there the woman of his dreams, a woman who looked at him the way no other woman has ever looked at him: his "idealized, unattainable beauty."

He raises his eyes toward the top of the patio stairs, but there is no one there, just emptiness.

Don Manuel's voice wakes him from his reverie. "Is it about the members of the Clerical Party that you want to talk to me?" Julián looks at him, astounded, and nods his head. They enter Don Manuel's library and Don Manuel continues. "One of their friends came to see me at El Ateneo yesterday. They claim they are innocent, and I am inclined to believe them. Yesterday afternoon I sent a note to Rubios, asking for clemency, but—" He offers Julián a seat, goes to his desk, opens a drawer, and hands Julián a note in Rubios's own handwriting.

"Here," the general says. "I got this yesterday evening. From Rubios himself."

Julián reads it.

Guatemala cannot allow insurrections of any kind. Nor treason. Guatemala must use a strong hand. The time has come for Guatemala to prove herself. How else can Guatemala step out of the past and open new roads into the future? Those who do not agree are against Guatemala.

Julián shakes his head.

"I know what you're thinking, Julián," says Don Manuel. "Rubios has gone crazy. Notice that he did not even sign the note, and that it sounds as if *he* were speaking for Guatemala. As if he, and only he, *is* Guatemala. A bad sign, a *very* bad sign. Have you reread your Cicero lately?"

Julián nods his head.

Don Manuel continues. "It happened then, it is happening now. And the worst thing about it," Don Manuel adds, "is that our Americas need men like him. He has already done so much good for Guatemala! Look at the roads, and the schools, and the hospitals, and the railroads, and the telegraph service. And now he's even thinking of sending a delegation to the Paris Exposition, to let the whole world know about Guatemala. I don't know, I just don't know what to do." He pauses. "It's Caesar again, isn't it?" he says, almost to himself, as he opens a mahogany humidor with silver hinges, "Caesar, letting all the power go to his head so he can then begin to misuse it, or abuse it, as he likes."

He offers a cigar to Julián and takes one himself.

"But we cannot give up hope," he adds, striking a match against the pumice stone on his desk. "As long as those men are alive there is still hope for them, and for Guatemala." He pauses for a brief second. "But, *damn it!*" the general then says, enraged, suddenly hitting the top of his desk with his closed fist, with all the force that he is capable of, shaking the entire desk, the entire room, with his violent gesture. Julián has never seen Don Manuel like this, with so much anger burning inside, so much anger exposed in his gesture. *"I"*—the general starts to say, then he looks at Julián and corrects himself—*"We* have got to do something for those men. At least make sure they get a fair trial. If they did conspire against Rubios, well then, let the legal codes of Guatemala decide what to do with them. That's why we have those legal codes. That's why Rubios *himself* created those legal codes, no?" He asks Julián, but is really asking himself, "What good are those legal codes if Rubios himself does not follow them, eh?"

He draws on his cigar once, inhaling, only to put it down immediately in the large ashtray on his desk. He shakes his head. "I'm sorry, son," the old man continues. "This is not your headache, but mine. You have other concerns with your new wife and all." He pauses. Then looks Julián in the eye, his own eyes filled with a sadness Julián has never seen before. "You know, Julián," he says, "for a while I thought that you might have become my . . ." He lets his voice trail off, not finishing his sentence. Don Manuel places his arm around Julián's shoulders and smiles. "Funny, I forgot what

I was about to say," he adds, apologetically. "This entire thing concerning those men of the Clerical Party is making my head spin," Don Manuel adds. But Julián understands what Don Manuel meant to say, as, to himself, he fills in ". . . might have become my son-in-law."

"We'd better get back to the ladies," the general says. "Come, Julián. Let's get you back to your pretty wife." And with that the old man escorts Julián out of the library and back into the patio.

DON MANUEL crosses the patio, his head lowered, as if he were carrying a tremendous weight on his shoulders. Julián has never seen him look so old. He pauses and watches the general, who, walking very slowly, is not even aware that Julián paused in the center of the huge patio.

Julián begins to follow the general but, suddenly, he stops, turns, and looks again toward the top of the stairs. Seeing no one there, he just sighs and shakes his head. He then turns to follow the general again, when, out of the corner of his eye, he thinks he sees a white shadow. He raises his head again and looks at the side balcony. And there, on the second floor, is Sol, who is peering down at him, a look of painful disbelief filling her eyes. He looks up at her, and without his realizing it, his shoulders sag and his chest sinks as tears well up in his eyes: tears of rage, tears of self-hatred.

Tears of impotence.

But then he sees this angel, woman, goddess who is looking at him, her eyes also filled with tears, smile at him. A smile making her tear-filled dark eyes sparkle and shine. A smile that seems to be saying, I know, I know.

A smile that says, I understand now, Julián. *Now*, I understand.

Slowly, keeping her kind, understanding, smiling eyes fastened on him, Sol backs into her bedroom. Julián wipes his eyes. Don Manuel is only a few steps ahead of him. It all had happened so quickly. Desperately, he looks up again at the balcony, but he sees no one there. He takes a deep breath and then, limping ever so slightly, follows Don Manuel into the parlor, his stooped shoulders mirroring the carriage of the general, who precedes him.

. . .

BACK IN HER BEDROOM, Sol is shaking her head in disbelief. It all happened so suddenly that Sol herself did not realize when, at what instant, it actually happened. One moment she was looking at Julián, deeply hurt, her questioning eyes avidly looking to find his, and yet fearing it at the same time—and the very next moment, when she saw the hurt in his eyes, she understood, all at once, that he was going through the very same pain, the very same agony she was going through.

In the merest fraction of a second she understood everything:

What that first glance of his, filled with divine love, with human desire, and at the same time with immense despair, was telling her. What words like, "A man whose hands are tied behind his back," or "Tied by a promise," really meant. What verses like, "How different my song would sound should I dare use a harp made of your hair," or "Today I have a need of singing, but . . . I cannot finish my song," were really saying.

And, above all, she understood what that kiss of his meant. That fiery kiss of his with which he had elected to brand her forehead forever when she had offered him her lips instead.

Oh, Julián, what you must be going through, she thought, as she was looking at him.

It was then her eyes smiled at him, filled with love and with understanding. Eyes that did not have to forgive him, because there was nothing, nothing at all, to forgive.

"IT WAS A NEW STRAIN OF MALARIA." Doña Rosaura answers Lucía's question as the general enters the parlor. "'Malignant malaria,' that's what the doctor called it, but everybody here in Guatemala calls it 'Galloping Malaria,' that's how fast it kills. And my little son, weak from a bad cold, did not have the strength to fight it. He had a very high fever, soon followed by hallucinations, and in less than two days he was gone. I guess God wanted my little boy by His side," Doña Rosaura adds. "But He has allowed me to keep three precious daughters. Gabriela and Carola, the two girls you just met, and our oldest, Sol, who is not feeling very well today and who asks of you to please excuse her."

"Nothing serious, I hope," says Lucía.

Julián enters the room. His face is paler than normal, and his eyes sadder than usual, but the ladies, involved in their conversation, do not seem to notice.

"Oh, no, no. Nothing serious," Doña Rosaura continues. "You know how stubborn young girls can be sometimes," she adds. "Three days ago, when it was so hot here in the city, she decided to go and bathe in the river late in the afternoon, and what happened? The temperature suddenly dropped and by the time she got back home she was shivering and shaking all over. But Xenufla, an older Mayan Indian woman who lives with us, makes an herbal tea—'Cakchiquel tea,' she calls it—a delicious potion made with mushroom buttons and secret herbs. Believe me, Lucía, there's absolutely no sickness that tea cannot cure, absolutely no problem that tea cannot solve, no matter how big. Whatever it is that girl of mine has, she'll get over it, I'm sure," Doña Rosaura says, with strong determination. "And now," she adds, "how about another cup of Mexican hot chocolate? Three days ago it was stifling here, in the city, and today, look at the four us, shivering in this room." She is about to stand up to ring for service when a young Ladino man, totally dressed in white, appears at the doorway holding a small silver tray with a sealed letter on top.

"It's for you, Don Manuel," the young man says. "The gentleman who brought this said it was urgent."

"Excuse me," says Don Manuel as he crosses to where the young man stands, and takes the letter. "Thanks, Folcano," he tells the young man, who leaves.

Still standing by the door, Don Manuel rips the envelope open and reads, while everyone looks at him. Suddenly the color leaves the general's face, and his knees bend. It seems as if a hundred years has fallen on Don Manuel's shoulders in just one second. He catches hold of a side chair next to the door and sits. He seems to be unable to breathe as the letter in his hand begins to shake.

"What is wrong, Manuel?" Doña Rosaura asks, deeply concerned, just as Julián stands up and goes to the general.

Don Manuel hands the letter to Julián, who quickly scans it, while Don Manuel, trying to regain his composure, takes a deep breath. Doña Rosaura rushes to her husband and kneels by his side. "What is it, Manuel? What has happened?" she asks, holding his hand in hers. When she realizes that her husband cannot say a word, she turns and faces a dejected

Julián, who is holding the letter in his hand, his face ashen. "Julián, please, I beg you," she demands, urgently, "tell me. What has happened? What has happened?"

Don Manuel takes Doña Rosaura's hand, which has suddenly become icy cold, in his own hands, and warming it, he answers her. "This morning, at dawn . . ." But he cannot finish his sentence. Doña Rosaura turns to Julián, a question in her eyes, which Julián answers by handing her the letter.

"All the Clericals were shot to death, Doña Rosaura. Executed. At dawn," Julián says, his voice still filled with disbelief. "Every one of them. Without a trial, even a mock trial."

A long, long silence fills the room.

Lucía, who does not know who these men, the Clericals, are—were—is totally disconcerted. Her eyes dart from her husband to Don Manuel to Doña Rosaura and then back to her husband again.

Don Manuel looks at his wife and shakes his head.

"After all the years we have spent trying to bring a new life to our country, a life of law," he is finally able to say, "here we are again, back at the beginning. No law but the law of the sword. We are back to being barbarians under the hand of a despot, a tyrant, who will not allow anything or anyone to get in the way of *his* sword." He sighs. "This is the end of the Guatemala we fought for, Rosaura," he says. "The end."

Still kneeling by her husband's side and still holding his hand in hers, Doña Rosaura looks deeply into her husband's eyes for the longest time. Then she smiles at him. "The Old Guatemala City, Antigua, was destroyed twice, Manuel," she says. "Once by a volcano, the second time by an earthquake. And what did Guatemala do?" She tightens her grip of her husband's hand. "Guatemala rebuilt the city a *third* time." She looks at her husband with immense pride. "Well, Manuel, this is nothing but another earthquake. A shattering one, maybe. But Guatemala can and must be rebuilt again. And if anyone can do it, *you* can do it," she adds. She stands up, defiantly. She crosses to the doorway and decisively tugs the bellpull. "No, Manuel," she says as she looks at her husband with eyes beaming with confidence, "as long as you are still the man I married, this is *not* the end of Guatemala."

As Doña Rosaura began to speak, Julián, who had been looking at Don

Manuel with a deep concern in his eyes, turned his gaze toward her. At first surprised by the energy and the determination he detected in Doña Rosaura's words—something that has always been there, but something Julián had never seen before—his eyes were puzzled. But as he listened to her beautiful words, his eyes became filled with boundless admiration. So *this* is Sol's mother, he tells himself, as he looks in detail at Doña Rosaura, seeing in her the same fearless and passionate courage he has often glimpsed in Sol.

Meanwhile, Lucía, who at first was looking at Doña Rosaura, has turned her head and is now looking at Julián. But her eyes seem perplexed, as if she was totally unable to understand the look in her husband's eyes.

The young Ladino man is at the door in answer to the bell.

"Folcano," Doña Rosaura says, "please ask Xenufla to make a large pot of Cakchiquel tea, and tell her to make it *really* strong."

The young man begins to leave, when she stops him.

"Oh, Folcano," she adds, "and, please, tell Xenufla that this time the tea is not for Sol, but for *us*."

CHAPTER XXIII

AFTER JULIÁN COMPLETES his scheduled morning lectures at the university the following day, he travels across the city to the Escuela Central for his afternoon session there. As he enters the office that he shares with Saavedra he finds the professor packing his belongings.

"Saavedra," Julián asks, "what is going on?"

"Did you see this?" Professor Saavedra asks, holding up a copy of the morning issue of *El Progreso*. There, on the front page of the paper, is an open letter addressed to President Rubios, signed by Don Manuel. Saavedra points to this published letter written by the man who liberated Guatemala from Spain and who is also one of the leaders of the Reform Party—a letter that surprised Saavedra, as well as many others, because it supports the same priests Don Manuel had once expelled from Guatemala.

In that letter Don Manuel says, vehemently,

I may not have agreed with what those members of the Clerical Party had to say. But I would have defended them—and to the death, if necessary—for their right to say it!

Julián looks at Saavedra and nods.

"Why, yes. I saw that letter in the newspaper this morning. And I was very impressed by it. But—" Julián cannot finish his sentence.

"Apparently," Saavedra interjects, "that letter got President Rubios so incensed that he sent his men out to incarcerate *more* people—not only additional members of the Clerical Party, but even Rabbi Mordecai, who had been here only yesterday to ask me for my help. It must have been Mordecai who gave Rubios my name."

"What do you mean?" Julián asks.

"Early this morning I was called into Rubios's office. When I got there, Rubios was fuming. He told me that he knew that I had spoken to Rabbi Mordecai about this affair with the members of the Clerical Party, and he added that I, a Cuban man, had absolutely *no* right *whatsoever* to express my views on the internal affairs of Guatemala. And then, in the presence of all of his cabinet ministers, who would not even look me in the face, Rubios called me persona non grata and told me that my presence in *his* country was no longer welcome. He gave me a week to leave Guatemala. He said he could not be responsible for my life, nor for the lives of my relatives, after that, if I were to stay here."

Julián shakes his head.

"This is unbelievable," he says. "You haven't done any—"

"There's no quarreling with Rubios, Julián. I think he knows he made a big mistake with his purge of the Clericals, and now he is looking for a scapegoat of some kind. If I am the scapegoat, so be it, provided those two dozen men just incarcerated are not executed like the others. God knows what Rubios thinks I have said, or done. But you and I know I have done nothing I should be ashamed of."

"This is outrageous, Saavedra," Julián answers. "This is not only an insult to you, and to me, but to all civilized people." He sits at the desk, pulls out a piece of paper from the drawer, and begins to write.

"What are you doing, Julián?" Saavedra asks.

"Writing my resignation."

"Don't do it, Julián . . . It's not worth it."

Julián raises his eyes to the old professor's and tries to speak, but Saavedra will not allow it. He places his hand on Julián's shoulder and says, decisively, "No, Julián, don't. Please, listen to me. Look at this office. You will probably be named the head of this school, and I cannot think of a better person to take my place and occupy this office than you."

Julián looks around the fancy office, his eyes taking it all in: the expensive leather chairs, the silver-and-ebony humidor, the splendid mahogany partners desk. And he remembers when, not so long ago, he thought of the possibility that he would one day end up like Saavedra, sitting behind a desk like this, smoking the best Cuban cigars, his waist getting thicker and his hair getting thinner as he did nothing but sit there, waiting for someone else to act and make the world change.

Saavedra, seeing Julián looking around the room, continues, "So, please, I beg you, Julián, for the good of the school, for the good of Guatemala, and for your own good, don't do anything rash."

It is then Julián's eyes focus on the magnificently bound books on the shelves. And those books—his friends—speak to him, reminding him that someone else, Rubios, has already acted and that someone else is making the world change, and for the worse. And that the time is now for Julián himself to act and make the world change, and for the better—no matter how insignificant that act of his may seem to be.

"No, Saavedra, I can no longer teach in a country where men do not keep to their word, where human rights are no longer respected, and where men are condemned without the decency of a trial. The other men, the ones Rubios executed, they may or may not have been innocent of conspiring against him. We'll never know that. But you, like those men just taken to prison, are totally innocent of anything, and neither you nor they deserve what President Rubios—"

"Julián, please, calm down and listen to me," Saavedra interjects. "I'm an old man. My wife and I have saved enough money to last us for a long while and I am sure I can go back to New York and teach again in a school there. But you, Julián. You have just gotten married. What would you live on? You have nothing, and—"

Julián stands up, irate and deeply hurt at the same time.

"*Nothing* . . . ? I may have nothing, Saavedra," he says, his voice loud and defiant, "but I still have my honor. And my honor is intact! Years ago I gave my word of honor to myself that, above anything, I would fight injustice to the death, and, Saavedra, I *am* a man of my word!"

Saavedra smiles at him and pats him on the shoulder, trying to calm him down. "I know that, Julián. I know that. All I am asking you is not to think of me or of your honor for a minute, and just think about your wife." He pauses. "And about that child she is carrying." Julián looks at him, puzzled. "She told my wife," Saavedra adds, shrugging his shoulders, "and, well, you know how women are . . . My wife told me. So, please, Julián, think of that child first. Think of your child."

Julián smiles at the old man. "It is precisely *because* I am thinking about my child that I must do what I must, Saavedra. For the *good* of my child." He sits down and with broad strokes completes his letter, which he signs. Then, standing up, he hands it to Saavedra. "Professor Saavedra," he says, "I beg you to accept my resignation, effective at once."

Saavedra sighs deeply and takes Julián's letter in his hand. Then he moves to Julián, and embraces him. After a while, Saavedra finally breaks the embrace, turns away from Julián, and continues to empty his desk and pack his belongings.

Julián, hurriedly, writes a second letter, resigning his post at the University of Guatemala, signs it, seals it, places it in an envelope, calls Pancracio, the gardener's son, gives the young Mayan boy a couple of reales, and asks him to take the letter immediately to Minister Andrújal, at the Ministry of Public Instruction. Then, after the boy leaves, he begins to clear his half of the partners desk.

Saavedra looks at Julián, who is systematically going through his things.

If I were in his shoes, the old professor asks himself, with no money and a pregnant wife, would I be doing what he is doing? Silently he shakes his head, answering himself. He raises his eyes and sees the white marble bust of Cicero that stands on a black granite pedestal in one corner of the office. Then he looks at Julián again, and as he does, a broad smile of admiration breaks across his face.

"WHAT DO YOU MEAN we are moving from Guatemala?" Lucía asks, agitated and angry. "We have just *arrived* here at the hotel, Julián. I have not even unpacked what I brought and now you're telling me we have to leave Guatemala?" She frantically paces all over the hotel room. "I cannot understand you, Julián. Don't you realize that I am pregnant?" she asks, circling her waist with her arms, "that I am expecting your child?" She moves close to him and stares at his downcast eyes. "Julián, tell me the truth." She pauses. "Did you even think of your child before you did what you did?"

Julián, who has been looking down at the floor, raises his eyes to her and nods his head yes.

She then adds, demandingly, "And, did you think of *me*?"

There is no answer.

How can Julián answer Lucía? Can he tell her, "No, I did *not* think of you?" Or, "I thought that my wife would never question my actions?" Or, "I just assumed that my wife would feel that I was doing the right thing, that my wife would *demand* of me that I do as I did, just as Doña Rosaura did when she demanded of her husband that he act as a man ought to, at whatever the cost?"

There is no way Julián can answer Lucía's question with anything but the truth.

And the truth is that he had not thought of her at all. And that the glass wall separating Lucía from him has gotten thicker and thicker every day of their life together. A glass wall, Julián knows, he himself built. With his cowardice. And with his lie. The only lie he has ever told in his life. Because when the bishop at the cathedral asked him, "Do you, Julián, take Lucía as your lawful wedded wife?" he answered the bishop with a lie. He simply did not have the courage to tell the bishop the truth—*his* truth—and say, "No, I do *not*. I can*not*."

That is what he should have said.

How could he have married Lucía when Almighty God—not the Church, but God!—had already joined him in spirit to Sol for eternity even before their eyes met that first night on the patio? And, "Those whom God hath joined together let no man put asunder." Isn't that what the Bible says? Isn't that what Jesus *himself* says?

"No, I do *not*. I can*not*."

That is how he should have answered the bishop at the cathedral, because that was the truth.

But that was not how he answered.

Forgetting the little bit of wisdom that Chirilingo, the organ grinder's monkey, brought to him—a tiny piece of pale cream paper that said: "When honor and truth are at odds, let truth prevail"—forgetting it totally, he did what he thought was honorable.

He bowed his head, said, "I do," and lied.

A cowardly lie.

.   .   .

LucíA, tired of staring at him, and still waiting for an answer, encircles her waist with her arms once again and collapses into a chair.

There follows another long pause, broken by a knock at the door. A Mayan boy dressed in a plain brown uniform is there. He hands Julián a letter. "They are waiting for an answer, señor," the boy says. Julián rips open the envelope and reads. It is a formal letter in which Minister Andrú-jal accepts Julián's resignation from the university but begs Julián to remain there, teaching until a suitable successor can be found. Perhaps two or three weeks, he says, at most until the end of the month.

At the bottom, Minister Andrújal added, in his own handwriting:

Julián, please.

Julián tells the boy the answer is yes.

After the boy leaves, Julián closes the door behind him and faces Lucía. "That was from Minister Andrújal," he says. "He asked if I would stay in Guatemala until the end of this month, and I said yes."

Lucía says nothing.

She rushes behind the screen, where Julián hears her vomiting.

CHAPTER XXIV

W HEN SOL'S DOCTOR came to visit her tonight, hours ago,
right after dinner, before the family retired to their rooms, he
told Sol to remain in bed and under the covers until her high
temperature subsided. "A cold must be sweated out," the doctor said as
he left.

But Sol has not listened to him.

Wearing nothing but her sheer, almost transparent nightgown, she is
drawn to the window, where she stands looking out at the river, the same
way she has been standing there night after night, unable to sleep, ever
since Julián went away. But tonight, as she looks at the distant river, her
face is no longer twisted with the doubts she once had, because now she
understands.

Now she *truly* understands.

And now she knows beyond doubt that Julián loves her, just as she
knows that she will never see him again.

As she looks at the river, she remembers the many times she and Julián
walked by its banks, the many times they sat in the white gazebo, the
many times she listened to his words, his magical words, there, by the
river's edge. The many times she caught his eyes, those piercing deep blue
eyes of his she loves so much, staring at her, telling her that he desired her
as much as she desired him.

Suddenly her feverish eyes begin to sparkle with a vision.

Julián is in the white gazebo, beckoning her. She doesn't know how she knows, but she knows it. Her heart is telling her.

Elated, she rushes to the trunk that is at the foot of her bed, opens it, and pulls out a white lace shawl, the same one she wore over her shoulders the night she met Julián. She covers herself with it and, ecstatic, radiantly jubilant, she rushes out of the house, toward the river, toward the white gazebo, toward her place of power, her *Katok,* toward that magical place that allows the soul to travel ahead and move forward.

Toward him.

Though she knows the path to the white gazebo with her eyes closed, the moon seems to be lighting her way, guiding her steps.

The night is exceedingly warm, she thinks.

Or is it her?

She feels her body is burning.

Still rushing, she lets her lace shawl fall on the path as she makes one more turn.

And then, the minute she is able to hear the violent uproar of the rushing river, she finds herself shivering with excitement all of a sudden, for she knows—feels—that she is close to him. Her heart begins to beat so strongly that it seems it wants to burst out of her chest. She makes one final turn and she sees it, the white gazebo, its gauzy, diaphanous drapes untied, delicately billowing in the gentle breeze.

She was right. Julián is there. Waiting for her. It had been he who called her.

She can see him, in his black suit, a silent silhouette, expectantly waiting for her.

She rushes to him and before words begin to pour out of his mouth— words of guilt, words of shame, words of apology—she seals his mouth with her own, for this time, this time words are not needed at all.

She feels him embracing her, caressing her with his strong, virile hands, as his mouth avidly searches for hers while hers searches avidly for his.

Oh, how long has she waited for this incredible moment, a moment they can both now enjoy thoroughly, for now the truth is out, and the truth is that he is and has always been hers, just as she is and has always been his.

She tastes his mouth, his lips, his neck, just as she feels him taste her

mouth, her lips, her neck, the delirious smell of his body intricately interwoven with the delirious smell of hers. She feels his hands on her breasts,
her nipples erect, hard, as hard as his body is, pressing hard against her as
he kisses strand after strand of her hair. And then she finds herself opening her body to him, her body and his body pressing hard against each
other, their two bodies pulsating to the same wild, violent rhythm of the
rushing river surrounding them until there comes a moment, a magical
moment in which all thought ceases, in which time suddenly stops, in
which she sees, hears, smells, tastes, feels nothing else but the exhilarating
warmth that envelops her and makes her erupt into shattering wave after
shattering wave of incredible power, the violent outbursts of forces she
didn't even know—didn't even suspect—were hidden inside her body, her
body, which has finally come alive responding to his, just as his body has
finally come alive responding to hers, their two bodies finally becoming
one, just as their two souls have always been one, in a moment of ecstasy
beyond belief, beyond limits, beyond comprehension.

And when she feels more than sees a light, the light of his poems—a
light so immense that it surpasses all the stars—she finds herself bursting
into a prolonged, agonized moan, matching the prolonged agonized
moan that is his, that cannot be drowned, not even by the violent song of
the rushing river enveloping him. Her.

Them.

CHAPTER XXV

L UCÍA MOVES TO THE WINDOW of the hotel room and opens
the shutters, letting the beams of the early sunlight stream into the
room.

It is a glorious morning.

The mere fact that Lucía woke up without morning sickness makes
her feel confident. Perhaps all is not lost. Perhaps things can change. Perhaps she can convince Julián to stay in Guatemala. After all, she thinks, he
has already said he would stay in Guatemala until the end of the month,
hasn't he?

She is determined to change her attitude toward Julián. She remembers the Cuban saying, *Más se consigue con azúcar que con vinagre*—A lot
more can be achieved with sugar than with vinegar. She has been using
too much of her vinegar, she thinks. The time has come to try some of
her sugar.

Lucía sits on her chair at the breakfast table and starts to read *El Progreso*, the only newspaper still being published in Guatemala City. Rubios
forcibly closed *El Estandarte*, the newspaper of the Traditional Party,
claiming he had to do it for the good of Guatemala, since, according to
him, they published nothing but lies and distortions.

Lucía takes the paper apart, leaving the front section dealing with politics on the breakfast table for Julián to read, while she takes the society

pages in her hands and begins to scan through them, until something catches her attention.

"Isn't that a shame?" she says, almost to herself, as she shakes her head. "We were there, what? Only two, three days ago."

"What is it?" Julián asks, from behind the screen, where he is shaving.

"I cannot believe it," Lucía says. "Listen to this," she adds and reads.

"Soledad Menéndez y Peláez, the eldest daughter of our great patriot, General Don Manuel, died yesterday at her home of malignant malaria, contracted while bathing at the river. She was not yet nineteen years old."

"Isn't that a shame?" Lucía repeats, shaking her head. "She was just a child. Did you ever meet her?" She hears no answer. "Julián?" she asks again. Julián steps from behind the screen, his face white. "Julián," she asks again, concerned, "what is wrong?"

Julián looks at her, stunned. "What did you say?" he asks.

"Anything wrong?" Lucía asks again.

Julián stares at her for a long, long time and then shakes his head. "Oh, no, no. I . . . I just nicked myself with the razor," he says as he rushes back behind the screen.

And this time it is Lucía who hears him vomit.

THAT NIGHT, after staying up for hours in the parlor of the hotel suite doing nothing but pondering, unable to sleep, unable to think, unable to breathe, Julián steps out of his room and goes to the stables, where he finds his horse, awake, as if waiting for him. He saddles and cinches it, working automatically, as if under someone else's control. Moments later, he climbs on the horse and starts galloping at full speed, aiming for nowhere, going nowhere.

But the horse, as if by a will of his own, goes to where he has gone so many times.

Toward Sol's house.

When Julián realizes where the horse is going, he pulls up on the reins, and then, unconsciously, almost unwillingly, he changes course and goes toward the river. He makes one more turn, and there Julián stands in the stirrups, looking at the little gazebo in the distance, a pale, white vision in the pale, white light of the moon.

Never before has he seen the gazebo like this, at night.

It looks so magical, he tells himself.

But then he remembers the last time he was there, weeks ago, the Friday before he left for Mexico. While Xenufla stayed inside the gazebo, knitting, Sol and he had sat on the steps, by the shore of the river, in total silence, just looking at the river rushing down the side of the mountain, while he kept throwing little stones at the placid pool in the bend of the river and watched them skip across the surface until they finally sank.

The gazebo was equally as magical then, he thinks.

Or even more so, because Sol was there, by his side.

He gets off his horse, ties the reins to one of the Greek pillars of the gazebo, and enters it, finding himself as if in a world of dreams, for the gazebo's thin, vaporous, virtually transparent gauzy white drapes, untied and billowing ...ly in the cool night air, seem to encircle him, almost as if they were trying to caress him. Never before has he been inside the gazebo like this, with the drapes untied. It feels wonderful to be here, he tells himself, inside this wonderful white world that he finds so peaceful, so soothing, so calm. The delicately billowing drapes that occasionally brush against him feel like gossamer wings that try to envelop and embrace him, making him feel something he has never experienced before, something he cannot name, because he wouldn't know how. A wonderful feeling that warms him inside. That makes him feel welcome. At home. What makes it so? It must be the silence, he thinks, for the world about him is quiet, incredibly quiet. He hears no crickets, no frogs, no birds, no singing of any kind. Even the river seems to have stopped flowing.

He raises his eyes and looks around the gazebo, turning his head slowly, scrutinizing it in detail, carefully studying it as if he were trying to memorize it, as if he were trying to engrave that vision deep within his heart: the tall, slender Greek pillars, the delicate drapes that quietly dance in the gentle breeze, the clear pool of water so close by, the rushing rapids, the glittering river, the view of the distant city, the faraway volcanoes.

And then he remembers the first time Sol brought him here, to her

Katok, to her place of power. How filled with excitement and adventure her musical voice sounded as she said to him, *"This is my favorite place in the whole world. Isn't it wonderful?"*

Remembering those words of hers make him smile to himself, and as he does, he feels Sol's presence there, by his side, smiling back at him.

He kneels by one of the benches inside the gazebo, pulls out the tiny notebook he always carries, and, using the bench as a table, is about to scribble something when the first light of dawn awakens him.

He raises his eyes.

There, behind Xenatopilcho, the most distant volcano to the east, he sees the fiery edge of the rising sun welcoming him to a new day.

The warm red light of the sun, filtering through the delicately billowing gauzy sails of the gazebo and casting long playful shadows all around him reminds him of Sol, his sun, telling him, *"Here you can always find me."*

He takes his pen and, almost without thinking, scribbles the first thing that comes to his mind in his notebook. Then he looks down at what he wrote, and he is amazed at his own words, words that had just poured out of his mind and onto the page almost on their own.

> *Shaded by a silent wing*
> *I must write of a love in full bloom . . .*

He looks again at the notebook, rereading the words that he just wrote.

And then, abruptly, he hears himself utter an uncontainable cry, a cry of the most unimaginable pain, the deep, wailing cry of a man beyond control, as he urgently shouts Sol's name again and again, calling and calling her at the top of his lungs almost in anger, the desperate reverberating words loudly echoing all over the silent valley, while his tears, falling on his notebook, make the ink of his words run.

"Sol! Sol! Sol! Sol!"

"Sol . . ."

As if answering his disconsolate call, a beam of the rising sun momentarily startles him, suddenly quieting his urgent crying, and making him reexperience the wonderful feeling he felt only moments ago, when he first entered the white gazebo—a magical feeling that warms him inside. That makes him feel welcome. At home.

It is only then that he can understand—that he can name—the wonderful feeling he is experiencing. For all of a sudden he realizes that he is no longer—and will never again be—alone.

He raises his grateful eyes to the rising sun and stares at it until he sees it detach itself from Xenatopilcho and, now free, begin its ascent into the sky.

PART FIVE

THE SUN

CHAPTER XXVI

AFTER YEARS of incessant traveling—first, from Guatemala to Venezuela, then to Honduras, then to Mexico, then to Florida—Lucía, Julián, and their five-year-old boy, Ismaelillo, now make their home in two small rented rooms on the uppermost floor of a tenement building located within a small Cuban enclave in Brooklyn, New York. This new home of theirs is not too far from the home of Professor Saavedra and his wife, who also live in Brooklyn, though in a much more elegant and exclusive section, called The Heights, located within walking distance of the recently completed Brooklyn Bridge, a marvel of modern engineering that, suspended from two monumental stone towers, seems to float over the East River as it ties Brooklyn to the island of Manhattan.

Julián and his family arrived in the United states just two months ago and are now living through their first real winter ever.

The winter of 1883 is one of the harshest the northeast coast of the United States has ever experienced. Somber days are followed by more somber days; snow—which at first the three of them took to be something amazing and wonderful—has not ceased falling and has quickly lost its magic; and the temperature outside has stayed well below freezing for the last two and a half weeks. Lucía finds that it is only Ismaelillo who brightens the gray, cold, desolate winter days of the city, days that are as gray, as cold, and as desolate as she finds her own life.

She has long ago ceased complaining to Julián about their constant moving, and their constant packing and unpacking, just as she has ceased complaining to herself about her broken dreams and has learned to accept her life—if anyone can call hers a life. Her relationship with Julián, her husband, is almost nonexistent. They do share a bed. But that seems to be all they are able to share.

And yet, she has never been able to say a harsh word about Julián. He always looks at her with kind eyes, has nothing but comforting words for her, and always treats her with the respect and love a husband should show his wife. But she can barely remember the last time that she and Julián embraced. Thank God for her boy, Ismaelillo, she thinks, every time she embraces her child and feels his warmth.

Ismaelillo is Lucía's hope, her only reason for existence.

JUST AS ISMAELILLO has brought a beam of sunshine into the dreary, gray life of Lucía, the boy has filled the emptiness of Julián's existence.

It is his boy, with his long curls and with his perennial smile, who makes Julián's days bearable.

His boy—and his dream of freeing Cuba—keep Julián alive.

Julián spends long, long hours working each day, Sundays included, in a tiny, barely heated office that he keeps on Front Street in Manhattan, where he tries to eke out a living by writing. Luckily, he has just become a New York correspondent for newspapers in Argentina, Uruguay, and Mexico, countries that are eager to know what is happening in the United States, the nation they all think is quickly becoming the center of the New World. The editors of those papers keep demanding from Julián articles about life in a country they both fear and admire. And Julián is spending more and more time answering the desires of those editors. He is writing about everything, from corruption and political scandals in the administration of New York City and Tammany Hall, to the latest fashion in the design of ladies' feather fans, now all the rage—and his writings are always replete with details, which is what he knows his readers want.

He has little time to write intimate thoughts and poems in his diary anymore. Any free time he finds during the day is spent writing letter after letter, asking, begging, anyone, everyone, for money to buy weapons to liberate Cuba—letters which for the most part are never answered. At the end of each day, when totally exhausted, he finally arrives at the two rooms he calls home, it is his boy, Ismaelillo, who makes him smile. His boy climbs on his back, playing horsie, and together they fight battles against invisible dragons, and invisible ogres, and invisible tyrants.

Julián no longer writes poems to the woman of his dreams. But he still dreams of her, always seeing her as he saw her last, her eyes glittering with love as she smiled at him from the balcony of her home. And every action he takes, every letter he sends out in pursuit of his dream is dedicated to her, to Sol, his sun. He does write poems, very late at night, in his diary— short poems dedicated to his son. In those poems he calls Ismaelillo his muse, his little prince, his knight.

Ismaelillo is Julián's life.

The boy is taking a nap. Lucía has just finished cleaning the back room, which has a bed and a cot, where Ismaelillo is asleep, and has started to clean the front room, whose faded wallpaper is heavily stained by grease because all the previous tenants before them have used the coal heating stove in the corner for cooking, just as Lucía does. She begins to pile Julián's books on a chair so she can clean the top of the small table against a wall that Julián uses as a desk, as always crowded with books and papers, when a small something that was inside his latest diary falls on the floor. She bends down and picks it up. It is a small sepia photograph of a beautiful young woman with light hair and dark eyes. On the back of the photograph there is something written.

"Always," it says, that is all. No signature, no name underneath.

That night, after Lucía puts Ismaelillo to bed, she partially closes the door separating the back room from the front room, leaving it ajar, so some heat will enter the back room, and handing Julián the small portrait, she confronts him.

"Julián," she asks, her voice bitter, "what does this mean? Who is that woman? What does that word, 'Always,' mean?" She looks him in the eye. "Is she your mistress?" she adds, accusingly.

Julián looks at the photograph in his hands and shakes his head. Then, his truth, which he has held inside himself for so many years, just seems to want to burst from his lips. Never raising his eyes from Sol's photograph, he tells Lucía everything. *Everything.* From the moment he first met Sol till the moment he said good-bye to her at the funeral.

"You are *disgusting!*" That is all Lucía can say after Julián has totally poured out his soul. *"Disgusting!"*

She stands up and faces him, staring with utter contempt into his deep blue eyes.

"I always *knew* I had a rival. But I thought my only rival was Cuba. *Your* Cuba. Your *damn* Cuba! And I was willing to live with that rival. Willing to live in poverty, willing to live a loveless life, and willing to follow you, *my husband,* wherever you went, from one country to the next, from one city to the next, from one cheap tenement building to the next, as a good wife must. But how wrong I was! All this time, during all of these years, it was not Cuba who was my rival each time I got into the bed with you. But *that* woman"—she says as she looks at the photograph in Julián's hands—"that woman was there in the bed with us since the first time we made love." She raises her eyes and looks at him. "How could you have lied to me? The truth would have hurt. Yes! But truth only hurts once. A lie hurts over and over, day after day. For five years, Julián, for five *long* years, I've been hurt by this cowardly lie of yours! Wondering all the time what was I doing wrong, thinking all the time that *I* was the one to blame, that *I* was the reason we have not had relations in bed for so long!" She bursts into tears.

Julián tries to come close to her, but she won't let him.

"Don't you touch me!" she barks, with utter disgust. "Don't you ever *dare* to touch me again!"

She moves away from him just to turn back and face him again.

"And now, after all of these years, now you dare tell me what you didn't have the courage to tell me then? Now you tell me that you didn't have the courage to break our engagement? You were more concerned about what other people thought of you than what you thought of yourself! And you were so concerned about them that you were willing to sacrifice me—not you, but me, *me!*—for what other people thought about *you?* Now you tell me? Now? What kind of a man are you, Julián? All my life I thought I had married a courageous man, an honest man. A *real* man. But a real man would not have lived this lie! A real man would have told the truth whatever the cost! But you—You are not and have never been a real man in your entire life!" she spits out at him, venom in her voice. "And if you are a real man, then real men *disgust* me!"

Awakened by his mother's loud voice, Ismaelillo in the back room suddenly begins to cry. "Now see what *you* have done!" Lucía screams.

Then she rushes into the back room and loudly slams the door behind her.

THE NEXT DAY, unbeknownst to Julián, Lucía goes to Señor Rómulo Gonzalo, the Mexican consul in New York, a friend of her father's, and begs him to get passports for her and for her son so they can leave the United States as soon as possible. "And, please, I beg you, do not say a word of this to my husband," she tells Señor Gonzalo. "My life and the life of my son depend on it."

LESS THAN A WEEK LATER, at the end of another one of Julián's long, exhausting days spent writing letters to raise money for weapons to free Cuba and writing newspaper article after article to make a living, Julián returns to the two tiny rooms in Brooklyn, only to find them empty.

Not knowing what to make of this, he goes downstairs and asks the landlady if she has any idea where Lucía and his son are.

The landlady goes inside her room, and after a moment, she returns and hands Julián a letter.

The letter is from Lucía.

Julián rips the envelope open and reads.

When you receive this letter, my son and I will be on the Cataluña *on our way to Cuba, the only place in the world where I can be certain that my son and I will never see you again, because the Spaniards will never let you enter Cuba alive. I'm taking my son away from you, to save him from you. You, who are no man, are certainly not fit to be a father. I give you my word that Ismaelillo will never see you again and that he will never ever become the kind of a man you are.*

Just as he is, without a coat, without even a jacket, in the worst of winter, Julián runs out into the street, his slight limp aggravated by his emotion, climbs into a carriage he knows he can barely afford, and asks the driver to, please, please, rush him as fast as he can to the southernmost piers in Manhattan.

But by the time he gets to the piers, it is too late.

As he stands there, in his shirtsleeves, snow falling heavily around him, Julián can barely see the distant silhouette of the *Cataluña,* already going past the partly completed colossal statue the French government has given as a present to the United States, *Liberty Enlightening the World.*

The irony of the whole thing is not lost to him, when he realizes that his son, who will soon be living in Cuba, a country enslaved by the Spanish Crown, is passing by and moving away from liberty.

It is then Julián makes an oath—a sacred oath he is determined to keep, no matter what.

My son will not die in an enslaved Cuba.

Then, decisively seeing no reason to go back to the empty rooms he left behind in Brooklyn, shivering as he is, he walks to the building on Front Street and climbs the steep stairs, up to his little office on the uppermost floor. There, after he has spent an entire night writing letter after letter, the early morning sun catches him, still sitting at his desk, still writing one more letter, the opening line of which reads like the opening line of all the other letters that preceded it: *For Cuba, who suffers . . .*

His son will *not* die in an enslaved Cuba.

CHAPTER XXVII

THAT IS THE REASON a much older but exhilarated Julián is here today, May 19, 1895, in this small encampment in Dos Ríos, at the east end of Cuba: to make that sacred oath he took twelve years ago come true.

His son will *not* die in an enslaved Cuba.

Julián is inside his army tent, impatiently waiting, as are the rest of the men of this improvised volunteer army. Guns have been polished and repolished; their triggers, checked and rechecked. But the men have yet to see any action. They have been given strict orders by General Torres, the commander in chief of this military operation, not to move or attack until they receive further orders from him. And yet, the men in this encampment are celebrating, because Julián, the man who through his unflagging exhortations and passionate writings, assembled, planned, organized, and brought to fruition this invasion, that man, Julián, is now *here,* in Cuba, in *this* camp, ready to fight with *them.*

Only six months ago Julián spoke at a reunion of Cuban tobacco men in Tampa, and his powerful words were so stirring that the men, trusting Julián completely, emptied their wallets and gave Julián all they had in them, every bit of it, to buy weapons to free Cuba. When word reached the Cuban tobacco men in Cayo Hueso—as Cubans call Key West in Florida—Julián was invited to speak at the Club San Carlos, and the oration he delivered there was so brilliant and so passionate that it made everybody cry and cheer at the same time. This time, not only did the men empty the contents of their wallets, giving all they had to Julián, but their wives took off all the jewelry they were wearing—all of it, even their wedding rings—and gave it all joyfully to Julián, so he could buy the weapons that were badly needed to free their beloved homeland, Cuba.

Those weapons are now in this encampment, smuggled from the United States, brought by Julián, who arrived here in Oriente province, at the opposite end of the island of Cuba from La Habana, barely minutes ago, after having evaded the Spanish Army for days.

As soon as he arrived and the men in the encampment recognized him, he was unanimously chosen by them to be their commanding officer. *El Comandante,* they call him. Julián's hairline may have receded a lot, and his face may look a lot thinner. But his eyes are refulgent with excitement, because at last he is here, back in Cuba, to fight for freedom, as he promised himself he would do years ago.

Julián, El Comandante, is a man of his word.

OUTSIDE JULIÁN'S TENT, the hot sun of the tropical Cuban afternoon shines relentlessly, even though it is only May. The army cook is roasting a *jutía,* a large Cuban rodent, the only animal the men have been able to find, and the air is filled with its pungent aroma. The faint echoes of distant gunfire and agitated voices are heard all over the encampment, and horses are heard whinnying. The shadow of the guard standing outside Julián's tent can be seen projected on its translucent canvas walls.

But Julián smells nothing, hears nothing, sees nothing.

As he waits, sitting on his cot, he is lost in his thoughts, thoughts of his son, Ismaelillo, trying to imagine what the boy, now a young man, is like. A boy who—Julián has heard—*despises* his father. A boy Julián has not seen since he was taken away twelve years ago by his mother, when he was five. A boy Julián barely remembers. A boy Julián would give anything to embrace. But that is impossible. His son has been living in Cuba with his mother, Lucía, all these years. Ismaelillo is now almost seventeen, the same age Julián was when he was sent to prison here in Cuba, when he first stated his belief that Cuba had a right to be free from Spain. Julián wonders, had they not been separated, would Ismaelillo be here, next to him, in this encampment? He shakes his head and sighs, one of those deep sighs his friends always make fun of, the kind that comes from deep within his soul. In my play, Julián thinks, the man's wife courageously urges her son to go with her husband, so the two of them can fight for freedom side by side, hand in hand. But here I am, without my son, in this tent. He shakes his head as he carefully rips the last two pages from the small note-book he always carries, where he has written a letter to Ismaelillo. He folds the letter, writes ISMAELILLO in capital letters on the outside, and places the folded letter in one of the pockets of his vest.

Suddenly a tall, muscular black man carrying a rifle in his hands enters Julián's tent.

"Comandante, Comandante," he says, his voice tense with excite-ment, "one of our men has sighted the enemy nearby, less than two miles away. Should we wait for orders from General Torres?"

Julián stands up at once. "No. If they are that close to us, then we must attack, orders or no orders. Right away. Before they find us here. Go tell the men. Quickly. Go. *Go!*"

The black man rushes out of the tent, a smile of purpose crossing his face.

Julián grabs his brand-new rifle, one of those weapons he has just smuggled in, checks that it is properly loaded and that he has enough ammunition for it, and starts out of his tent, when he remembers some-thing. He turns around, places the gun on the ground, opens his old leather suitcase, which was lying on his cot, and rummages through it, hurriedly searching for something until he finally finds it. Neatly hidden for safekeeping inside his latest diary is the most sacred object he pos-sesses: the small sepia photograph Sol gave him years ago. Julián looks at the cameo photograph in his hands and smiles. Eighteen years is a long, long time, he tells himself. Those years have gone by so slowly. And yet— so quickly! He remembers the words of Panoplo, his good friend Panoplo, the wrinkled old Mayan man who was the bartender at El *Último* Adiós. *If you really found the woman the gods mean for you to have . . . then Ginebrita . . . if you truly found her, no matter what you do, no matter what may happen, she will always be by your side. . . .* Always. And then Panoplo had said it again, firmly, as to corroborate it. *Always.*

Panoplo was right, Julián tells himself.

"Always," he says aloud.

He kisses the small photograph of Sol and places it in the inner pocket of the black coat of the old black suit he is wearing, where it belongs, over his heart. Then, carrying a gun he has never fired, Julián rushes out of his tent, climbs on a horse he has never ridden, and heroically spurs it on, defiantly rushing into the enemy lines, determined to free the land that he loves beyond belief, his homeland, his Cuba.

As Julián leads his men in a fearless charge up the hill amidst Spanish bullets whistling by him, his eyes become the most exultant eyes in the world, totally enraptured with joy, when he feels more than sees a light so immense that it surpasses all the stars. And then comes a moment, a magical moment in which all thought ceases, in which time suddenly stops, in which he sees, hears, smells, tastes, feels nothing else but the exhilarating warmth that envelops him and makes him erupt into shattering wave after shattering wave of incredible power, the violent outbursts of forces he didn't even know—didn't even suspect—were hidden inside his body, his body, which has finally come alive. He opens his eyes to this light, and then they freeze in an immense moment of boundless ecstasy.

His last vision is of the sun.

His sun.

Sol.

EPILOGUE

WHEN THE AMERICAN BATTLESHIP USS *Maine,* moored in the bay of La Habana, was blown to pieces, the United States entered into war with Spain. This war resulted in the liberation of Cuba, which became independent on May 20, 1902, seven years and one day after Julián's death.

A statue of Julián depicting him at the moment of his death—victim of a Spanish bullet, his head back, looking up as he falls from his rearing horse—was placed at the southern entrance to Central Park in New York City, at the head of the Avenue of the Americas, then called Sixth Avenue.

Neither Lucía nor Ismaelillo accepted the invitation to attend the unveiling.

ABOUT THE AUTHOR

JOSÉ RAÚL BERNARDO is the author of the lavishly praised novel *The Secret of the Bulls*, which was named one of the best works of First Fiction for 1996 by the *Los Angeles Times*, and which has already been translated into five languages, including Greek.

Also a noted composer, Bernardo—born in Havana, and educated in Cuba and the United States—now lives in the Catskill Mountains in New York State.